D0371559

The Original
COLORED HOUSE
OF DAVID

The Original
COLORED HOUSE
OF DAVID

Martin Quigley

Houghton Mifflin Company
Boston 1981

Rejoice in thy youth
and let thy heart cheer thee in the days of thy youth
and walk in the ways of thine heart
and in the sight of thine eyes
and whatsoever thy hand findeth to do,
do it with thy might.

Ecclesiastes

Library of Congress Cataloging in Publication Data
Quigley, Martin, 1917–
The original Colored House of David.
Summary: A seventeen-year-old boy convinces a black
baseball team to take him along on their tour as a re-
lief player, but he must pretend he is a
deaf-mute albino.
[1. Baseball—Fiction.   2. Afro-Americans—Fiction]
I. Title.
PZ7.Q4155Or   [Fic]   81–6447
ISBN 0–395–31608–1   AACR2

Printed in the United States of America
V 10 9 8 7 6 5 4 3 2 1

Author's Note

━━━◄◆►━━━

Although I have made up all the characters and happenings in this story, they are based on my memories of the way things were when I was a boy in the 1920s. There *was* such a Fourth of July celebration in a Minnesota town that was much like the Indian Springs of my story. It *did* include a ball game with a team of itinerant blacks from the South. The kind of racist attitudes reflected in this story *did* exist. That is one of the things this story is about.

In a history of baseball (*Baseball*, published by Simon & Schuster in 1947), Robert Smith describes how things were before black players were able to take their natural and rightful places in professional (and high-school and college) baseball:

> In the earliest days of colored baseball the Negro player, who was unblushingly described by white sports writers in the public prints as "coon," "nigger," or "darky," often accepted his role as ambulating joke and spent a

good deal of his time clowning on the bases or in the field to draw laughs from white customers.

He might well have included such racist epithets as "shine" and "stovelid" that were used by ignorant defenders of so-called white supremacy. It is interesting that in 1947 Mr. Smith, reflecting *those* times, used "colored" and "Negro" instead of "black," which then seemed derogatory. Times — and people — change.

In many years as an amateur baseball and softball player — with more love for the game than ability — I have known and been able to play with and against a good many black players. A little bit here and a little bit there, the players of this story are drawn from those buddies of the diamond.

Martin Quigley

Contents

The Original
COLORED HOUSE
OF DAVID

1

Into the Camp of the Black Wizards

In the dawning of the Fourth of July of 1928, Timmy was listening for the boom of a firecracker that would start the day's celebration. It seemed to come from Main Street, where Mr. Pete, the town marshal, would be raising the flag on the east side of the Square. It was followed by booms from all over town. As Timmy thought about all he must do that day, his cozy bed became a cage, and he sprang from it.

Stealing past the other bedrooms into the bathroom, he splashed his face with cold water. Back in his room, he admired his baseball uniform — its pin-striped pants and shirt, its yellow and brown stockings, its cap with an emblem of a brown beaver gnawing through a yellow bat. Its shirt identified him as number 17 of the Indian Springs Beavers. It was clean for the game at two o'clock against the visiting Colored House of David for a prize of $200, winner take all.

Should he put it on now? He felt both eager and scared. He was eager for the game. He just hoped for a decent chance to show Donna what he could do, a man among men,

1

against the best ballplayers this town would ever see. If he could work up the nerve to do it, he was now going to march alone into the'r camp to find out for himself what these black wizards of baseball from the Deep South were really like. Were they religious fanatics who had vowed not to cut their hair until the Second Coming? Were they the descendants of runaway slaves who had turned to piracy? Or was all that just a lot of hooey to stir up interest in paying to see them play? So far the only dealings the town had had with them were by mail and long distance through Druggist John Olson, chairman of the whole celebration.

He decided to put the uniform on now. It would show them he was an official representative of the town team, not just some nosy kid. His spikes and glove were in the iron strongbox in the home-team dugout. Until game time, he would wear his all-purpose Grip-Sur tennis shoes, laced to the toe.

Downstairs in the kitchen, in her nook by the wood-burning stove, Minnie was sucking coffee through sugar lumps.

"Breakfast is the same as on Sundays," she warned him. "I'm putting on the pancakes at eight o'clock sharp." She had come to Timmy's family from the Lutheran Orphans' Home twenty-five years ago as a homely, skinny girl of sixteen. Now this was as much her home as anybody's, and she was boss of the kitchen and laundry.

"I know the Law of the House," he told her. In the pantry, he cut a muskmelon open and spooned its orange fruit. He sawed a slice of bread from a fragrant new loaf and spread it thickly with butter. He washed it down with a dipper of cold buttermilk from the crock in the icebox.

He went out through the windowed back porch where

outdoor clothing and equipment were kept — rain slickers and lumberjack coats, the shotgun and fishing gear, skis and snowshoes, oars and paddles, boots and overshoes . . . There, hanging from its peg by the door, was his old two-gallon tin pail. He paused at the door to consider taking it with him. He had not picked it up since early that spring, on Good Friday, when he was still sixteen.

Minnie had given it to him when he was a kid of twelve. "You that's young on your feet, get me a dozen brown eggs from Mrs. Ebeltoft's hen house for my devil's food cake." "Run to the creamery for a pail of fresh buttermilk for your dad's lunch." "Take this leftover chicken stew to poor old Annie Munson in your lucky pail."

He began taking it wherever he went on his rambles around the town and through the countryside. Old people and busy housewives would call to him: "Yoo-hoo, Timmy! I need a dime's worth of salt side pork for these beans I've got ready for the oven." "Could you spare a minute to fetch me a can of Prince Albert smoking tobacco?" And he would get a penny or two, sometimes a nickel, just for running there and back.

And it came in handy for bringing home all kinds of things he hunted for or came upon in his explorations — wild plums for a pie, chokecherries for jelly, black walnuts for the fudge his mother made on a winter's night, baby sunfish to be fried in butter for Sunday breakfast, pretty stones from the bed of the creek and pussy willows from its banks . . . "Look what I've got in my lucky pail!"

At fourteen, when he was reading and reliving in play the stories of Sir Launcelot and the other knights of the Round Table, he began, secretly, to think of it as his Magic Vessel . . .

3

There was a curfew in Indian Springs. Kids under sixteen had to get off the streets when Mr. Pete tolled the bell in the fire station at nine o'clock.

One summer night, stretched out in the dark at the back basement window of Silver Fox Hanson's pool hall, he watched the town sports play their big Wednesday night snooker game till way past curfew. As he ducked into the alley to run for home the back way, he was caught by the beam of Mr. Pete's flashlight.

"Good evening, Mr. Pete," he said, knowing that town law required he be locked up until his father came to get him. Then there would be hell to pay at home.

Instead, the marshal nodded sociably. "How's Old Billy getting along these days, Timmy?"

Mr. Pete and just about everybody else in town knew that Timmy earned two bits a week running errands for Old Billy Nicholson, the retired locomotive engineer who was living out his time in a third-floor room of the Indian Springs Hotel. Timmy was careful not to tell a fib. "He's not getting any younger, Mr. Pete. Good-night, sir."

"Good-night, Timmy."

Running home, the truth about his pail dawned on him. Its magic was that *grownups trusted a kid carrying a pail.*

After that, he walked boldly into places forbidden to other kids in short pants — such as the lobby of the hotel at night when the traveling salesmen gathered to swap yarns and tell stories considered too raw for the ears of females and growing boys. On a winter's night, when their own stories were their only entertainment, he would duck into the nook under the stairwell and seem to see on the isinglass of the wood-burning heating stove the stories he heard.

Often, in summer, he would take his pail down the tracks to the hobo jungle between the stockyard pens and the great

4

coal dock where the fast freights and transcontinental passenger trains paused to gulp coal and water. No other kids dared go there. The hoboes were mostly footloose laborers looking for work. They followed the harvests and chased rumors of construction work Out West. But some were bums running from work, and some no doubt were crooks on the lam. They would crawl off the blinds under the car floors or jump out of the empties for food and water in their own jungle.

The pail worked its spell in the jungle as it did in town. "You from around here, kid? Where kin we get us some stew meat?" "Has your ma got a bar of laundry soap she kin spare?" "Know anybody got any work to do for a handout?" "When does the next fast freight for Fargo go through?"

Timmy knew the answers. Any bum willing to work an hour on its woodpile could get a hot meal at the hotel. The next fast freight west would coal up at ten in the morning. For four bits he could get them a pail of stew meat, potatoes, and onions, or a slab of bacon and a dozen eggs. Ground coffee was fifteen cents a pound.

From their lingo of the road, Timmy would see in their fire the far places they were coming from or heading to out there in the world beyond his own . . .

And so it was this morning that he paused to consider taking the lucky pail of his boyhood with him into the camp of the black wizards. He took it from its peg. But why? He had outgrown its need. He hung it up. But why not? It might come in handy. He took it down again. But it was just an old empty lard pail. He hung it back up. But it swung easily from its handle and was no burden. It might just . . . He took it with him.

Outside, the pale blue eyes of his dog, Snow, were gazing

steadily into his own for a sign that he might come along. An albino cross between Grandpa Tim's setter and Uncle Hans's elkhound, he was silky white and long-haired. His haunches were lean, but his chest was broad. His forelegs seemed shorter than his hind legs. "I doubt me the need of you, old friend," Timmy said, moved by the silent pleading to a lapse into the storybook talk of the rambles of their younger years, "but come if ye will." And they were off together at the easy run that could take them the eight miles out to Uncle Hans's farm in less than an hour. But this morning they had only a mile to go to the ball park on the outskirts of town.

From the lilac bushes along the road, he could see across the infield into their camp in the oak grove, beyond right field. They had a fire going — twelve black warriors and an old man tending the skillets. They were bearded and mustachioed. A few wore their hair knotted behind, like pirates. Most were naked to the waist.

They had moved in at night, after yesterday evening's game in Staples, a town a hundred miles to the south. Their 1926 red Packard touring car and high-wheeled 1923 Dodge flatbed truck with a canvas hood took them and all they needed to live and play ball from town to town. They had set out north from Kansas City in May, up through Iowa and on into Minnesota, north and west to Indian Springs. From here they would go west across North Dakota into Montana, all the way to Billings for the Labor Day celebration and rodeo.

The diamond of the Beavers was in the corner of Tillie Johnson's forty-acre pasture. The infield, as good as any between Minneapolis and Fargo, was the town's boast and the labor of Ed Mulligan, a hobo who had chopped wood for a meal at the Indian Springs Hotel thirty years before and had stayed on to become the town's handyman. He had spent yesterday dragging and watering down the base paths; pruning the edges of the infield grass; lining the batter's and coach's boxes, the on-deck circles, and the foul lines; doctoring up the pitcher's mound; cutting, with a hand mower, the outfield grass to one and three-quarters inches; helping the ladies decorate the lemonade and watermelon stands with red, white, and blue bunting. Everybody knew that Ed was getting all his work done the day before because he was going to tie one on on the Fourth of July. A teetotaler in between, Ed drank moonshine till he could drink no more every New Year's Eve, St. Patrick's Day, Memorial Day, Fourth of July, Labor Day, Halloween, and Christmas Eve.

The outfield was as level as a pool table into center field, but the far reaches of left field ran a little uphill to the rise on which Tillie's white house overlooked her domain. It ran a little downhill along the right-field line into the big oak trees where the House was camped. A snowdrift fence that arced from 325 feet at the foul lines to 370 feet into center kept Tillie's cow, calf, and mare and their droppings out of the field of play; a ball hit clean over the fence was a home run; one that bounced over was a ground-rule double.

The grandstands could seat eight hundred spectators. For this occasion the hundred seats behind the backstop were reserved for Congressman Youngdahl, visiting mayors, the leading bankers and merchants of the county, and their ladies. Others of the expected attendance of three thousand would sit and stand on the grass inside a rope stretched twenty feet outside the foul lines, behind the outfield fence, and on the fenders and hoods of cars, buggies, and wagons parked on the road. There was no admittance gate, but every adult (reckoned as those who had left school to go to work

7

or get married) was expected to pay twenty-five cents for a Beavers Booster tag; any adult without a tag was regarded and spoken of as a pauper or a cheapskate.

Though it was not yet six o'clock, there was already heat in the sun's clear stare, and it was going to be a scorcher, a regular barn-burner, a hundred or better on the diamond before that day's winner walked away with the stakes. (A dollar could get you five from the sports at Silver Fox Hanson's pool hall if you wanted to put your money where your mouth was on the Beavers. Druggist John Olson was the only known taker, for $10. His bet was regarded more as a rich man's gesture of civic pride than as a smart man's gamble.)

A good many people who came to that day's game would be seeing Negroes for the first time in their lives, but Timmy had spent an hour with one in the hobo jungle. So he felt he knew that they were people just like anybody else, except for the way they looked and talked and acted and where they came from.

He set his cap and strode forth, Snow at his side. He tried not to look as nervous and scared as he felt. What was he afraid of, for cripes sakes? Still, they got meaner looking every step he took. He made his face smile to show that he was friendly.

They paid no more attention to his approach and entrance into their camp than if he and Snow had been two stray dogs drawn by the fragrance of the steaming pot of stew and the crackle of grease in the frying pan.

He stood among them like an invisible white spirit. They went right on eating, laughing, talking, and lolling around. Their voices were as thick and high and rich and strange as the food on their tin plates.

"I guess you must be the Colored House of David," he said, and his voice sounded accusatory to his own ears.

8

Now they saw him. They stared at him. One of them spoke up: "Damn if he don't look jes like his dawg! Light hair, blue eyes, pointed ears, an' all."

"He do! He do!" They shouted and cackled their glee, and Snow barked joyful assent.

He had been teased before about his pointed ears, but he wore them with pride. In his Grandpa Tim's yarns about their ancestry, the pointed ears they both had were proof of their descent from the Firbolgs that had driven the giant Fomorians out of Ireland in the dawn of time. His hair, white as a child but now a light brown, was from his Viking ancestors on the Nelson side. The blue eyes were common in both lines.

"Quiet, Snow!" Timmy commanded and looked at his dog with appraisal. Damn if he didn't look like him. No one in town ever had remarked on the resemblance. "He oughta look like me," he blurted out. "He's half Irish and half Norwegian, same as me."

This set off another burst of cackles and laughter. "Hey, boy, come ovah heah." He was small, naked to his belt, with a wispy goatee, a tied mane of long hair, and a scarred face. He was sopping up his gravy with an end of corn bread. Timmy was reminded of the Oak Tree Priest and his twelve merry men of evil from a story his Grandpa Tim had told him about the dangers in the forests of Ireland in the times before Cuchulain. "Yes, sir?"

"Where you get the idea we the Colored House of David?"

"You were here, so I figured it was you."

"You ain't gonna put nothin over on this white boy."

"He one smart white boy. How you figger that out all by yourself, white boy?"

Timmy stood straight against their laughter. "The way I figured it, it's the Fourth of July. We're going to play the

9

Colored House of David. You're here. So you must be the Colored House of David."

"You wrong, boy. We is *not* the Colored House of David."

"That white boy not as smart as he make out he is."

The old man at the fire, as white-haired as Snow, stood up from tending the pot and the skillets and smiled to ease Timmy's concern. "We the Original Colored House of David. The *Original* — make no mistake, son."

"I won't make that mistake again, sir. And I'll tell the other guys on our team that you are the *Original*."

"I take it you they bat boy?"

"His shirt don't say he BB, his shirt say he seventeen."

He had chosen the 17 on his back as a secret talisman. Both he and Donna were seventeen years old. There were seventeen letters in each of their names (Donna Louise Miller and Timothy Hans Nelson). He had checked the books of mythology in the library and had found no identification of 17 with god or mortal of myth or legend. It was his alone, for love and for fortune on the field. The secret of it (undisclosed yet even to Donna) gave him now an inward calm as he faced these black warlocks.

"I asked you, you they bat boy?"

"No, sir, not this year. Was for seven years. This year I'm on the official roster."

"What you play?"

"I'm second relief pitcher, and I pinch-run, pinch-hit, and serve as utility infielder-outfielder."

"You don't do no catchin?"

"No, sir," Timmy said through their laughter, which he set off again by adding: "Except to warm up the other pitchers."

"How old you, boy?"

He wished it were this time next year when he would be a man of eighteen, out of high school, able to go into the pool hall by the front door, getting the Chandler to take Donna to the dance at Cormorant . . . "Seventeen," he said boldly, "same as my number."

"What you, six foot?"

"Not yet. Five eleven and a quarter. My dad says he figures I'll make it by fall and will more'n likely go to six two, same as him. My uncle's six four and weighs three hundred pounds."

"What you weigh?"

"I wear a size forty uniform shirt."

"I ask what you weigh, not how big your shirt is."

"Nearly one forty, sir."

They were taking turns with the questions, easy and laughing.

"Zackly how much?"

"One thirty-six and a half."

"Soakin wet?"

"No sir, stripped on the scale in my dad's office."

"He got it all down to the fractions."

"The opposition does not appear to be too formidable today," said one, a tall man of dignified bearing, nearly as big around as the oak tree he leaned his back upon. "I doubt that we shall require the services of our redoubtable Merv to pick up these marbles."

"I be ready if Bofey needs help," said the one called Merv. He was sitting cross-legged, eating left-handed, awkwardly.

"This ain't even no double-header. I won't need no help today," said the one called Bofey. He was also tall, though lanky. His light brown skin was heavily freckled.

"You pitched nine innings right-handed yesterday an' a

double-header both ways on Sunday," the man called Pops told him.

"I'll pitch left-handed today," Bofey said.

Then it came to Timmy that he was in the presence of the hero of legend. The sparkles of sunshine in the deep shade seemed to hallow the oak grove. Bofy! The great Both Hands Wilbur! Reverend Larson, who had actually seen major-league baseball while attending the seminary in Chicago, had proclaimed, during the town's discussions of the caliber of these Negro opponents, that Both Hands Wilbur was the greatest left- and right-handed pitcher in the history of the game.

"Both Hands Wilbur!" said Timmy in the awe of recognition.

"Why they call me Bofey," said the Man of Legend with a smile of human warmth. He was nearly as old as Timmy's father. "How come you know 'bout me?"

"Reverend Larson, he's our manager — sept he'll be umpiring behind the plate today —"

"Your manager, he gonna umpire! When we playin for all the marbles?"

"Don't worry about a fair shake from Reverend Larson. They say that he and God see every play the same way. He says you're the greatest ambidextrous athlete in the whole history of sports," Timmy said to Bofey. "He saw you pitch against a team of American League all-stars years ago after the World Series in Chicago. He said you struck out Babe Ruth!"

"Twice, I struck him out."

"But he said he didn't think you were still playing. He said you must be retired by now."

"I ain't retired or dead, neither one," said Bofey. He looked out at the field. "Still workin at it." The applause and cheers of countless thousands on a hundred faraway ball fields were distantly sounded in the rustle of the morning breeze through the oak leaves.

"May I?" Timmy asked. "May I shake your hand?"

"Which one you like?" And the laughter of his mates drowned the distant sounds of his days of glory.

Timmy took both of Bofey's hands.

"It come to pickin up the marbles, I be ready to go, Pops," Merv called. "We don't go again till Sunday in Fargo."

Timmy stooped to look at Merv's swollen right hand and forearm. "How did it happen?"

"Jest a bitty scratch, cleanin fish Sunday mornin."

He picked up Merv's hand and felt along the forearm for the extent of infection. "This has got to be taken care of, maybe cut open and sterilized. These infections can be dangerous."

Merv jerked his hand away. "What you, boy? You think you some kinda doctah?"

"No," said Timmy defensively, "but I got a merit badge in first aid before I quit the Boy Scouts."

"A Boy Scout doctah! A real honest-to-God Boy Scout doctah, gonna cut my arm open."

" 'On my honor,' " quoted the big man against the tree, " 'I will do my best to do my duty to God and my country and to obey the Scout laws.' "

Against the wave of their laughter, Timmy turned to him. "How come you know the Oath? You musta been a Boy Scout yourself!"

"Our Mistuh Tetley," said the old man smiling to himself at the fire, "he know everything."

"And my dad," Timmy went on, "he's the town doctor. He'd tell you how dangerous these little infections can be if they're not taken care of."

13

"I agree with our Boy Scout," said Mr. Tetley, "that competent medical attention would be advisable. There must be a hospital or clinic in a booming metropolis the size of this one — what's its name?"

"Indian Springs. But the nearest hospital is in Detroit Lakes, fifteen miles south of here. And since Old Doc Anderson died, my dad's the only doctor in town."

"You kin get him to come out here?" Pops asked. "Or I take Merv to his office? Will he treat him?"

"It's a holiday," Timmy explained. "And his office is closed. He only goes out on real emergencies on Sundays and holidays."

"No white doctor gonna come out here to treat a colored man."

"Perhaps this Boy Scout will see it as his duty to his God and country to remind his father of his Oath of Hippocrates," Mr. Tetley suggested.

"If I ask him," Timmy found himself saying, "you can bet your boots he'll come."

"You tell 'im we pay his price."

But it wasn't going to be easy. His father would let nothing short of a dying mother keep him from Big Breakfast on a Sunday or holiday morning. And nothing short of hell or high water would keep him from the morning's Great Automobile Race, in which Grandpa Tim was entered with his Model T, or from the Tug-of-War Championship, in which Uncle Hans was anchor man for Indian Springs. And the devil on horseback could not keep him from gathering unto himself his grandchildren when Marilou and the folks from Detroit Lakes got off the Winnipeg Flyer at 9:32 this morning. Timmy looked up from these calculations: "I'll bring him over as soon as he drives up with the kids to see me in the Fastest Human race before the game. Right now I can tell you what he'd say. He'd say, 'Soak that hand in hot salt water half an hour out of every hour until I get here to lance it open.'"

"Can't pitch wif my hand in no bucket," Merv said.

"Forget pitchin'," Bofey told him. "I gonna dipsy-doodle 'em left-handed."

"Let's get some water heated." Timmy raised the tin pail. "We can use this." He had been right to bring it, and it was fitting that this last practical use of it would bring to an end his boyish need for it. "Where is the water? And I'll need a cup of salt." He felt the way he did as a quarterback, calling the signals. He followed the old man with white woolly hair to the water in the twenty-five-gallon milk can on the truck's tailgate. Holding the pail while the old man dipped it full, he peered into the traveling home of the Original Colored House of David. From a rod along the left side hung the uniforms. Locker boxes contained gloves, spikes, and personal gear. Along the right side were crates and boxes for the bats, balls, and bases and for cooking and camping gear and supplies. At the rear were rolled canvas tarps for lean-to shelters. On the floor was a scattering of mats and blankets.

The back seat of the Packard, parked alongside, had been converted into an office, which held a heavy iron safe and storage space for an ice chest and containers of perishable food.

As he took all this in, he saw himself tossing in his own gear to hit the road with them. The urge seemed to grow out of all the stories his Grandpa Tim had told him about how their ancient Irish ancestors had set out every spring to entertain and instruct the country people with story, song, and magic. And it fit right in with the stories his Uncle Hans had told him about their direct descent from Sigurd the Joyous, the first and greatest Viking of them all. Ah, yes, it was in his blood. But, oh, it was another fantasy.

He returned to put the pail in a nest of embers.

Several of the players had pulled mats and blanket rolls out of the truck and were stretched out upon them, like fallen bronze castings of Roman gladiators. "We done drove most the night long," Pops said, "an' the boys will ease theirselves till they suit up." The others were finishing their meals in a cluster at the fire. Timmy never had seen or smelled anything like their food. Pops saw his twitching nose and smiled: "Dig in to what you see. Lotsa base hits left on that fire."

Big Breakfast at home was nothing to sneeze at, but he could get blueberries and sour cream rolled in Norwegian pancakes, bacon, little pig sausages, butter-fried sunfish, scrambled eggs, and Minnie's oven-fresh cinnamon rolls most any Sunday morning. At this fire was food that a man around here could be baptized, confirmed, married, and buried without ever tasting or knowing anything about. He would be the only one in the county, maybe ten counties around, able to tell that he had sat down in a camp with Negroes and eaten the genuine food of the bayou.

"Yes, sir," he said. "Much obliged."

As he heaped a tin plate, something of everything and all running together, the high fragrance seemed to inflame him. He dug in, spooning it up and sopping it down. He could feel the juices of the food surge into his blood and fuel his muscles. His face glowed, and his forehead sweat. He let out a little Viking snarl of gratification, and Snow demanded his share.

"That boy eatin way back into yesterday."

"Give that dog some leavins, his beggin keepin me awake."

16

The old man scraped up a plate of leavings for Snow. Heads turned and eyes opened to watch the disappearance of the food.

"Damn if they don't *eat* alike." There were murmurs of agreement. "He tol' you, man, they related."

After wiping the gravy from his chin with his sleeve, Timmy helped himself to a tin cup of the strong coffee, loaded with sugar and laced with canned cow.

"How hot you want this water to be?" Merv asked. Timmy stuck a finger in it. "Little bit more, as hot as you can stand it."

He helped himself to a final chunk of the hot corn bread and ladled over it a modest portion of the pork and greens, which he ate with the supervised table manners of his home, as if it were strawberry shortcake. Snow went chasing after a rabbit and what other excitement he might stir up.

The water in the pail was steaming. "It won't scald you," Timmy told Merv. "Put it all the way down."

"Do like he say," said Pops.

The black hand went down and came quickly out. "Again," said Timmy. Down again and out again. "Keep it in this time." Down it went the third time and stayed in the hot brine. How like the story of King Arthur's Excalibur, Timmy was thinking — the third time was the true time — and now the Magic Vessel was again just an old lard pail.

The huge man of dignity eased a blanket roll under his head and addressed Timmy: "How big a crowd, in your no doubt humble estimation, can we expect for this afternoon's performance?"

For the last month, the main town topic had been the plans and preparation for this great Fourth of July celebration. Timmy believed he was better informed about all of its details than anybody else. Now, taking his ease in the center of these strangers who had only one part to play in the events of the day, he saw himself as an ancient Druid priest of an oak grove to whom the fearful faithful came for interpretation of dreams and the wheelings of the stars.

"We're figuring on three thousand or better out here for the races, the band concert, the singing, and the ball game. It's gonna be," he said, and the awe of it inflected his tone, "the biggest crowd ever assembled in Becker County."

"That's more people than you *got*."

"We're not talkin about just Indian Springs and the farmers who trade here, Mr. —?" There was that about him that compelled respect.

"Tetley. William P. Tetley, the Second."

"Mr. Tetley. They're coming from the better part of all the counties around. See, it's our turn to have the big Fourth of July celebration. Last year it was at Lazy River. Year before, Pelican Rapids. Before that Height of Land, and before that I think it was Tamarac, or was it Detroit Lakes? Let's see, that was the year the cyclone hit the —"

William P. Tetley II raised a catcher's hand of crooked fingers. "And this year, I take it, it's your turn?"

"Yes, sir, and Indian Springs is gonna put on a celebration they'll be talkin about for years to come. There's gonna be all kinds of things. Smokey King, the daredevil aviator, is gonna loop the loop over Bergerson's pasture and then is gonna take people up for rides, *five dollars for fifteen minutes*, and there's gonna be a lot of takers, just to brag they've been up in an aeroplane. But the main things start this morning with a band concert on Main Street. Then, at eleven o'clock, the Great Automobile Race right down Main Street to the flagpole."

Again Mr. Tetley raised the hand of crooked fingers.

18

"Please, young man, tell me if you can, how in the name of Jesus, Mary, Joseph, and Moses can you have an automobile race down Main Street? It ain't but two blocks long."

"It's a slow-moving race, you see," Timmy explained. "The car that stays in high gear and finishes last is the winner."

Mr. Tetley nodded his understanding and let his head sink back so he could gaze at the oak leaves above him. "Then what?"

"The big tug-of-war contest between our team and the lumberjacks from the tie camp at Loon Lake. Four men to a side. My Uncle Hans is anchor man for Indian Springs. The losers get pulled through a pit of flour, water, and chicken feathers."

"These folks don't need *us* to entertain them," Mr. Tetley said.

"Out here, what time do the game start?" Pops asked.

"The rolling-pin-throwing contest for the ladies starts at one."

"I reckon your mother the favorite in that one."

"No, but Minnie, who works for us, finished third last year."

"Why do they *need* us?" Mr. Tetley asked of the leaves above him.

"Then we play ball?"

"After the races."

"What races?"

"All kinds of races. The Scrambled Shoe race, the three-legged race for girls, the Bachelors and Old Maids Relay . . . The final event is the hundred-yard dash for Fastest Human of Becker County. I won it last year, and you'll see me going again to keep my championship."

"Then we play ball?"

"At two o'clock. After the choir sings 'The Battle Hymn of the Republic' and joins the band in leading the crowd in 'O Say, Can You See.' "

"Why did they send for us?" asked Mr. Tetley.

"The ball game is the main event of the afternoon."

"Then people go home?"

"Heck, no. After the ball game, there's the chicken dinner and speeches at the Cooperative Creamery, then the big fireworks display. We got the same professional pyrotechnicians who put on the Burning of Rome at the state fair last year."

"What they gonna put on for you?"

"The Battle of Gettysburg, featuring Pickett's Charge."

"Then people go home?"

"After that there's the big dance out at Lake Cormorant where they won't play 'Three O'clock in the Morning' until dawn."

"Where they have this fireworks?" Bofey asked.

"Over the pond — the original Indian Springs — between the creamery and the stockyards. People will bring blankets or sit in their cars or wagons along the road."

"Is it free?"

"Sure, it's free. Everything's free except the Beaver Booster tags and what you buy at the stands."

"Is everybody welcome?"

"Sure, everybody's welcome. People come from miles around."

"We welcome?"

In the sudden quiet, Timmy understood the question. "Gosh." He looked around at the open eyes. "Gosh, I don't know. I never heard it — this is the first time —" Then he saw the light of an answer: "One place I know you'll be welcome — on the roof of the stockyard sheds. That's where the Indians go, the Indians that come in from the reservation. They're allowed to sit on the stockyard fence and on the sheds. They get as good a view as anybody."

"The Indians of Indian Springs know that their place is in the stockyards," said Mr. Tetley.

"They can be troublemakers," Timmy said, "specially if they get ahold of some moonshine and get likkered up. Some people around here, specially the farmers and storekeepers, don't like the Indians hanging around with their thieving ways. That's why they've got their own reservation."

"Way up North in freedom land," said Mr. Tetley.

Timmy felt his ears go red. "It's just —" he started to say, but no words in his town's defense came to him.

"Just what?" Mr. Tetley persisted, but not unkindly.

"Just the way we do things, I guess," he said. His view of himself as the oracle of the oak grove went out of focus.

Mr. Tetley nodded, however, as if Timmy had cleverly explained a perplexing riddle.

"What about this likker?" one of them asked. "Where you get this moonshine? You know where, boy?"

"Sure I know. Silver Fox Hanson, who owns the pool hall. He'll sell you all you want. It's good stuff. I take a snort or two myself, once in a while. It's made back in the woods at Height of Land near where the Mississippi rises."

"Ain't that a dog? Mississippi River water whiskey, make me feel I down home."

"What he get for it, you know how much?"

"Dollar a pint. Seven dollars a gallon with two bits extra for the jug."

"Give him the money, Pops."

"This boy git in trouble, buyin our whiskey. How I get ahold this Silver Fox a your'n?"

"I'll give him your order. He delivers purchases of a gallon or more, except out to the Indian reservation where his minimum is five gallons and the price is ten dollars a gallon."

"How come he charges Indians ten dollars?"

Timmy often had heard the hangers-on at the pool hall discuss the economics of Silver Fox's bootlegging. "There's a special law against sellin booze to Indians, so he's gotta break two laws instead of just Prohibition. He runs it in the same Reo Speed Wagon he's gonna drive in the race this morning."

"I have a premonition that this Silver Fox philanthropist is going to charge us the Indian rate," Mr. Tetley observed.

"Why?" Timmy protested. "You're not Indians."

"We ain't white neither," said Bofey.

"If we have got to go to the stockyards with the Indians to see the Battle of Gettysburg, featuring Pickett's Charge, it stands to reason we will be charged the Indian rate for moonshine," Mr. Tetley observed.

"I didn't say you *had* to, I just said I knew you'd be welcome there."

"Have you asked the Indians if we would be welcome there?"

"It's not *their* stockyards; it's *our* stockyards." Timmy was trying to get them to see the straight of it. "We certainly get to say who's welcome at our own stockyards."

"We go to the stockyards, with the Indians, we pay the Indian price for rotgut booze," said Bofey. "Maybe we decide we play ball only with the Indians."

"Size a the crowd, all these doin's, we got euchred for two hundred," the one called Scrappy said to Pops.

"Two hundred a good price a town this size. Who knew they was gonna have the whole county in?"

"We've got big expenses," Timmy explained. "We're paying out four hundred for the fireworks display alone."

"Four hundred for fireworks and two hundred for us, and we are, by this young man's admission, the main attraction of the day."

"An' they don't have to win the Battle of Gettysburg to collect. We got to win to get our measly two hunnerd."

"We never had no trouble up this way an' we not gonna have no trouble now," said Pops.

"Gimme a run, we got 'em beat," said Bofey.

"We do no clownin'," said Pops, "till we got this game on ice."

Timmy could see it their way. "Maybe if I talked to Druggist John Olson — he's in charge of everything — he would cough up another hundred or so."

"You don' talk to nobody 'bout our business," Pops said. "We play what we bargained for. An' we give 'em our good show," he told the others, "after we got the game in the bag."

"The boys in the pool hall can't find any takers on us at five to one," Timmy told them, "but we'll do the best we can to make a real game out of it."

"Pay us to get a hundred down on the home team an' figure out some way to let 'em win."

They laughed and cackled. "How about that? Wouldn't that be a dog if we had some way to get it down?"

"You wouldn't do it if you could," said Timmy.

"Why wouldn't we?"

"Because that would be crooked, and I know you're not crooks."

"You're right 'bout that, son," said Pops. "We play to win an' we haven't been beat in near three years."

"Our two hundred and sixth consecutive victory will be at

23

the expense of the Beavers of Indian Springs, where cattle, hogs, Indians, and niggers are welcome at the stockyards," said Mr. Tetley.

"We'll do the best we can," Timmy repeated, hoping that Big Ole, their coach, would give him a chance to show his stuff against them. Suddenly all he must do this day seemed to swell up inside him and stop his heart. He had to be moving into the day. How could one day hold all that would happen? He had to run ahead into it and hurry it along. "I gotta get back to town."

"We gotta get us our rest."

He squatted to raise Merv's hand from the brine in his old pail. "Seems to be coming more to a head. Keep the water good and hot — and I'll bring my dad to lance it when he comes to the races."

Only last year, he would have seen himself as the Fastest Human in Becker County running back into town with news from the camp of the enemy. Now, with the Magic Vessel tucked away in his boyhood, he saw himself as Timmy no more, but Tim, Tim Nelson; Timothy Hans Nelson or Timothy H. Nelson for formal and legal identification, but Tim Nelson, Tim, just plain strong Tim.

"Who's that Number Seventeen?" the stranger would ask.

"That's our Tim Nelson," the townsman would say.

"Who is that stunning girl?"

"That's the Miller girl from Detroit Lakes, engaged to our Tim Nelson."

He would begin with the simple announcement at breakfast that he was now Tim and would so be called.

2
The Battle at the Livery Stable

"Timmy! Timmy!"

It was Karen Larson, the twelve-year-old daughter of Reverend and Mrs. Larson. She was as quick and wiry as electricity. She wore brown coveralls like a boy, and her feet were as dirty and tough as any boy's. Her long brown hair made her a girl. It flowed free from her orange skullcap, and no boy dared pull it for fear of her fists and nails. The skullcap was decorated with pop-bottle caps of every flavor. She wore it like a helmet.

There were tears in her wild grey eyes. "Come with me, Timmy. You've got to stop them."

"Tim," he said gently.

"What, Timmy?"

"Tim," he said. "I'm just Tim now."

She shook her head in angry puzzlement. "They're blowing up frogs with firecrackers in the horse pond behind the livery stable."

"They're doing what? Who?"

"It's Snorry Snot Rag, Larry Erickson, and the three Norman cousins. They catch these big bullfrogs, see? Then they —"

She clutched the back of her coveralls and shook her head and stamped her feet. Timmy saw in her face that she could not find decent words for what they were doing. "You've got to stop them, Timmy."

They were the meanest kids in town. Nori Jensen, their leader, was proud to be known as Snorry Snot Rag. He had quit school in the eighth grade, as soon as he had turned sixteen. Larry Erickson was a star basketball player and a good outfielder, but a troublemaker on the high-school teams. The others didn't amount to much on their own, but they made a tough gang.

Timmy looked up and down the street. There was nothing stirring on this holiday morning except the distant clatter of breakfast preparation in the kitchen of the Indian Springs Hotel. Karen shook her head. "There's no one around except Old Walt at the livery stable, and he just laughed when I told him what they were doing. I was hoping to find Mr. Pete . . ."

Even while he looked up and down the street, Timmy knew that only a girl could run to the marshal for help on a case like this. No boy had a right to interfere at all; a boy would be expected to join the fun or be branded a mama's boy. A man could go busting in on them: "What the hell you God damn kids think you're doin? You haul your asses outta here an' don't let me catch you doing anything like that again." That's the way Uncle Hans would handle it. Grandpa Tim would go sailing in with his silver-handled walking stick and start beating them over the head and shoulders. Roan, the harness-maker, would scatter them with a horsewhip. Reverend Larson would command them to stop, take their names down in his book, and mention them in his remarks before next Sunday's sermon, to the disgrace of their parents. He was now Tim the man, and he must find a man's way to send them flying.

Karen's bright face shone with her trust in him.

"Well," he said, "let's go take a look." She danced ahead. He strode after her as purposefully as if he had been called to the mound to relieve in a tough situation.

"Karen." He called her to his side. "What kind of firecrackers you got with you?"

She opened the brown paper bag. "Just ladyfingers and two-inch salutes."

Without breaking stride, he took three red salutes and a few kitchen matches from her bag and dropped them into the big back pocket of his baseball pants.

"What you want them for, Timmy?"

"Just in case," he said.

"I'm so glad you were there. What if you hadn't been there, Timmy? I didn't know what to do."

If he had not been there, he was thinking, he would not be dreading this encounter. "Show me where they are," he said, and she could not contain a squeal of excitement as she led the way through the airy livery stable, where Old Walt was readying the horses with harness for the day's business. Many visitors would come by train and rent buggies to take in the events of the celebration.

The gang was out back beyond the corral at the edge of the pond, squatting at its edge around Snorry Snot Rag. "Stay behind the fence," Timmy told Karen, the very words Uncle Hans had used last summer when he had crawled through the pasture fence to get a rope and a halter on Iffy, the old bull that always went mad in the dog days of August. Now he advanced alone until he could see what they were concentrating upon.

Snorry was working a dandelion stem up a bullfrog's hind end. "That's good, that's good enough." "Give it an easy blow now. Easy, it don't take much." Larry gently puffed into the stem to inflate the frog. "That's enough." "Whoa." "Plenty." "No, a little more." "We always lose air before we get the firecracker set." "That does it," said Snorry. "Give me one with a long fuse." Larry eased the stem out, and Snorry, with the deftness of practice, worked the firecracker in to replace it. Then he held the frog out over the water until Larry lit the sizzling fuse. He tossed the frog out into the pond. With shouts and cries of expectancy, they stepped back to watch the frog's efforts to dive to safety. The gang howled its glee as the frog, fighting its buoyancy, propelled by its own efforts and the back-thrust of the fuse, became a living torpedo. Then frog, water, and the early morning were shattered by the explosion.

"He really put up a good fight, that one did." "How many more we got?" "The three biggest ones." "This time we set off all three at once." "That's the berries." "Get me three fresh straws."

Timmy strode into their midst. "What you guys doin?"

"We got these frogs, see," said one of the Norman cousins. "We blow 'em up with dandelion stems an' put firecrackers up their assholes. They go just like torpedos before they blow up."

"Suitin up a little early, ain't you, sonny boy?" said Larry, a sarcastic reference to Timmy's uniform. Larry had tried out for the town team. He had been put on standby in case of need and had been offered a last year's uniform without a number. He had disdained the offer.

"Make them stop, Timmy!" It was Karen's anguished yell. They all turned to look at her, perched like a falcon on the fence.

They waved and hollered their derision.

"Who's gonna make us stop?" Snorry said, getting a good grip on the frog's legs. He looked up at Timmy. "You wanna try to make us stop?"

"How would *you* like a firecracker up *your* ass?" Timmy asked him.

"You an' ten like you ain't man enough to stick no firecracker up my ass." He was a powerfully built eighteen-year-old, a head shorter than Timmy but forty pounds heavier. The problem, fighting him, would be to keep him from getting a hold on you.

"Have your fun," Timmy said, turning away, "and I'll have mine."

"Be blowin this one," Snorry told Larry, "while I get a stem up the next one's ass."

From ten feet away, Timmy took one of the salutes from his back pocket, lit its fuse with his back to them, and turned to toss it a foot from Snorry's squat. The force and surprise of the explosion pitched Snorry forward into the muddy pond and scattered the others. Timmy lit the second and threw it into their midst. Over their howls and shouts came the shriek of Karen's vengeance. Timmy ran forward and threw the frog box into the pond, and Karen shrieked again to watch the frogs leap free into the water.

Snorry came out of the water. "I'll get you for this, you son of a bitch." But he was confused and in pain from the burns on his arms.

In the moments before the gang could form a purpose, Timmy held the third salute in his left hand and clicked the match into flame with his right thumb.

"You want me, I'll be waiting in the corral," he called to them. "Any of you or all of you, one at a time." He lit the firecracker and hurled it high in the air so that it would come down among them. They scattered to get away, and Snorry stumbled back into the pond.

Timmy ran back to the fence to Karen. "Get into the stable. Tell Old Walt to bring a buggy whip if more than one of 'em jumps me."

"Serves you right, serves you right, serves you right," she was screaming at the gang as she darted for the stable.

Old Walt had come out back to see what the commotion was all about, and Timmy knew that he would get a fair fight. Only Snorry was a threat. Larry would not fight, and the others were no match for him. They crowded to the fence.

But Old Walt, tugged along by Karen, advanced with a buggy whip. "That's enough now, you fool kids. Gettin my horses all worked up with your noise an' commotion. Beat it. Get the hell outa here 'fore I come after you."

"I'll get you, you son of a bitch, get you if it's the last thing I ever do."

"Any time," Timmy said. "You know where to find me."

He followed Old Walt into the cool dark of the stable. He was breathing hard, and his arms and legs felt trembly. At the door, against the sunlight, Karen put her hands to her mouth to give carry to her threat: "I'm going to tell my father and the marshal what you did to those poor frogs. And how Timmy gave you a taste of your own medicine."

They hollered something back, rough and obscene. She caught up with Timmy and took his arm and clung to it as they walked back toward Main Street. "Oh, Timmy, I love you. I really do."

"Tim," he said and patted the little girl's head.

3

The Law of the House

————◄◆►————

Running homeward his thoughts kept swinging forward to that night, after the fireworks, when he and Donna would be strolling downtown, probably holding hands by then, for the special Fourth of July banana split at Mollestrom's ice-cream parlor. He would explain how, from his studies of mythology, he had calculated 17 as their own talisman . . .

They had made their date for the Fourth back on Memorial Day. The Nelsons (except Freddy, who was away at college) had driven to Detroit Lakes to visit Marilou, Timmy's sister, who had married Donald Miller of the department-store people. Since Donna was Donald's kid sister as Timmy was Marilou's kid brother, the families had kidded them about the possibility of another interfamily romance. Until then, Timmy had thought of Donna as just another shirttail relative he was supposed to be nice to at family gatherings. But they had spent most of that holiday together. Timmy had rowed her clear across the lake into a secluded bay and taught her how to cast for bass, though he had to take them off the hook for her. They had talked about the mean teachers they had and the crazy things they did at school. That night, on the porch swing, Timmy realized that this was no family joke: He was in love with Donna and had reason to believe that . . . When he had suggested that they go to Mollestrom's after the fireworks, when the Millers returned the visit on the Fourth, Donna had given him the sweetest smile: "Sure, Timmy," she had said, "that sounds swell." They had actually shaken hands on it.

Now, stepping up his pace lest he be late for Big Breakfast, he was supposing that she would, however subtly, dare him to kiss her good-night. They would caution each other, of course, that theirs must remain a secret Understanding, at least until after their high-school graduations next June . . .

As he ran up the walk to the screened porch of his home, he renewed his determination to make his announcement that from now on he was Tim, Timmy no more. Under the Law of the House, as his father called it, he was still treated as a child. His father, Harold, was a despot from whose rulings there was no appeal. His mother, Ellen, was influential but without superior authority except in household matters. The rest of them — Timmy, Freddy, and Minnie — were bound by the Law of the House, which gave them no authority over one another. Marilou, now with a home of her own, was accorded the courtesies and rights of a visiting lady.

Before going into the dining room, where all evening meals and Big Breakfasts were served, he went to the sink on the back porch to wash and comb.

From the kitchen, Minnie was reporting to his father and mother already in the dining room: "That squirt of a Timmy is here now. The fish and the bacon are ready. Should I put the pancakes on now, or do we have to wait for that lout of a Freddy?"

"Go ahead with the pancakes, Minnie," his mother called. "No telling how long Freddy will be primping and fussing up there this morning."

"He will not eat at this table unless he is here for grace," his father declared. "Just because that lout, as Minnie so aptly calls him, lives in a frat house nine months a year does not excuse him from the Law of the House when he is at home."

Mother put down her napkin and scooted to the stairwell. "Freddy, pancakes are on, and Daddy is about to say the Preamble."

"Be there in a jiff, Mom."

Timmy was hoping Freddy would have to eat in the kitchen with Minnie, but the big lout made it just as Minnie came in with the platters. He was wearing an open-necked pongee shirt, a sleeveless sweater and matching stockings of a yellow, black, green, and blue Argyle pattern, white plus-four knickers, and white and brown oxfords.

Mother broke merrily into song: *"Collegiate, collegiate, oh, yes, we are collegiate!"*

But Father sarcastically changed the tune: *"That's where my money goes, to buy that loafer clothes . . ."*

"It was ever thus," thought Timmy, his glance expressing the contempt of warrior for courtier.

Freddy bowed an acknowledgment. He had neither the pointed ears nor any Irish intensity of spirit. He was a pleasant, comfortable boy, most people thought, to have around. Minnie wiped her hands on her apron and folded them. Father checked to see that all hands were folded and heads bowed. (Timmy liked this article of the Law because

33

he knew that it galled Freddy, especially when a college friend was a guest.) Father's preambles to prayer were addressed to the family, not to God. "Today we celebrate the birth of our democratic republic and the principles of justice and freedom that govern and bless our lives, both in this republic and in this home. We welcome Marilou and her children and kin into our midst, as we anticipate the good times and excitement of the day's events. For this food upon our board, Timmy now will thank the Lord."

Timmy had been thanking the Lord since Freddy had been confirmed. His own confirmation had not relieved him of the duty because there was no one younger to take his place.

"Heavenly Father, bless our food for your glory and our good, amen."

Before Freddy could reach for the pancake platter, Timmy raised his hand. "If my brother will delay his assault upon the pancakes, I have an announcement to make."

This was protocol; all announcements (usually assignments of duty or of disciplinary punishment) were made in family silence immediately following the grace. Timmy had their attention.

"From now on, I will be addressed as Timothy or Tim, not as Timmy anymore."

This again froze the movement of Freddy's reaching hands. "Oh, for cat's sakes!"

"What's this about, Timmy?" his father asked.

He would not explain. "I will not be called Timmy anymore."

"We named you Timothy so we could call you Timmy," his father said. "You are Timmy. Your grandpa is Tim. You will be Timmy as long as he is alive or until you are out on your own."

34

"For cat's sakes, I like being called Freddy. Who wants to be called Frederick or Fred?"

"If he wants to be called Tim, we should call him Tim," his mother said. "I'll call you Tim, Timmy."

Her slip set off the laughter.

"So will I, Timmy," his father said. "I'll call you Tim, too, Timmy."

"Who him?" said Freddy. "Him Tim too Timmy? Or him Timmy too Tim?"

Except for the obligation to fuel himself for the day's action in the hot sun, he would have left the table. The energy from the bayou meal had been mostly consumed at the livery stable and on the run home. He ate steadily without looking up. His mother put a hand on his shoulder, but said no more.

The matter of meeting the folks from Detroit Lakes at the depot came up. "There won't be room for them if we all go," Ellen said, "so Timmy and I will stay home."

"I'm going," Timmy said.

"There won't be room for you in the Chandler," Freddy said and counted them out: "Marilou, Donnie, and the kids is four. Donna and I make six, and Dad makes seven. It's only a seven-passenger car, for cat's sakes."

"Timmy can ride the running board and help with the baggage," their father decreed.

Ordinarily, Timmy liked to ride the running board — balanced easily, his right arm curled around the window post, his face set into the wind, like riding shotgun on a stagecoach. "You and Donna," he said bitterly. "That's what he's been fussin and primpin all morning for."

"I'm dragging her to the dance at Cormorant tonight."

"We'll see about that," Timmy said. "When I was there, she said she'd sit with me at the Battle of Gettysburg and

35

have a banana split at Mollestrom's ice-cream parlor afterwards."

"Oh, mercy me, I forgot to tell you," his mother said. "Marilou called on the long distance to ask if Freddy could get the Chandler to take her and Donnie and Donna to the dance at Cormorant. Your father gave his permission. Besides, Timmy — Tim — she's more Freddy's age than yours."

"She is not!" Timmy said hotly. "She's my age exactly." Seventeen, their talisman.

"But she's so grown up. All the Miller girls grow up early, with a whole store to choose their clothes from."

"I'm going — and not on the running board," Timmy said stubbornly.

"Sez who?" Freddy demanded.

"Sez me."

"Oh, yeah?"

"Yeah!"

"Two's company, three's a crowd," their father said. "You've got plenty of time to get girl crazy, Timmy."

Timmy left the table and went out the back door. He must somehow find a way to win the day and Donna from Fat Fart Freddy. He was on the point of setting off for the depot when he remembered his promise to bring his father into the camp to treat Merv's infected hand. He waited for him to come out for his ritualistic inspection of the Chandler and to shine it up for the holiday. The Chandler was used only on Sundays and holidays and for trips to Detroit Lakes and Fargo; during the week, his father drove the Model T on his rounds.

"Dad?"

"Now what? For Pete's sake, son, you surely got to understand why I had to give Freddy permission to take the Chandler tonight. Your turn will come."

"I went out this morning to where the Original Colored House of David is camped by the ball field."

"The what? Oh, those coon ballplayers! The Colored House of David, they call themselves."

"The *Original* Colored House of David."

His father laughed and said: "Is it safe for a white man to go into their camp, Timmy? I hear they're religious fanatics who drink the blood of white folks in their communion cup."

"They've got long hair and beards, but they're just ballplayers, Dad. Reverend Larson says they're the best players people 'round here will ever get to see play."

"What I hear is that you Beavers don't have a chance." He opened the hood and tested the sparkplug connections.

To his father's back Timmy said, "Dad?"

His father lowered the hood and removed the radiator cap, an American eagle in flight. "What is it now?" he said, sticking his finger down for assurance of water.

"One of the House players has a bad infection in his hand from cleaning fish. I told him you would come and fix it."

"Streaks up the arm?"

"It's hard to tell how far up on the black skin, but his hand is all swole up. I got him soakin it in hot salt water."

"It's the Fourth, Timmy, my one day to be with Marilou's kids. I don't do anything but real emergencies on the Fourth."

"You will, won't you?"

"You had no call to go visiting with those stovelids."

It implied criticism of his father and was on the verge of defiance, but Timmy was damned if he would use any of the demeaning terms his father and the people of the town applied to Negroes. "I probably know more about Negroes than anybody in this town," he told his father, thinking back

37

to last Good Friday — four months ago — when he was still sixteen.

His father turned to challenge his statement. "There's no niggers ever lived in this county," he said, "so why would you be making up a story that you know more about them than anybody else?"

*

It was a Good Friday, a cold and sour day of early spring. Between noon and three o'clock, just about the whole town was in church meditating on the last words of Christ. Timmy had played hookey from the service and had taken his pail to the slough to catch a few pickerel to sell to the mink farm for a nickel each. It began to drizzle. On the way past the stockyards, he paused to look down upon the hobo jungle. There was only one bum there, kneeling with his ragged rump in the air, trying to blow the fire of life into twigs and leaves he had cupped against the smoldering tie. The cold mist put a damper on his efforts.

Timmy sauntered toward him. "Havin trouble getting her goin?"

The startled bum looked around, and Timmy looked into the first black face he had ever seen close up. For a moment, he stared his astonishment and the black man his fright. Timmy smiled, and the bum relaxed his shoulders with a deep sigh. "Don' even have a match," he said. "Ain't got nothin."

"I've got some union matches," Timmy said, crouching beside him. "You know," he went on with the joke, "the kind that strike anywhere." The bum didn't get it. He was staring at the string of fish.

Timmy was thinking how exactly, in his rags, he looked

like the illustration of Nigger Jim in his copy of *Huck Finn*. He could be as young as twenty or as old as forty. "Let's get the fire going." He shaved dry splinters from the tie with his Barlow knife. "There's plenty of dead sticks over in those woods. You could be getting an armful while I get her started up."

Soon the fire was crackling away, and the hobo spread himself around it to soak up its heat. Timmy now saw that he had only one shoe, a scuffed-up tan oxford with a narrow toe. His other foot was bleeding from running on the cinders.

"How'd that happen?"

"Them railroad bulls, they wukked the train ovah, some town back there."

"Did they get to you?"

"Los' mah shoe runnin to git away." His eyes were watery from cold and hunger. "Could you be a-sparin me one of them fish?"

Timmy knew just what to do. "I'll get some potatoes and stuff from home. We'll boil you up a nice fish stew. And clean up that foot . . ."

"I get some food in me, I be on mah way. You a good boy to hep me."

Timmy stood up tall. "Keep the fire going and heat the water. I'll be back in fifteen minutes."

"I be here."

Timmy ran home the back way. Everybody was in church. He felt like a thief in his own home. He filled a bag with potatoes and onions, cheese and summer sausage, bread and apple pie. From his father's office, he got a bottle of iodine and a roll of gauze. Then he opened the big closet on the back porch where the outdoor clothing was kept. It was a quarter to three, and he had to work fast. He selected a woolen shirt and his father's duck-hunting britches. From the boots and overshoes, he decided on a pair of brogans his father wore for dry-weather dove hunting. On the shelves were long underwear and socks. What else? He wrapped the bundle up with a length of clothesline that would serve as a belt. As he ran back to the jungle, the church bell was tolling for Christ's last words: "It is finished."

*

Since then he had thought much about the black man, homeless out there in a hard white world. He had got, somehow, to thinking of him as a Nigger Jim, running for freedom, and of himself as a Huck Finn, yearning to bust out from parental restraint. When his father had gone storming around the house looking for his hunting shoes, Timmy had kept his mouth shut. But he had told his Grandpa Tim and his Uncle Hans about feeding and clothing him and sort of wishing there were a raft and a river to take them to freedom and adventure.

He had to tell them separately because they had nothing to do with each other except to go at each other's throats in argument. Grandpa Tim was small and quick like a ferret, Uncle Hans big and ponderous like a mastiff. If one said up, the other said down; east, west; go, stay; it will, it won't. Tim did not go to church, but stood up for Catholicism; Hans went every Sunday to the Lutheran Church but often talked like an atheist. Tim was an Al Smith Democrat, Hans a Calvin Coolidge Republican. To others in the family and to the whole town, the schism between them was funny. It hurt Timmy that he could not share with both all the secrets and private talk he shared with each.

In his shanty by the depot, sipping his moonshine and

smoking his pipe, Grandpa Tim had said: "Isn't it like Martin of Tours himself, riding out on glorious adventure? Who got off his horse to feed and clothe the beggar in the snow? And wasn't the beggar the Christ Himself?"

Uncle Hans had nodded and poured Timmy a little swig of the home brew, now that he was confirmed and had a long pants suit. He told him the story of how Sigurd the Joyous had given all the food and wine and fine clothing of a Roman ship they had captured and plundered to the galley slaves and set them free.

His uncle Hans, with little schooling, had taken over the family farm. His father had left the farm to go to the university and become a rich doctor. Yet it seemed to Timmy that his uncle knew more about what was right and what was wrong than his father even thought about.

Now he knew that if he told his father about the black hobo, his father would forbid him ever to go near that hobo jungle again. So all he said was: "You will come out, won't you, Dad?"

"It's an imposition on a day like this. I work twelve hours a day and am on call the other twelve. I'm entitled to one day, especially today with all the fun that's going on and my grandkids to take care of, when I don't have to go running off to take care of some nigger's sore hand."

"They'll pay you, Dad, same as anybody else."

His father went around the car, kicking each tire.

"I promised them you would come."

His visit to the camp of the Original Colored House of David now seemed as unreal as a night dream. The reality was that his father went on inspecting the Chandler.

"I told them you were my father."

"All right, God damn it, I'll look at him."

41

"When, Dad? Now? We've got time before train time."

"No, not now. I don't know when. When I get a chance. I told you it was an imposition."

"When you come for the races before the game?"

"What races?"

"Before the game. The races. I'm running to defend my title as Fastest Human. The kids won't want to miss the races. It won't take you five minutes."

"All right then. Don't bother me with it now."

"I'll watch for you and take you to their camp."

Now his father took the polishing cloth and the chamois skin from their pegs. "You get the windows while I get the body."

"I'm going down to the depot now," he said. "Grandpa Tim might need some help with the Flyer crowd."

This was on the edge of insubordination, but his father shrugged it off. "God damn if I'll ever understand that kid," Timmy heard him tell his Chandler.

4

Donna at the Depot

Grandpa Tim was station agent at the depot on the Northern Pacific main line, just where it turned west to Fargo and points west and where a branch line continued north to Winnipeg. Now the noise of excitement was rising from the depot like the heat waves from the track bed. People would be coming on the Winnipeg Flyer from as far away as Wadena. The crowd at the depot overflowed the waiting room onto the planks of the platform. Kids were scooting in and out. Every minute was celebrated with bursts of firecrackers over the tracks.

Timmy knew how to do everything except sell tickets and work the telegrapher's key. While Grandpa Tim sent and received messages, answered the phone, sold tickets, and minded his candy, fruit, and tobacco counter, Timmy pitched in to help Perky Kittleson load the spoke-wheeled baggage wagon with outgoing mail, five crates of chickens, and a cream separator bound for Sundown, Manitoba. Timmy was as deft a wagon steerer as Perky and nearly as sharp with his turns as Grandpa Tim himself.

At 9:30, two minutes to train time, Grandpa Tim closed the ticket window and led the way outside to the platform. He gave Timmy, proud in his Beaver uniform, the holiday honor of running down the platform with the message hoop for the engineer to sweep up as he went by. Timmy ran beyond the platform to kneel on the ties and put his experienced ear to the hot steel. All eyes were on him as he ran back to the platform and cupped his hands to assure the waiting throng: "She just cleared the switch at LaBelle!" There was a cheer for the Flyer. A boy touched off a string of ladyfingers.

First her black plume, then white steam from her whistle, and now her thunder as the Flyer pounded down the line. Timmy raised the hoop aloft at exactly the height of the engineer's gauntlet. Women screamed and children shrieked as they pushed back from the heat and thrust of her mighty pistons. The platform shuddered. Her brakes took hold. Shaking the spine of her cars, she eased to a sobbing sigh and came to rest still seething her power, as if impatient to get on with her long run into Manitoba.

He caught a glimpse of Donna between the first and second passenger cars. Did she see him — his hand still aloft in perfect messenger-hoop position — as she blurred by? Was her smile for him alone, or was it the frozen smile of a queen for her multitude? The pack of the crowd impeded his dash up the platform to be first to greet her. He found himself on the edge, left out, beat out by his father and Freddy. His father pushed the conductor aside to grab his two granddaughters, one in each arm, and hustle them to the Chandler. It was Freddy, his big ass blocking the way, whose unhard-

44

ened hand guided Donna's descent to the midst of ordinary people.

Timmy's heart fell like a dead duck. He saw that she was unattainable — never again the laughing girl you could race to the diving dock. She was a female spirit in human form. He wondered that a mortal hand had been entrusted with fastening the rosebud buttons down the back of her dress, a wispy chiffon of palest pink. A maddening lavender seam on the sheer silk of her stockings hailed the perfect symmetry of her legs and rose from the heels of her white slippers. The upturned brim of her white hat was a halo over the ringlets of her black hair. From the depths of calm brown eyes, she looked out upon this day's bustle like a princess gazing over her subjects.

He moved into her path and touched the brim of his Beavers cap. "Oh, Timmy," she said. Her smile became laughter. "I didn't recognize you in your baseball suit."

He turned his shoulders to show her the number on the back of his uniform. "Seventeen," he said, and the words came out, not in the flare of bursting rockets or in a moonlit stroll, but here in this tangle of shoving people. "Our talisman. Seventeen letters in your name, Donna Louise Miller, and seventeen in mine, Timothy Hans Nelson, and we are both seventeen . . ."

She could not know what he was trying to tell her. She laughed again. "Oh, Timmy, you're so funny. You've always been the funniest boy I ever knew."

The horn of the Chandler blared his father's impatience to get on home with his granddaughters and on into the whirl of the day's doings. "Dad's tootin at us," Freddy croaked at Donna. "Shake a leg."

There were only seconds in the glare of day to plead a

moonlight cause. "You promised — remember on the diving dock? — that you would sit with me at the fireworks display tonight, and now —"

"Oh, Timmy, I didn't know about the dance then. You wouldn't want me to miss the dance, would you? My first big dance? And it's all arranged. Marilou arranged everything, so we could get the Chandler and Freddy could take me. But I'll sit with you at the ball game today . . . or something . . . Don't look so hurt, I'll *sit* with you. Coming!" she called ahead. "I'm coming!" And she was gone. As she bent to climb into the back seat, the staring world could see up to her purple garters.

5

The Automobile Race

Grandpa Tim's 1921 Model T touring car was the oldest and humblest of the six entries in the race. Timmy kept her polished and had learned to drive her and shared the old man's pride in her. Now, one on each side, they lowered the top and buckled it down.

"She's as ready as she'll ever be," said Grandpa Tim. "Now it's up to luck — and me."

It was a quarter to eleven, fifteen minutes from starting time. "Twist her tail," said Grandpa, pulling his goggles down and settling behind the wheel. Timmy engaged the crank and jerked it up, and her engine caught first time. They nodded their agreement that she sounded fit. Timmy climbed in, and they headed up the depot road to Main Street.

"She turned you down, did she?" Grandpa asked. No use trying to hide anything from him.

"So far," Timmy admitted. "Why would she want to go to that dumb dance with that big slob?"

"You got too much to do today to mope about a flighty girl."

"Seventeen," Timmy said. "I had no chance to tell her all it means."

"I never had any luck with girls till I was past twenty." And the luck he had didn't last long. The bride he had brought to Indian Springs had died of the flu when Timmy's mother was a little girl. Now, though, he had today's race on his mind. "You gotta run into the pool hall an find out from Bibleback how the betting's going. If you can get ten to one or better, here's five bucks to put on my nose."

Timmy looked at the money. "Hot diggety dog!"

"If we win, ten of it's yours."

Timmy rubbed the bill on the 17 on his shirt. He began to tingle for the start of the race. An hour ago he had thought he would never tingle again.

Four of the entries were in their places at the ready line, sixty feet back of the starting line. Grandpa Tim swung his tin lizzie around and backed into the number-three position between Druggist John Olson's 1927 Hupmobile coupé and Silver Fox Hanson's 1926 Reo Speed Wagon. In number one was the high-wheeled 1923 Dodge touring car of Moe Hundergaard, who ran the blacksmith shop; number five was the 1926 Overland Whippet of Matt Waldo, a farmer from near Twinkle; and number six, the favorite, was the 1927 red Stutz Bearcat of Doc Hayfield, son of the proprietor of the Indian Springs Hotel, now a dentist in Minneapolis. Doc, a fat man, had driven the 221 miles from the city the day before in four hours and forty-two minutes, a new record. Now he was taking a turn on the track, heading back for the start. Still wearing the dust it had raised over thirty counties on its record run, the Stutz was cheered by the jam-packed crowd. At the finishing line at the flagpole, the band could be heard under the booming of the firecrackers. Timmy didn't need Bibleback to tell him, as he dodged through the throng to the pool hall, that Doc and his Stutz were the popular and betting favorites.

Timmy squeezed through the sports inside the pool hall. The six pool tables and two billiard tables were covered with canvas for the day. The sports were milling in and out of the back room, where Silver Fox Hanson, a man of white hair and legendary cunning, was doing a land-office business in moonshine at two bits a shot. Bibleback, normally the rack boy but today the betting commissioner, was operating from atop a stepladder behind a billiard table. He was a sixty-year-old hunchbacked dwarf whose head seemed bowed in perpetual prayer, hence his nickname. He did not make book; he was a broker. "Here's another ten on Doc's Stutz," he was bellowing "What am I offered?" "I'll take it for ten." "I'll take it for fifteen," another sport shouted, and nobody went any higher. Bibleback took the money from the parties to that bet and scrawled a note for each.

Timmy had worked his way to the bottom of the ladder. "My Grandpa Tim wants to bet five bucks on himself," he called up to Bibleback. "What are we offered?" "Here's the first action of the day on Tim Coglan's Model T," Bibleback called out. "It's Tim his own self layin it. Who wants it?" "I'll take it for thirty." "In a six-car race, that tin lizzie should get a hunnerd," Bibleback shouted down. A sport from Hitterdahl raised a sheaf of bills. "I'll take it at ten to one — fifty bucks." Emerging from the back room, Silver Fox himself got into the action: "Sixty." "Sixty-five." "Seventy," shouted Silver Fox. "Gone for seventy." Bibleback scrawled the note for Timmy, who snatched it and pushed his way toward sunlight.

Down at the ready line, the drivers and their walkers, the

starting judges and clutch watchers, and a mob of advisers were creating the chaos essential to a fair race. Timmy sprinted to Grandpa Tim. "Fourteen to one, seventy bucks." "Who laid it?" "Silver Fox himself." "Good work, Timmy. All over fifty of it's yours if we win."

"God of Fire," Timmy shouted to the noisy heavens, "lend us your might!" It was an old Irish battle cry.

Reverend Larson was assigning the clutch watchers. Their job was to make sure no driver used his clutch to keep his engine from conking out once the starting line was crossed.

Silver Fox came striding up to his Reo. "Who's my watcher?"

"I'm going to watch you myself," said Reverend Larson. "One touch and you're out!"

This announcement was hailed with a great cheer; the way he was betting on himself by betting against the other entrants had heated up the notion that Silver Fox had some trick in his white thatch. Grandpa Tim's watcher was Einar Morken, a thirty-second-degree Mason who could be counted upon to stay alert for any Irish shenanigans.

Each driver was permitted a walker of his choice. The walker's main job was to help the driver keep track of his relative position in the race and to give advice and encouragement; he could either ride the running board or walk alongside, but he was not permitted to push the car, drag his feet, or handle any of the controls. Timmy was the youngest of the walkers.

The racetrack was 528 feet on Main Street, a tenth of a mile. The drivers would roll together the sixty feet from the ready line to the starting line, which they must cross in high gear. Then, in high gear all the way, they would nurse the gas flow into their engines to keep them alive while they raced to finish last.

Creamery John Olson, so called to distinguish him from Druggist John, a white flag in one hand and a red in the other, inspected the line-up from the starting line. Goofy Johnson, who had bayoneted three Huns before getting shell-shocked in the Great War, was crouched behind the town's Spanish-American War cannon, ready to touch her off to signal the official start of the race. "I packed enough gunpowder in her," Goofy shouted, "so you ain't gonna mistake her boom for no firecracker."

The band quit playing, and the crowd became silent. Creamery John's stentorian words could be heard by all the drivers and half the multitude: "Gentlemen, start your engines!"

All the cars except Grandpa Tim's Model T and Matt Waldo's Whippet were equipped with self-starters. Tim had chosen Roan, the harness maker, to be his crank man. Braced on his left leg, his left hand manipulating the choking ring, Roan, who could crack walnuts between his thumb and forefinger, spun the crank half a dozen times, and the engine vibrated into action. As their engines started, the drivers called "Ready here!" — all except Grandpa Tim, who called out: "The time to tinker and talk is past! Now may the best car finish last!"

Creamery John dropped the white flag. The cars moved forward together. Their drivers aimed to reach and hold five miles an hour as they shifted into high at the starting line. Standing on the line, Creamery John dropped the red flag to signal a fair start. Goofy touched off the fuse. The cannon's booming belch cracked the plate-glass window of Severson's dry-goods store. Fifty flashcrackers exploded over Main Street. Timmy walked alongside. Grandpa Tim's eyes were sparkling and his hands steady as he adjusted the gas and spark levers beneath the steering wheel. Only the twitching of his pointed ears betrayed his tension as he eased her back to three miles an hour.

In this race, where first was last, Doc's Stutz was out of it early. His backers groaned when he went off the throttle and the red beauty humped, coughed, sputtered, and nearly died. When he gave her gas, she spurted forward. The groans became taunts when he finished in last place nearly three hundred feet ahead of the field.

The field began to spread out. After a hundred feet, Matt's Whippet was in first place, a full length *behind* Moe's Dodge. Grandpa Tim was running in a tie for third, radiator to radiator with Silver Fox's Reo, half a length in front of the Dodge. Druggist John's Hupmobile, speeding along four lengths up front, was no threat.

Grandpa Tim was unable to get his spark down. Timmy saw the trouble. When Grandpa Tim raised the lever along the notched scale to retard the spark, the engine coughed and missed, and he had to jerk the lever down to keep Ol' Liz alive. "Your spark lever isn't giving you clean contact, Grandpa!" he called. "There's rust or dirt in the notches."

Grandpa Tim tried to clean the notches with his thumbnail. Meanwhile, he edged three feet ahead of Silver Fox into fourth place.

"I need a file! Get your mother's fingernail file from her purse. Run, Timmy! Run like the devil after souls."

Timmy was off in full sprint. He made the four hundred feet in close to fourteen seconds.

His mother was with the other wives of dignitaries in the row of seats in front of the bandstand. "Mother! Give me your fingernail file. Quick, quick!"

"My fingernail file? But I don't have one with me."

Donna was laughing at his tense urgency. "For goodness sakes, Timmy, why do you need a fingernail file?"

"Will an emery board do?" asked Aunt Clara, as cool and elegant as a swan. She was Uncle Hans's wife.

"Quick! Give it to me quick."

Her diamonds flashed in the sun as she poked into her purse. He snatched it from her and sprinted back. In the forty seconds he was gone, Grandpa Tim had fallen a full length ahead of Silver Fox, only two hundred fifty feet from the finish line.

Blowing the dirt and rust away, Grandpa Tim deftly and coolly filed the notches until the brass shone clean. Now slowly he retarded the spark. The engine settled down and held. He fell back, caught Silver Fox, and dropped steadily back toward the leaders. Silver Fox profaned the air with a mighty curse. His Reo humped under the strain of deceleration. He went to the clutch. Reverend Larson leaped from the running board to declare him out of the race. The Reo humped its last breath and died.

Now, with a hundred feet to go, Grandpa Tim challenged the leaders. He caught Hundergaard's Dodge fifty feet out and went after Matt's Whippet. Slowly, he fell back. With twenty-five feet to go, he cut the margin to half a hood. Both cars began to hump. Could either hold on under the punishment? With fifteen feet to go, Grandpa Tim shouted out: "In you, Dear Liz, I put my trust to win it all or now go bust!"

And he gave her full gas and jammed the brake to the floor.

She leaped a foot forward and came to a dead stop while Matt's Whippet rolled ahead of her. Then Grandpa Tim released the brake and gave her full gas, just in time to keep her engine from dying. She gave a final leap that carried her front wheels onto the finish line, where she died, six inches behind the Whippet's headlights.

The crowd cheered. Goofy touched off another charge. A hundred flashcrackers responded. Twenty cheering sports carried Grandpa Tim into the pool hall where his money was no good. The band struck up "Hail to the Chief," and a shout of ecstatic excitement pierced the din: "Hooray for the Fourth of July!" It came from Karen Larson.

6
The Mighty Oaks

Uncle Hans was anchor man for the Mighty Oaks of Indian Springs in the tug-of-war with the Loon Lake Lunatics for championship of the county.

Donna was squeezed between Freddy and Marilou four rows up in the stands. Over the noise, she called down: "They say it was Aunt Clara's emery board and your quickness that won the race for Grandpa Tim." Timmy touched the visor of his Beavers cap and produced the roll of bills from his back pocket. "My share of our winnings, twenty dollars." Then he shouted his plea: "I've got a good place, right at the edge of the pit, where you'll be able to see everything."

"Hey, son," his father demanded, "what are you doing gambling on a sporting event?"

"It wasn't me, it was Grandpa Tim, just a little sporting bet, five dollars at fourteen to one."

"Somebody said you marched into the pool hall as real as life."

"For Grandpa Tim, Dad. I just laid it for him. He gave me all over ten to one I could get. I got fourteen to one."

"You know you've got orders to stay out of that pool hall till you're eighteen. You're beginning to talk like a pool-hall bum. Hand that money over to me."

"But, Dad. This is mine, fair and square. Grandpa Tim . . ."

"I didn't say it wasn't yours. I said hand it over. I'll put it in your savings account when I go to the bank tomorrow."

There was no compromise in his father's eyes. His mother came in with her two bits' worth of sweet reason: "It's just for safekeeping, Timmy. Running the way you do all day, you could lose it right out of your pocket." She turned to her husband. "Timmy can keep a dollar of it for spending money."

Timmy ignored her and handed his winnings over.

"It's so dusty and dirty down there," Donna decided. "I better stay right where I am."

There was no way he could quench the humiliation burning the tops of his ears. "I don't think the judges would allow a girl down by the pit anyway." He turned away and headed for the pit.

Ed Mulligan's clean overalls were already sloshed with paste up to the rubber bands he wore below his knees. He had dug the pit — ten feet long, four feet wide, and a foot deep — in front of the flagpole. He had filled it with flour, feathers, and water and was working them into a mixture as thin as pancake batter with a long-handled hoe.

Timmy knelt to test the consistency through his fingers. Ed leaned on his hoe and took a pint from his back pocket and raised it to the sun, as if making an offering to the God of Fire, before tipping it into his mouth. Watching the Adam's apple on the old red neck, Timmy counted four big swallows before the gurgling was silenced by an explosive sigh of immense satisfaction.

"Timmy, my boy! How does it feel to ye? Is it of championship quality in your view of the matter?"

"The feathers are just right," said Timmy, testing another handful, "but I think maybe it's a little on the thin side."

"Isn't it the same I was thinkin myself? You that's young on your feet, now would you be the one to fetch me another twenty-five-pound sack of the flour that's there under the north end of the bandstand? An' the rest of the feathers while you're at it?"

In front of the bandstand, inside the rope that held back the throng, there was harsh argument going on between the teams. The Mighty Oaks were protesting the hobnailed logging boots of the Lunatics, all Finnish lumberjacks and sawyers from the tie camp and lumber mill that were Loon Lake's reason for existence. Otherwise, both teams were dressed, as the rules required, in their Sunday best, the blue serge suits that were standard wear for workingmen at church services, funerals, weddings, Saturday night social functions, and when going to the bank to pay debts or borrow money. The Oaks were wearing straw skimmer hats.

The captain and anchor man for the Lunatics, who were feared for their Finnish tempers, was Mickey Mikkelli, who was built like a stove. A foot shorter but not a pound lighter than Uncle Hans, he had to lean back and shout up to make his points. Uncle Hans was making his points loftily and simultaneously. Boiled down, Mickey's argument was that there was nothing in the rules that said you couldn't wear hobnailed boots, and Hans was countering that you wouldn't be allowed at the communion rail or on a dance floor wearing them.

Reverend Larson stepped forward and separated the contestants. "Gentlemen, gentlemen. Stand back, and we will consider this dispute in the light of what is fair to both and fun for all. That is what we are here for, to have fun on the Fourth of July. Now then, the way I look at it is, firstly, that you are all properly attired to assure fun for all as the losers are dragged through the obnoxious pit, and, secondly, that there is merit both to the argument that the rules do not specifically prohibit hobnailed boots, as well as to the argument that hobnailed boots are not generally accepted as part of Sunday-best attire. Thirdly, since there is nothing in the rules about footwear, there is equal merit to the argument that no footwear at all is required. The doctrine of fun and fair would be enhanced if all contestants took off their shoes and socks and pulled barefooted, and I so rule."

The groans and grumbles of the contestants, none of whom did anything barefooted except go to bed, were drowned by cheers and laughter from the throng as word of the ruling was passed back and around to its farthest edges.

As the Mighty Oaks took off their shoes and socks, Timmy gathered them and took them to the wives of the owners for safekeeping. "I never saw such silliness," said Aunt Clara, refusing the responsibility. "It would serve that big galoot right to have to go home and change his clothes." Timmy tied the shoelaces together and hung the shoes around his neck.

Creamery John lined the teams on either side of the pit, the lead man of each team braced exactly eight feet from its edge. The inch-and-a-half rope, knotted at two-foot intervals, was stretched over the pit to the contestants. "Gentlemen, the rules require that you maintain the grip you begin with until all members of one team are in the pit."

"We know the rules," said Mickey with his crooked grin.

The Lunatics seemed more primitive, unsoftened by the ease of town life, than the Mighty Oaks. But the confidence of the Oaks was reassuring. Roan was as massive and agile as a gorilla; Sletton could tear a tennis ball apart with his bare hands; Hundergaard had lasted nineteen minutes against Strangler Lewis; and Uncle Hans was reckoned the strongest man in the county.

"Ready, take up slack, brace, tug!"

Muscles bulged against the seams of coats. Grunts of exertion could be heard at pitside. For thirty seconds not an inch was given, but then — and the hometown crowd marked it with a mighty cheer — the Mighty Oaks began to inch the Lunatics toward the pit, now a foot, now two feet, and now more steadily, until the lead man of the Lunatics was not a foot away from the white muck. Then Mickey the Finn uttered a wild cry and called to his mates: "Now, boys, now! On the count of three, let 'em have it! A one and a two and a *three!*" Suddenly, in perfect synchronization, the Lunatics leaned forward and gave the Mighty Oaks two feet of unexpected slack. Only Uncle Hans kept his feet as the Oaks fell to their butts. The Lunatics put full power on the rope. The Oaks, three of them down and unable to find footing, were like logs in a sluice. Roan got to his feet but only in time to be pulled headfirst into the pit, where he floundered, blowing feathers from his nostrils. Sletton went in feet first, and after him Hundergaard, both struggling to keep their heads above the paste. Now Uncle Hans, unmindful of the hide being scraped from his stubborn heels, was at the brink. His mighty Viking curse of rage penetrated the howling laughter of the crowd. Still leaning with all his might against the rope, he was skidded in. Tripping over his fallen mates, he flopped into the white muck. The Lunatics, howling derision, tossed their end of the rope into the pit atop their fallen foes.

As his uncle rose a taunted and feathered clown, Timmy sprinted out of hoot range to the hotel to borrow towels for the fallen Oaks, his uncle's shoes flopping on his neck.

7

"Do it with thy might"

————◀◆▶————

The twelve o'clock whistle on the brick factory was blowing when Timmy got back with wet towels and his uncle's shoes. Looking like a sick white rooster, Uncle Hans was the only one there. Donna had gone with the others to the picnic in Druggist John Olson's big yard. Timmy had planned how he and Donna would spread a blanket under the willow tree, away from romping kids and chattering grownups . . .

What a big boob he was. The private pain of his busted hopes for Donna and the public humiliation of turning his rightful winnings over to his father could not be scrubbed away with a wet towel. Watching his uncle get the worst of the paste and feathers from his face and head, he said: "They won by trickery."

Uncle Hans nodded. "They tricked us, and they won."

"They cheated. We should have protested."

Uncle Hans shook his head. "Then they'd have had two laughs on us. The preacher's doctrine of fair and fun applied. We were fair, and they had fun."

61

"I would rather lose than win the way they did."

"I would rather win than lose the way we did."

"But right makes might," Timmy said stubbornly. The quote from "Sir Galahad" came to him: " 'My strength is as the strength of ten, Because my heart is pure.' "

His uncle's sudden smile was of sympathy, but his words were derisive. "With a pure heart, you're gonna need the strength of ten, Timmy. I've gotta get home and change clothes. Will you drive me out, Timmy?"

The chance to drive the LaSalle sedan, which had a speaking tube from the back seat to the driver, was itself a considerable temptation. Besides, watching Fat Freddy pawing around Donna would gag him . . . But . . . "The thing is, I've gotta be back for the races . . ." And to take his father into the camp of the Original Colored House of David.

"Just a few minutes out, a few minutes there, and a few minutes back. If you don't dawdle," Uncle Hans went on, "there's time for everything."

The farm, nearly a thousand acres, was about half in lake and wooded pasture and half in rolling rotations of wheat, oats, barley, and potatoes. The red hay-and-horse barn, white dairy barn, grain silo, tool and work shop, woodshed, chicken coop, pigsty, bunkhouse, and outdoor privy had been built many years before by Grandpa Nelson, who had come as a homesteader from Norway. But the three-story house — with its cupolas and huge screened porch — was the only farmhouse in the county equipped with running water, an indoor toilet, central heating, and a steam-powered laundry. It had been built and added on to by Uncle Hans and Aunt Clara. When Grandpa Nelson died, long before Timmy was born, twenty-year-old Uncle Hans took over running the farm. A few years later, he married Aunt Clara, a city girl from Fargo. She toiled not in the fields, neither did she spin, but she bossed the household and kept the books. Uncle Hans admitted he was in charge only when he stepped off the back porch in the morning.

They had no children. Their social life was a compromise between Aunt Clara's love of parties and Uncle Hans's contentment with evenings at home. They went to church every Sunday and never missed the Every Other Thursday meetings of the Indian Springs Whist Club in the church parlor.

When nothing interfered — such as a ball game — Timmy went out to the farm Every Other Thursday for supper and a ride back to town. Because Timmy was on hand to help, Uncle Hans scheduled his production of home-brewed beer for those afternoons and evenings. He would come in from the fields an hour early and clean up for the evening. Then, with Timmy's help, he would bottle the setting batch, move the new batch into the cooler to set, start a new batch, and move the bottles of the drinking batch into the cellar cooler. The job Timmy enjoyed most was syphoning the setting batch into the bottles. Every time he had to suck the tube to activate the syphon, he got a good swallow.

Today the farm was drowsing. The hired people were in town for the celebration. The horses on the shady side of the barnyard showed the life in them only by an occasional swish of their tails. The cows were browsing a distant pasture. The chickens were clucking more than scratching.

Uncle Hans stripped off his floured Sunday best in the barnyard, and Timmy sluiced him with buckets of water from the horse trough to get the paste and feathers out of his hair and ears. "Again!" he called. "And yet again."

Timmy, fascinated by his uncle's four tits, sluiced him again.

*

63

Timmy had first seen his uncle's four tits on an Every Other Thursday when he was fourteen, after his confirmation in church. Then, for the first time, Uncle Hans poured a small glass of beer for him. Timmy raised the glass to admire its amber clarity before taking his first swig and smacking his lips.

"I suppose *he* gives you a taste now and then of that rotgut moonshine he's always swilling."

"Just a sip now and then out of the tin cup. But I shouldn't be telling. Grandpa Tim says my dad will raise holy hell if he ever finds out."

Uncle Hans nodded in rare agreement. "The same here. People can't get it through their heads that a boy is better off learning the taste and pleasure of drink with the menfolk of his family than sneaking it with the pool-hall bums."

"Grandpa Tim has ancestral memory, you know," Timmy found the nerve to say.

"He's got *what?*"

Timmy told him about his Irishness and the ability of his grandpa to recall the past, back to the Firbolgs themselves.

Uncle Hans snorted Norwegian contempt not for Grandpa Tim's claim to ancestral memory but for the sneaky and tame lives it conjured, compared with the glorious adventures of their ancestral Vikings. "Shoot, boy, that's just like all Irish bullshit — it's thin and it stinks of rotgut moonshine. Us Vikings was the best fighters in the history of the world. We didn't need any of your fancy dwarfs and tricky magic to steal sheep from the poor. We went roaring in with our swords and shields, and there was nobody anywhere in the world that could stand up against us."

"Do we — the Nelsons — do we have it, too? Ancestral memory? Do some of us — do you? — have the power to remember way back when we were Vikings?"

64

"Shoot, boy! Ancestral memory is as common among us Nelsons as true blue eyes, six-foot men, and beautiful womenfolk. Now look here, I'll show you something you won't find on any Irishman that ever lived." He undid the buttons of his shirt and of the B.V.D.'s beneath to expose the white mountain of his belly. There, peeping up from tufts of light brown hair below the barrel of chest and on either side of his bellybutton, was an extra pair of tiny red nipples.

"I'll be dinged!" said Timmy.

"You're darn tootin you'll be dinged. Them there are an extra set of tits, no more use to me than my regular ones, but they go back hundreds and thousands of years to when us humans had as many tits as cows, long before those dwarf ancestors your famous Irish grandpa is braggin about was ever born. These extra tits," he went on, buttoning up, "is proof I know what the hell I'm talkin about when I tell you stories about the olden days when we was the terrors of the sea and the scourge of the land. Up to now, before you was confirmed in the church and got your first long pants suit for Sunday wear, I've held back from telling you about the ways we used to do things back in the Viking days, because — well, son, the facts of life is involved, and they ain't, not by any means, the kind of stories I'd tell to a kid who didn't have his long pants suit for Sundays and who couldn't drink a glass of beer without puking."

Uncle Hans seemed to see in his glass, as if it were a telescope into the past, the long-lost respectability of pillage, plunder, and rape. "Tell you the truth of it, we didn't amount to diddly-shit as Vikings after we turned Christian."

"You know, Grandpa Tim says it was the same with my Irish ancestors. In olden days, we worshiped the God of Fire by day and the White Goddess by night. One was for strength and courage out there against your enemies and the wild beasts, and the other for the love and safety of your home and family. After we turned Christian, we never did amount to much as a clan. He said the Golden Rule did us in."

"But don't get the idea that Christianity isn't the best religion there is, nor that being a Lutheran isn't the best kind of Christianity there is," Uncle Hans said sternly. "Or you'll have the whole damn town on our necks. I'm not going to tell you another family secret unless you promise to keep it to yourself, until maybe you got a son or nephew of your own you want to pass it on to, like I'm doing to you. If it ever got to Reverend Larson that I'm preaching against Christianity, he would kick me and your Aunt Clara right out of the Whist Club. There's already talk against us for sticking up for Darrow against Bryan in the Monkey Case and for her saying that if Jesus Christ came to a church social she would ask him for a dance. Another thing, don't you go blabbin around about my four tits. Good God Almighty! If Silver Fox Hanson knew I had four tits, he'd want to put me up as a side show and charge a dollar to see them."

"You never heard me blabbin 'bout anything, did you? Grandpa Tim told me if I ever snitched about the stories he was telling me about when we worshiped the God of Fire and the White Goddess. . ." Timmy broke off, afraid he had already invoked the terrible curse.

"He'd do what?" Uncle Hans demanded. "I showed you my four tits, didn't I?"

"He said my ears would lop over, my hair would turn green, and my pecker would shrivel away."

Uncle Hans considered the punishment and nodded. "I wouldn't take any chances if I was you, son. But I can take you back further on the Nelson side than any Irishman that ever lived could take you on his side." He tapped the side of his belly. "And I've got four tits to prove it."

Together they had built a two-foot replica of the original longboat of Sigurd the Joyous, as Uncle Hans remembered it. The pictures Timmy brought from the library were remarkably accurate, Uncle Hans said, but many details were missing or wrong. As they cut and sanded and polished each piece and fitted the rigging, Uncle Hans described life aboard the boat on raids and the great adventures they had under Sigurd the Joyous. "The main thing Sigurd taught us was that, by God, if you got something to do, do it *hard,* whether it's working or having fun, laughing or crying, fighting or praying, whatever it is, if you're gonna do it, do it, by God! If you got to do it, don't be sighing and moaning about your bad luck or that you got more than you can do or that you're being put upon, poor you, the hell with all that, do it! And while you're doing it, have fun doing it. When you get up in the morning and breathe the air, you're *alive.* You got a *day* ahead of you."

" 'Whatsoever thy hand findeth to do, do it with thy might,' " Timmy offered. "That's from Ecclesiastes."

"Damned if I thought they taught you stuff like that reading for the minister."

"That wasn't required. I found that and learned it on my own."

*

Now, while Uncle Hans was upstairs putting on his second-best suit, Timmy went into the parlor to admire again their longboat. It had become a community pride — first displayed in a glass case in the school, then at the county fair, now on the fireplace mantle.

The figurehead was a demon woman with flowing hair of gold and spearheads for nipples on her thrusting breasts. With her in the lead, who could fear the unknown?

Uncle Hans laid out a spread of cold chicken and potato salad, with home-brew for himself and buttermilk for Timmy.

"You've got a race to run and a ball game to play in the hot sun."

Timmy nodded acceptance of the buttermilk. "Against the Original Colored House of David," he said in the awe of things to come.

Being with his uncle had renewed in him the confidence that he was a special Somebody from long lines of Somebodies, destined to venture far and boldly into that big world out there. Meanwhile . . . "Let's get going," he said.

8

The White Doctor

———◄◆►———

The band was playing, the children's races had started, and the tide of the multitude was still coming in. There were still twenty minutes of minor races and events before the hundred-yard dash to determine the Fastest Human. The family was there in the choice section reserved for Celebration Officials, Visiting Dignitaries, and Honored Guests. Donna was with Freddy and others of the Fast Set in the top row. Uncle Hans doffed his skimmer in response to the sarcastic cheers and laughter as he made his way to his place beside Aunt Clara. She gave him a hug and a kiss to welcome him back to the society of noncontestants.

Timmy, a uniformed contestant, looked up to Donna. She was laughing at Freddy's chant:

> *She doesn't drink,*
> *She doesn't pet,*
> *She hasn't been*
> *To college yet.*

When she saw him, he touched the 17 on his back. She smiled vaguely.

He had work to do. "Dad! Will you come now?"

His father, wiping strawberry ice cream from a granddaughter's white pleated blouse, had forgotten.

"The House of David guy I told you about? Your promise? The infected hand?"

"Dammit, son, don't say I promised what I maybe might have said we'll see about."

Timmy stood mute. His mother saw without knowing. "Whatever it is," she told her husband, "he needs it."

He made the best of it with a joke: "I'm just a tough ham, but my sugar cured me." He got up and worked his way down. "Excuse me, folks, I've got to make a bedside call."

"I'll get your bag from the Chandler," Timmy said and ran ahead.

The House was in uniform, still lolling in the deep shade of their camp, looking out upon these North Country goings on.

"Here he be now," called Pops. "I tol' you this boy do what he say."

"This is my father," Timmy said proudly. "Doctor Nelson."

No one offered to shake hands. "Yes, sir, Doctor, much obliged you comin. He ovah here."

Merv, suited up, was leaning against the tree by the embers of the fire in which Timmy's tin pail was steaming. He held his hand up. "Tain't much. This soakin took some a the soreness out."

The doctor crouched beside him, looked, felt, squeezed. "Nothing to fool around with. President Coolidge's son died of an infection that started out no worse than this."

He opened his bag and worked quickly and surely, lancing

and cleansing the infection, dosing it with disinfectant, bandaging it firmly and neatly. "Leave this on until tomorrow morning. Then soak it an hour or two in hot salt water. I'm going to leave you this bandage roll and bottle of medicine to paint it with. Keep it clean. Ought to clear up in a day or two. Meantime, you rest it."

"I won't need no help today," said Bofey.

Pops was opening a leather pouch heavy with silver and bills. "Much obliged, Doctor. How much we owe you?"

"No charge for a case like this."

"We like to pay."

The white doctor looked around the camp and shook his head. "I don't charge Indians or darkies for professional services." He picked up his bag and strode away.

"Shit," said William P. Tetley II.

"That's what I say, too," Timmy said, looking after the white doctor. "Shit."

"Thas okay, son," said Pops, "you fetched 'im, like you said."

"I'll be back after the game, to see about your moonshine," Timmy said. "Now I gotta go run for Fastest Human of Becker County."

9

Snorry Snot Rag's Revenge

Timmy got back in time to watch the finals of the rolling-pin-throwing contest in which the four division winners were competing. Minnie, winner of the Old Maids Over Forty Division, didn't stand a chance for the championship against Ugly Hilda, but her toss of 87 feet was better than both Married Ladies Under Forty and Married Ladies Over Forty. Ugly Hilda, so known by everyone but by no one to her face, was the headmistress at the Orphans' Home. Her throw of 138 feet cleared second base and broke the old record by nearly 30 feet. Timmy felt sorry for the poor kids in her charge.

He got his baseball spikes out of the iron strongbox beside the Beavers' bench and laced them on. The race was one hundred yards along the left-field foul line.

Creamery John Olson called the event through his huge megaphone, first to the left then to the right. Twelve entrants responded. Creamery John ordered that the event be run in two heats of six each, with the first three in each heat competing in the final race for Fastest Human of the County.

Timmy knew that no one could beat him. The only two trained runners were high-school sprinters from Detroit Lakes and Big Toad Springs, whom he had beaten during the track season; the others were an assortment of farm boys and town sports, two of whom were charging themselves with nips from a pint of moonshine.

Timmy drew the first heat and didn't bother with a sprinter's crouch. He was out front after twenty yards and coasted in. The other entrants were so badly beaten that all dropped out of further competition. In the finals it was Timmy against the two sprinters, who had run a close one-two in the second heat.

He went into the crouch, lifted his tail on set, and was off with the others in a perfect start. Running on the inside, he had a one-yard lead and the race in the bag after forty yards. Suddenly a giant firecracker exploded five yards ahead of him, another behind him, another in front of him. He stopped, swerved, leaped to his left. Now ten yards behind, he dug in again but could do no better than pick up a few yards and finish a poor third.

In the turmoil around the finish line, the judges were debating whether to declare the results official or order a rerun of the heat. The noise of the crowd was mostly laughter. "Funniest thing I ever saw," he heard a sport, "that smart-aleck kid dodging firecrackers like a Hun in no man's land."

Into the cluster around Reverend Larson burst Karen, tears coursing down her angry face. "It was Snorry Snot Rag and his gang. They did it to get even. You can't let 'em, Dad. You *can't!*"

"It wasn't fair," said the second-place runner. "I'll run it over."

"It just happened," said the winner. "I coulda been the one it happened to."

Reverend Larson knelt beside his daughter and heard her story. Then he called Timmy and shook his hand. "I'm proud of you, Timmy. You deserved to win." Then to the judges: "It's the Fourth of July, and the rule of fun supersedes the rule of fair. The results are official. I will make the announcement to the crowd." He took Creamery John's megaphone to the pitcher's mound and waited until the crowd hushed.

"The race for Fastest Human of Becker County was marred by malicious interference on the part of a gang of young ruffians whose parents shall hear from me from the pulpit. However, we have decided to let the results stand as official. In doing so, it behooves us all to contemplate these words from Holy Scripture: 'I returned and saw under the sun that the race is not to the swift, nor the battle to the strong, neither yet bread to the wise, nor riches to men of understanding, nor yet favor to men of skill, but time and chance happeneth to them all.' "

"Oh, Timmy," said Karen.

He put his hand on her shoulder and held her against his side. "If your heart is pure, you need the strength of ten," he told her.

"Oh, no, Timmy. Never, never! Right always conquers might . . . in the end," she added. "It always does in the end."

"The day isn't over yet," Timmy said, more to himself than to her, for she was scampering away to keep watch on Ed's generosity with his pocketful of coins.

Grandpa Tim and Uncle Hans came to him with just what he needed — a paper cup of ice-cold lemonade.

"It's a bit of rest ye'll be needin now," said Grandpa Tim.

"And forget about getting cheated out of the championship," said Uncle Hans, leading the way to the privacy of the LaSalle. The three of them were alone together for the first time. The memory of who he was did more to cool Timmy down than the lemonade.

10
The Game

The game was scheduled to start at 2:30 with the playing and singing of "The Star-Spangled Banner." At two o'clock sharp the Beavers got the field for fifteen minutes of infield drill and fungoes to the outfield. Big Ole Olafson, the Beavers' catcher and field manager, hit the grounders for the infield drill. Timmy caught for him. He was proud of the professional ritual of their infield drill. Big Ole, now coming on to forty, had played professional ball with the Minneapolis Millers in the American Association, just one step below major-league baseball itself. Ole had had major-league power at the plate and defensive skill behind it, but not enough speed to take the step up.

Timmy didn't muff a throw, and he threw as sharp and hard as any of the men playing infield. The drill concluded with grounders that the infielders charged and threw home; Timmy tossed simulated bunts at their feet and took their snap throws back. The crowd applauded their precision.

The House drill made the Beavers look like old people waltzing. Their acrobatic pepper game had the crowd marveling out loud. Keeping half a dozen balls in play, they caught and flipped them in crazy patterns from behind their backs, between their legs, and from off their heels and biceps. Their runty shortstop, juggling three balls, fielded the batted ball, flipped it between his legs back to the batter, and kept on juggling the other three.

"That's Scrap Iron Davis," Big Ole said. "I saw him play against the Slaughterhouse Nine in Fargo last year, best shortstop I ever saw, and a switch hitter that hits nothing but line drives. And that outfielder out there, that's Busy Ike Miller. Him and Scrap Iron and that big catcher . . ."

"That's Mr. Tetley," Timmy supplied. "I was in their camp this morning."

". . . and that pitcher of theirs, Both Hands Wilbur — they'd all be in the majors if it wasn't for the color line."

Timmy was on the bench between Big Ole and Billy Herfendahl, the Beavers' left-handed starting pitcher.

"You'll see some crazy baseball, once they get a safe lead," Big Ole went on. "You can't believe the tricks they can do."

"Don't we have a chance?" Timmy asked.

"We got sticks in our hands, same as them, Timmy."

Bofey began his warm-up. "He's throwing lefty today," Big Ole said. "Against Pelican Rapids two years ago, I seen him throw the first game righty and the second game lefty. He throws mostly fast balls righty an' mostly curves and dipsy-doodle stuff lefty."

"He don't throw as hard as me," said Billy Herfendahl.

Watching him throw, Timmy felt the rise of cowardice in his belly. If he got a chance to hit, how would he stand up there against a pitcher of major-league caliber? Would he cringe against the fast ball, step back against a curve in on him? "Think you'll have to call on me today, Ole?" he asked.

"Expect I will, sooner or later, dependin on the way it

goes." Ole looked at him and smiled. "You got the guts to stand up to Lefty, you can stand up to this Bofey man if I need to call on you. Keep in mind, Timmy, that this Bofey man doesn't waste no pitches. He won't waste a pitch knockin you down. He'll throw strikes. Go up there an swing hard."

At 2:30, Reverend Larson took the megaphone out to the pitcher's mound. "We will now stand while the town band and the church choir lead us in the singing of our National Anthem. Now, folks, the Fourth of July is more than a day of fun and sports. It is also a day for meditation upon the meaning of the Flag of the United States of America and the Republic for which it stands. As you sing our anthem, I remind you that it is not a statement that we can take for granted, but a question. Yes, a question, folks. It begins with a question: 'O say, can you see?' Is our flag still there? And it ends with a question: 'Does that star-spangled banner yet wave o'er the land of the free and the home of the brave?' Those are questions, folks — not statements we can take for granted. As you sing, let each of you ask in your heart if our flag and all it stands for is still there. Let each of you answer from your heart what you are doing to make this the land of the free and the home of the brave!"

In the silence, a clear bugle over the roll of the drums asked the first question, and then the full band, the choir, and the multitude burst into an affirmative response that seemed to stop time itself.

Big Ole and Pops were summoned to home plate to hear Reverend Larson, who would umpire behind the plate, and Creamery John, who would umpire the bases, review the ground rules. Then Reverend Larson evoked another thunderous response from the crowd: "Play ball!"

For the first four innings it was a tensely scoreless game. Billy Herfendahl was at his wildest left-handed best, putting all the mustard he had on every pitch. He intimidated every batter. None could stand firm against his awful speed and wildness. He walked two and struck out two. The Beavers routinely handled the grounders and fly balls. In the third inning, Scrap Iron Davis poked a sharp single to the opposite field and stole second, but Billy fanned Mr. Tetley himself, after twice forcing his dignity to the dust.

Pops strode forth from the House bench. "Umps," he said, "that man out there, he either crazy wild or he trying to kill my players. He don't quit, we got ways to take care a him."

"I assure you that he's crazy wild," the Reverend replied, "and that he is doing his level best to throw strikes."

"Your assurance is of no comfort to us," Mr. Tetley said. "In fact, it increases our apprehension."

"Billy," the man of God called out to the pitcher, "I have given these gentlemen my assurance that you have not, are not, and will not throw at their batters and that if I even suspect you of throwing at them, you are . . ." His dramatic arm thrust finished the sentence and let Billy and the crowd know that he meant business. The crowd snarled its disapproval of this intimidation of its hero.

His delivery as easy and limber as the flick of a buggy whip, Bofey was astounding the Beaver batters with his left-handed dipsy curves and sudden shoots. His curve would break sharp and quick into right-handed batters, or loop out toward first base, hover like a chicken hawk, and come shooting down into Mr. Tetley's big mitt for a gentle strike. Now and again, Bofey would hum a fast ball past a curve-expectant batter. Some of the fast balls tailed up, some down, some in, some out.

Big Ole, wise in the ways of deception, appealed to Reverend Larson: "You know as well as I do, Reverend, that those ain't no natural pitches."

"There's something devilish about them," the man of God admitted, "but what?" He called for the ball, examined it, and showed its untampered purity to Big Ole.

"It don't act like a spitter or a Vaseline ball — more on the order of a mud ball or a emery ball, but I ain't never seen any doctorin that would give it a break both so wide an so sudden at the same time."

"Until we determine otherwise, Ole, we must act on the assumption that this man has powers over a baseball that are undreamt of in our pitching philosophy." He tossed the ball back to Bofey. "Fun and fair," he kept muttering as he called the unholy strikes. "Fun and fair."

After the third scoreless inning, the hopes of the crowd for a close contest rose. If only Billy could continue to mow down the clever strangers, the Beavers might somehow become unbaffled and win the game. Every pitch became an *oh* or an *ah* and every batted ball a hope or an anxiety. So it went into, but not through, the fifth inning. Billy struck out the first batter on six pitches and walked the next two on twelve more. Then Little Ole, the Beaver second baseman, made a sprinting leap to catch a line drive up the middle and snapped a throw to second base to double up the runner, but Maynard, the shortstop, still gaping his admiration of the catch, failed to cover second. The House runners kept running, one to score and the other to third base.

Billy, cursing his luck and Maynard's apology, threw twelve consecutive balls, forcing in another run and loading the bases. Now, aiming the ball down the middle, he threw a strike that Mr. Tetley popped far over the right-field fence for a home run. Four more runs made it a nigh hopeless 6 to 0.

Timmy, up and down on the bench, was making sure that Big Ole knew he was there and ready.

Big Ole called time and walked out to inspect the tamed

left-hander, who now slumped like a lathered plow horse at the end of a hot day in the field. On his way, he called to the bench: "Timmy! Get Trigger warmed up." Trygve Jacobson was nearly as old as Reverend Larson himself. As Timmy trotted by, he heard his father's voice: "Hurry up and get in the game, son. The girls are burning up in this hot sun."

Trigger had good control and a roundhouse curve, but his fast ball was only a memory of nineteen aught four, when he had pitched an undefeated season for St. Olaf College. Timmy could handle his best stuff with his fielder's glove.

Trigger's first batter was Scrap Iron. He slammed the first pitch into left center field and took off the wrong way for third base on his twinkling bandy legs. Mistaking the shrieks of the crowd and the yells of his teammates for applause, he doffed his cap in acknowledgment and slid safe into third base. Pops stepped out of the coaching box to turn him around and head him back the way he had come. Slapping his head for the dunce he was, Scrap Iron headed back to home plate, and dug in for first. Little Ole made a perfect relay to throw him out at first base by half a step. It took the shrieking crowd a few moments to realize that they had seen a batter with a sure triple thrown out at first base. Their shrieks became laughter. With the game in the bag, the House was about to replace the excitement of an even contest with entertainment from its bag of tricks.

After Bofey again set the Beavers down one-two-three, the House batters put on a dazzling bunt-and-run show. The first batter up bunted down the first-base line. Trigger made a game effort to get over to field it, but the runner easily beat his throw to first. The runner was off to second with the next pitch, and the batter bunted toward the pitcher's mound. Old Trig fielded it cleanly and wheeled to throw to second but much too late to beat the runner. With both runners off with the pitch, the next batter bunted down the third-base line. Trig's old right leg crumbled under him as he braced to throw to first, and the bases were loaded. All three runners taunted Trigger with big leads, and the Pin Wheel spun again as they took off with the next pitch, bunted down the first-base line. Both Trigger and Chuck Stevenson, the first baseman, charged this one and collided and went down together as the runner from third scampered home. With the bases still loaded, the next batter dropped a bunt in front of the plate. This time Old Trig coming in for the dribbler was hit by Big Ole going out and went down under him.

Timmy darted out to help Reverend Larson get Trigger to his feet. The crowd sensed that the old competitor had gone down on the last play he would ever make. The band struck up "For He's a Jolly Good Fellow," and the crowd stood and sang its farewell tribute as Reverend Larson and Timmy walked Old Trig off the field. "They were too quick for me," Trigger muttered. Big Ole said, "It's up to you now, Timmy."

He got his glove and strode to the mound. He was greeted by the crowd as another butt for the tricks of the black demons. The bases were still loaded. As he made his warm-up throws, Timmy saw the vulnerability of the Pin Wheel. He called Big Ole and the infielders to the mound to give them their parts. "The key guy is you," he told Little Ole. "Start your count when I give Ole the nod for the sign. Break for the bag on three, take my throw on four. If the runner comes back, tag him and fire to first. If he keeps going, fire home to Ole."

They nodded their understanding. "It might work," Big Ole said.

Timmy looked in at Big Ole's sign, nodded, and went to

set position. On his count of three he whirled and threw the ball over second base. Little Ole was there on four and swept the returning runner with a tag — "Out!" He threw to Chuck, who put the ball on the runner diving back to first — "Out!"

Timmy had engineered a double play without throwing a pitch. Along with its cheers for him, the crowd hooted the House runners, caught in their own device.

The House, now leading 8 to 0, opened a new bag of tricks. The first Beaver batter hit a sharp one-hop grounder to the shortstop. Instead of throwing to first, Scrap Iron tossed the ball through his legs to the second baseman, who tossed it behind his back to first, still in time to catch the Beaver runner. The next batter raised a fly ball to center. Busy Ike, playing close behind second, turned his back on the ball and raced into center. Instead of turning to catch it, he kept running and caught it in his back pocket. Big Ole and Timmy argued that, pretty though it was, it was an illegal catch. "Fun and fair," said the Reverend, and confirmed the out.

In his turn at bat, Timmy pushed a bunt down the first-base line. Mr. Tetley scrambled after it and made a quick throw to first, but the speed of the rightful Fastest Human of the County beat it out for the first Beaver hit of the game. Standing nonchalantly with a safe lead, Timmy took off with the pitch and slid into second, safe under the hard throw. Then Chuck Stevenson, the lead-off batter, got the end of the bat on a descending curve and blooped it into short right field. Timmy rounded third and sprinted for home. In the dust under Mr. Tetley's big mitt he laughed his joy to see Reverend Larson's palms-down blessing that he was safe with the first Beaver run of the game.

The game took another turn. The House, having entertained with its tricks, now played to finish the game as quickly and mercifully as possible. Bofey didn't waste a pitch. Only Big Ole got a hold of one — a drive high and far over the left-field fence into Tillie Johnson's front yard.

In his three innings on the mound, Timmy had good control on his entire assortment of pitches and deliveries — overarm, sidearm, and underarm. He struck out two, walked none, and gave up singles to four batters, none of whom got home. The Beavers, responding to his poise and leadership, played good ball behind him. They came in for their last at-bats in the ninth to standing applause. They had made a game of it anyway, 8 to 2, and there was talk in the stands that they might have had a chance if Timmy Nelson had been brought in before Billy dished up that disastrous grand-slam home run in the fifth.

*

She was gone. The place she had graced was just a bare pine board. They were all gone except Uncle Hans and Aunt Clara.

"The girls were hot and fussing, and your dad took them home," Aunt Clara called down to his bleak face.

Had she seen his pick-off play? Had she seen him beat out the bunt and steal second and come all the way around to score on the weak hit to right? Had she seen him strike out Busy Ike? "When did they go?"

"Oh, half an hour or so ago."

But Uncle Hans understood. "They saw you steal second and score the first run. That's all they waited for, to see you play. Baseball doesn't mean anything to them."

"They're all up at your house now, for four o'clock coffee. You come with us now," said Aunt Clara.

He shook his head. "I've got some things to do." He waved

so long and turned away and bumped into Grandpa Tim, whose pale blue eyes were bleared with moonshine and whose pale depot face was flushed with sunshine.

"Timmy, my boy, it's you that's the hero of the day, and never you mind the flightiness of girls nor the evil firecracker that took away your championship, entitled to both as you are."

"Grandpa, you've gotta help me with something."

"Isn't that what I'm here for, boy? Snap your fingers an' it's as good as done."

"Get Silver Fox to bring a jug of moonshine to the House camp over there. They've got the money."

"I'll see to that," said Grandpa Tim. "Them boys is entitled to light up on the Fourth same as anybody else."

"But at the white man's price. Not the Indian price."

"I hadn't thought he would spring the Indian price on them, but now ye mention it, he would. Sept now ye mention it, forewarned as I am, he won't."

"Is one jug enough for all of 'em?"

"How many they be?"

"Twelve plus Ol' Dan is thirteen."

"It's a taste."

"Make it two jugs."

"Two jugs it is, an' I'll fetch it myself in Ol' Liz."

"I'll go tell them now. I'll wait for you there."

"It is fitting," said Grandpa Tim out of some ancient insight, "that, like Cuchulain himself, you meet the enemy as friends after the battle."

"At the white man's price," Timmy called after him.

11

The White Crow

That morning he had fearfully entered the camp of the House. Now he strode across the ball field into the oak grove with assurance. Most of them were stripping off their uniforms to wash and douse away the dust and sweat and to change into the easy clothes of the road. "Here come de boy wit de smarts." "Hey, you showed us some good wheels out there." "Man, he come near makin a *game* out've it." "Son," said Mr. Tetley, "you may quote me as saying that you beat a good throw into second."

He basked in their acceptance of him. "Just glad you guys eased up and didn't make monkeys out of us all the way."

Suddenly there was the freeze of hush in the camp. Timmy looked where they were looking. A white stranger was approaching. It was Druggist John, coming from his car, walking awkwardly with a long fat watermelon under each arm.

"Here come Ol' Massa wit de sundown money." "Count it *twice*, Pops." "He totin our totin to us." "He knows there

86

is nothing we darkies enjoy more at the end of a hot day in the fields than a watermelon feast."

Pops went forth to meet him at the edge of the camp, and Timmy found himself stepping to his side.

"From what I hear," Druggist John said with his habitual heartiness, "you boys like watermelon, and these are still ice cold. We sold nearly a hundred of them today at a nickel a cut."

"Much obliged," Pops said and led the way out of the sunshine into the deep shade of the camp. Druggist John peered around as uncertainly as a blundering missionary. He almost stumbled into the embers. Timmy relieved him of one watermelon and took the white man's arm — "This way, Mr. Olson" — and guided him to the tailgate, now the counting table. The players edged around to watch the ritual. Druggist John took the leather pouch from the pocket of his seersucker coat. "You boys put on a great performance," he said in ceremonial terms, "and greatly deserve your victory and the monetary emolument to which it entitles you."

"Monetary emolument," Mr. Tetley was heard to say in ritualistic response, and there were murmurs of "Yes, yes! Oh, yes!"

"You'll find it all here, the two hundred as per our prior agreement," Druggist John said, taking the bills from the pouch.

"As per our prior agreement," Mr. Tetley responded, and the others sounded their affirmatives.

"Check," said Pops, gathering the money into a canvas bag for deposit in the safe in the Packard.

"The monetary emolument to which we are entitled as per our prior agreement," said Mr. Tetley.

Timmy escorted Druggist John out into the sunshine. "There's one other thing," he said.

"What would that be, Timmy?"

"Tonight at the fireworks, are these guys going to be welcome guests?"

"Why, of course, since there's no charge anyway." But then Timmy's question struck him. "Not to mingle with the folks, of course. That wouldn't be proper."

"On the stockyard roof?" Timmy said with cold contempt. "With the Indians?"

"We've got likkered-up sports here from three counties, don't you see, Timmy? We can't take a chance on any trouble from them that don't take it kindly for darkies to socialize with white folks."

"So the Indian rule applies?"

"It's got to be that way. Come on, Timmy, I'll give you a ride back to town."

From the edge of the shade, Pops spoke up: "He gonna stay help us eat up that watermelon."

Ol' Dan was building up the fire and placing stones around it to serve as props for a grill. "We gonna barbecue us a spring chicken for each. You wanna have one?"

"I sure do," said Timmy.

"An' beans an' rice an' everything nice?"

"You bet your boots."

Again there was a hush in the camp. This time it was a skinny old white man getting out of an old Model T. Timmy jumped up and shouted: "That's my Grandpa Tim, with the moonshine you guys asked me to get for you."

Busy Ike led the charge upon Grandpa Tim. "Whiskey man, Whiskey man! Where you got the whiskey, man?"

With a forefinger hooked in the ring neck of each jug, Grandpa Tim raised them in greeting and benediction. "For those who choose to pay the freight, I bring good booze to celebrate, With song and mirth our country's birth. Here's mud in your eye on the Fourth of July."

With whoops and hollers, the House hoisted the old man and his precious burden to its shoulders and carried them into its camp. Tin cups appeared like bubbles. And a cup for Grandpa Tim. "And Timothy, is he of drinking age?" asked Mr. Tetley. Grandpa Tim put it firmly: "He gets a taste."

The northern moonshine was judged to be as good as the white lightning of their hills of home. Grandpa Tim acknowledged their compliments. "It lightens each step and brightens each day, Makes the old feel young and the young feel gay."

"Seven dollars a jug. He didn't let Silver Fox stick us with the Indian price," said Timmy.

Mr. Tetley sipped and nodded his appreciation. "While there is no rational basis for it, the fact that we are not being charged the Indian price seems to improve the flavor of this rotgut."

Timmy raised his cup to Both Hands Wilbur. "When you going to teach me that tricky in-shoot pitch of yours?"

"Trick pitches is for ol' men to keep goin. You don' need no trick pitches, that arm of your'n. You don' need halfa what you throw. You throwin too much arm, not enough body. You gotta learn come down with your weight. Come down like this — pow — not standin up throwin with oney your arm."

"You could teach me."

Bofey raised his eyes. "I could teach you."

"Now, Timmy my boy," said Grandpa Tim. "They're expecting us at your house."

Timmy finished his taste. In its fire was born the crazy notion that he might just find a way to hit the road with them. "Tell 'em I'll be along in a little while."

Busy Ike was chording and picking a twelve-string guitar, his back against a tree, shouting the "Kansas City Blues":

Wish I was a catfish swimmin in the sea
And have some pretty momma fish after me.

She done moved, she done moved,
She done moved to Kansas City, honey baby,
Where they don' want you.

Walking on Broadway lookin down Beale
Lookin for the gal that they call The Seal.

She done moved, she done moved,
She done moved to Kansas City, honey baby,
Where they don' want you.

Timmy found a place between Pops and Mr. Tetley where they could keep an eye on Dan's eye on the chicken. "Where you guys goin from here?"

"We gonna make camp near a little town just across the Red River in North Dakota, get ready for a big double-header with the Slaughterhouse Nine in Fargo on Sunday. Then we heads west, playin four, five games on the way, till Sunday week we got a game in a good-sized town name of Valley City, then on west again, two weeks more, till we got another big double-header, two hundred a game, with them crazy bettin cowboy people in Mandan."

"Means you've got thirteen or fourteen games 'tween now and when you get to Mandan?"

"Sumpin like that."

"Till Merv's arm comes around, you're going to be short-handed," Timmy said.

Pops nodded. "Specially wif Bofey's right arm botherin

him. Moon kin pitch us ovah the small-town teams, but those double-headers . . ."

"Don' worry 'bout me none," Merv spoke up. "I gonna be out there earnin my shares of the take."

"I wouldn't expect a full share," Timmy said clearly.

They looked at him. *They looked at him.* They looked at him.

"What you do for us, boy?" Pops asked at last.

"Help around the camp. Help with the fishing. I know how to catch every kind of fish they got in the rivers and lakes in this part of the country."

Now he tasted the last few drops in his cup and waited for its courage. "Fact is, I could take a turn on the mound against most town teams round here. I could bunt and run that Pin Wheel of yours. Bofey could be teaching me some pitching."

Pops smiled and shook his head. "Be dogged. You know we can't carry no white boy on a colored team."

"His proposition is not entirely without merit," said Mr. Tetley. "When we bring Moon in from right field to pitch, we're gonna be short somewhere. Suppose somebody else gets hurt?"

"No question," said Scrap Iron, "he got the good wheels for our style game."

"I could put stove black on my face and arms," Timmy offered.

"And paint you mouf white like Eddie Cantor?" Pops said through their laughter. "Coon, coon, coon."

"What I have been cogitating," said Mr. Tetley, "is the possibility of playing him as an albino — a white coon, you might say. We were talking this morning how he looks just like that albino dog of his."

Now the entire House had gathered around, grinning and cackling the fun of it. "He could pass. He could pass," they agreed.

"What we gonna do 'bout that straight tan hair?" Busy Ike asked. "The only albino I seen had white kinky hair."

"We shave his head," said Scrap Iron. "Some a them albinos, they got no hair anywhere."

"His way a talkin give him away," said Pops.

"We make a deefy outta him," said Busy Ike. "That be his specialty. We talk to him oney by signs. He get em goofy all a time."

"It would certainly add a new dimension of comedy to our performance," Mr. Tetley remarked.

"He keep getting the sign wrong. Get the take sign, he swing. Get the hit-away sign, he bunt."

"Me'n him bofe run the wrong way," Scrap Iron put in.

"A new dimension of comedy," Mr. Tetley repeated.

"Speedy Deefy, the White Coon," said Busy Ike.

"I don' go fur dat white coon shit," said Ol' Dan, turning the chickens.

"There is this white comedy team, the Two Black Crows," said Mr. Tetley. "We could bill him as the White Crow."

"Speedy Deefy, the White Crow. Now we *got* it. Hone that razor a your'n, Dan, we shave his head."

Timmy laughed with the joy of it. He could see himself there. He could do it. He could see it happening as clearly as he could see the past.

But Pops raised a hand. "What your father, that doctor man, what he say 'bout his fine son runnin off ta play ball with these darkies, like he says?"

Pops was right. "That's too loony to discuss," his father would say.

Timmy felt the rage rising in him. "Damn him!" He pounded his right fist into the palm of his left hand. "Damn them!" Them? Yes, them! He saw in the after-flash of his anger that it was *them*, the whole damn town — everybody in it; not everybody, not Grandpa Tim, not Uncle Hans, not Karen . . .

"I could tell them I'm going fishing for a few weeks, up to a cabin near Ely where a friend of mine goes with his family," Timmy said desperately. "I can figure something out. The hell with them. The *hell* with them." He took another taste. "Hone your razor, Dan. I'm going to be your white crow!"

Pops stood up, the stern chieftain again. "Oney way we take 'im, he gotta get his say-so from his parents. That is the *oney* way. Some a the stories go 'round 'bout us up here, they have every sheriff they got out runnin us for kidnappin, if his parents they send out the call where is he." This silenced them. "And we got to have it in writin, so I got it in the safe all times."

So quickly was the joyous fantasy dispelled. There was no chance he could get it in writing.

"Who say he can't get it?" Busy Ike demanded and turned to Timmy. "Can you get it, boy?"

"In writing?" Mr. Tetley added.

"I'll try." He got up. "I'll go talk to him, see what I can do. But —" He shook his head disconsolately.

"You got a chicken here to eat," said Ol' Dan. "Things look better you got somethin in you to go on."

"That grandpa of yours, who negotiated the booze at the white man's price, you and he are pretty close, and he has been in our midst," said Mr. Tetley. "Could he not be of assistance in obtaining the required parental permission?"

Tim stared as at a revelation.

"Would he not be inclined to win the written parental

permission Pops so rightly insists upon as a condition of your hitting the road with us in the morning?"

Timmy, looking around at these black itinerant wizards of baseball, stood up in the light of his past.

"You bet your boots he will," he told Mr. Tetley. "And so will my Uncle Hans."

He *walked* home. The boy with the empty pail was gone forever from the streets of the town. The Fastest Human of the County was the boy of the morning. Timmy walked home in the late sunshine.

They were all there, in the parlor and out on the front porch. From the Victrola the sweet clear voice of Gene Austin penetrated the buzzing and laughter of their merriment:

Jeannine, I dream of lilac time . . .

He walked through the idle kitchen and, unseen, up the back stairs.

For you and I, our love can never die.
Jeannine, I dream of lilac time.

He closed the door of his room and took off his uniform. He held up the shirt and took a last look at 17. Then he went into the bathroom and dumped the bundle into the laundry hamper. He filled the tub and took his ease in the hot water.

He shaved and splashed his face with his father's forbidden Lilac Vegetal and rubbed pomade into his hair and combed it slick. He put on a starched white shirt and the Christmas necktie that Marilou had bought for him in Minneapolis. He had two suits, his Best and his Very Best. He chose the Very Best.

He went into the master bedroom to inspect himself in the full-length mirror. He smiled at what he saw. He was not dressed like a boy going to the Fourth of July chicken dinner at the Cooperative Creamery and to the fireworks afterward, nor like a lounge lizard all dolled up for the dance at Cormorant. He was dressed like a man for an Important Occasion.

His mother saw him first. "Where have you been, Timmy? I was beginning to worry. Not your Very Best? Your Very Best for finger food at the creamery?"

"I've had supper, Mom," he said.

And Donna tripped up to him. "It was so terrible, Timmy, the way they threw the firecrackers at you in the race. It wasn't *fair*. I felt just awful."

"Fun and fair," he said.

"I'm sorry about tonight, Timmy. I mean I really am."

> High brow, low brow, intermediate
> Make believe they are collegiate . . .

He was looking for Grandpa Tim and Uncle Hans. "Sure," he said, "have a good time with Freddy." Why should he care? Seventeen was a bust. He wondered how long the hurt would last.

"Seemed like every time I looked up all day long, there was my little brother, said Marilou, and everybody laughed in agreement that Timmy had been a part of just about everything all day long.

He nodded and grinned at them and went out on the porch. They were sitting together on the porch swing — Grandpa Tim with his tin cup and pipe, Uncle Hans with his glass of home-brew and cigar. Tim never had seen them together before, just the two of them.

Me and my shadow, strolling down the avenue

"I need a favor from you," Timmy said. "From both of you."

"Must be a mighty big favor, if it takes the two of us," said Uncle Hans.

"It's a big one," Timmy said.

They shifted apart to make room for him on the swing.

"Could we go into the little parlor, please?" asked Timmy. "It's something I've got to tell you about, away from all this noise."

All alone and feeling blue.

They looked at each other, the two who knew him best, and followed him through the people in the big parlor into the little parlor and slid the door shut behind them. Timmy pulled the footstool between the two easy chairs. The setting sun caught his face with purple and amber from the stained glass of the window. "Go ahead, son," said Uncle Hans.

"They drove all night, and I got to their camp early this morning while they were fixing breakfast," Timmy began. "Snow was with me . . ."

They were staring at him with as much marveling attention as ever he had given to their stories of olden times.

"The White Crow, is it?" Grandpa Tim said. "Well, I'll be dinged."

"Speedy Deefy," Uncle Hans said. "I'll be double-dinged."

"You'll do it for me? You'll talk to Dad and Mom for me? Get their permission?"

"Let's get a few things straight," said Uncle Hans. "You go only as far as Mandan."

96

"Yes, sir," Timmy said.

"And if anything goes wrong," Grandpa Tim put in, "you'll go into one of the towns on our right-of-way and have the station agent send me the message and put you on the next train home."

"Yes, sir," Tim said.

"We'll talk to them," said Uncle Hans.

"You handle your brother, I'll flamboozle my daughter," said Grandpa Tim.

"In writing. It's got to be in writing. And they've got to keep the secret. They can say I'm going fishing for a few weeks."

"Go get your father and mother," said Uncle Hans, "and you wait until we call you in."

His father looked up from his talk with Druggist John and said, "I hope you know why we couldn't stay for the whole game, Timmy. John here was telling me how you stopped those darkies in their tracks."

"Dad, can you come here a minute? Grandpa Tim and Uncle Hans want to talk with you and Mom about something."

"Tell you one thing," his father said to Druggist John, "you never know what this kid is up to from one minute to the next."

"You sure don't," said Timmy to himself as he went to get his mother.

He could hear that they were talking a mile a minute behind the sliding doors but not what they were saying until Uncle Hans came through like thunder: "Now, dammit, Harold, this is not an ordinary kid. There's more to that kid than either of you know. And, by God, he's going to do it. And you're going to sign right here." And the voices ceased their squabble.

His father slid the doors open. "Step in here a minute, son."

"Yes, sir," Timmy said. The room was in dusk, and they were like judges in a cave of lost time.

"I don't approve of this in any way, shape, or manner, and it's against my better judgment that I do it. But —" He handed him the TO WHOM IT MAY CONCERN envelope. Timmy opened it and read the note aloud: "Our son, Timothy H. Nelson, has my permission and the permission of his mother to travel and play baseball with the team of Negroes known as the Original Colored House of David. Should there be any question or difficulty in connection with his traveling and playing with them, contact the undersigned by telegram or long-distance telephone immediately. Harold F. Nelson, M.D., Indian Springs, Minnesota, July 4, 1928." Timmy put the letter in its envelope in his coat pocket. "Thank you, Dad. Thank you more than I can say." His mother was weeping. Suddenly the three of them embraced. "Okay, son. Now take care of yourself." "Yes, sir." "Take your Bible with you," his mother said. He nodded as they went out. "Yes, ma'am."

The three conspirators smiled on one another. "I'm sure lucky to have you on my side," Timmy told them.

"We're proud of you, son," Uncle Hans said.

"Isn't it just that?" Grandpa Tim raised his tin cup to him. "That we are?"

"I better get out to the camp and tell them the good news," Timmy said.

"Take Ol' Liz,"

"Or the LaSalle."

"I guess I'll walk, be thinking about what I'm going to take with me."

There's something wild
About you, child,
Let's be outrageous.
Let's misbehave.

Freddy and Donna were dancing the Bear Hug or whatever it was called that the lounge lizard had picked up in
the frat house. His left hand was damn near down to her
ass divine.

12

In the Oak Grove

Not even Minnie, who had got silly sipping her crock-chilled dandelion wine during the Battle of Gettysburg, was answering the red rooster's call to the dawn of the fifth.

He dressed quickly. His best suit (the Very Best of last year) was now short in the legs and tight in the shoulders, but it would be fine for going to town on a Saturday night to see a picture show and look at the girls in the ice-cream parlor.

He spread his yellow slicker on the floor. Only last fall he had printed funny things on it in India ink — "Oil Here," "Four Wheels No Brakes," "Danger! Man at Work!" . . . He had a smile for the boy of yesterday. He rolled up in the slicker a woolen sweater, coveralls, tennis shoes, a Jantzen two-piece bathing suit, and socks and B.V.D.'s and strapped it with his old Boy Scout web belt. Into the black traveling grip Grandpa Tim had given him he packed his spikes and glove, toilet gear, hankies, a writing tablet, and his Parker fountain pen . . . He had promised his mother he'd take his confirmation Bible; she would come mooning and snooping around his room, worrying that he was out and far on the road with the black wizards of baseball. He put it in . . . He considered the studio photograph of Donna, until yesterday his dearest possession. "Is that your girl?" they would ask. He put it back in the drawer under his winter underwear. What else?

He went out the back way. Snow came up to come along. Timmy crouched to pick a tick off his ear before commanding him to stay. He slung the slicker roll over his left shoulder and swung the traveling grip from his right hand and hiked down the back path. When he came to Grandpa Tim's shanty, he stopped and turned to its door. Would the old man be up yet or still sleeping off the moonshine? He opened the door to look in.

"There he is!" Grandpa Tim was sipping his tea — strong enough to trot a mouse — and smoking his breakfast pipe over an egg-smeared plate. "Is it a bit of breakfast ye'll have on your way into the world?"

Into the world — what he had been thinking himself. His grandpa's blue eyes were begging for a last minute more of the time together that had seemed so endless. "I'll be eating with them before we break camp," Timmy said, "but a cup of tea would be just fine."

"Into the world," Grandpa Tim repeated, nodding in his smoke. "And you'll not be when ye come back the same as leaves this door."

Timmy thought it kinder to pretend he did not sense that his grandpa was saying farewell to his being the little boy who believed his stories. "It's only for three weeks, Grandpa, and just to Mandan." He gulped the tea. "They'll be breaking camp early. I'd better be going."

"*Glohma loh sidh*," his grandpa said. "Go while the fairies are sleeping."

Timmy stood up and extended his hand. "So long, Grandpa. See you three weeks from Monday on Number Four."

The old man arose to catch him in a quick embrace. "May the hardness of the world put a shine on your goodness." Timmy hugged the old bones. Grandpa Tim turned him to the door and released him, and Timmy closed it on his whisper: "*Nah te foh, lah te foh.*" (Look not back lest ye come not back.)

They were at breakfast when Timmy strode into the dappled shade of the oaks. "Well," he said, "here I am." Their eyes followed him as he tossed his traveling stuff into the truck and came back to help himself to a plate of hot breakfast. He took his place among them.

"We been thinkin," Pops said. "We been thinkin, some of us been thinkin, that it not be good to carry you along."

Now Timmy sensed that their silence was ominous, and he felt his face muscles tighten. "Why? For heaven's sakes, why? You've got my father's letter."

"We acted too sudden," Pops said. "The moonshine was flowin an' not everybody had a chance to give his say. Some now say you won't help us that much, be worth a share. Some say you ain't gonna fool nobody, this white crow albino, make a fool outta all of us."

Their eyes were on him. "About the share," he said and paused to organize his points in logical order, as he had as captain of the debate team, but they got lost in a rush of red panic. "Yes, about the share. Well, I wasn't thinking about any pay except my keep. I want to go along and help any way I can, off the field and on. I can help Dan take care of the camp. I can do lots of things . . . Catch fish," he lit upon. "I can catch any kind of fish that swims in these lakes and rivers . . ."

"He can hep me get meals, clean up," Ol' Dan put in. "I need me a boy to hep."

"Trouble with that," Manny said to Ol' Dan, "is that you ain't got no vote."

"If he come, he gotta have a share," said Little Hoop. "I don' play no ball wif people who play this game for *exercise.*"

"Man, he ain't *worth* a share to us," said Moon.

Pops raised a hand to quiet the cackles and grunts of agreement and disagreement.

"Main thing," he said to Timmy. "The *main* thing that the people ain't sayin that's on their minds is that you a white boy an' this a colored team. Some don' want no white boy along."

"Thas right, thas right." "You hear?" "Thas right."

They looked at him. "I — I'm sorry I'm white. I mean I can't help being white, but I thought being an albino . . . I could be like one of you . . ."

"Sheeitt. What you know 'bout bein one a us?"

"We been back and forth, in and out" — Pop's hand silenced them — "and 'round and about all this since dawn. Let each man have his say and vote in turn, go right around, start with Mr. Tetley, then the infield, then the outfield, till it come to my vote last."

Mr. Tetley seemed to come back from thoughts of somewhere else. "I will reiterate my opinion that we can use this boy and that we need this boy, specially till we send back for a new pitcher and get him up here, which will take two maybe three weeks anyway. The fact that he is a white boy is no matter to me, as long as he passes himself as an albino and adds some comedy to our performance. He's here, ready to go. I vote we take him along and pay him half a share if he earns it. Okay, Nathan, your turn."

Nathan Black, tall and perpetually good-natured, played first base. "Me'n Clayton" — his twin brother who played left field — "we talk this ovah. We don' want no argument, we don' want no vote. Whatever way it do go, we go with it."

They looked at Clayton, who smiled and nodded. "We don' care."

Now it was to Little Hoop, the second baseman. He was thin and quick and had a long nose down which he sneered. "We make our livin workin together as colored. I don' want not even a little bit a white shit 'long with us."

"Little Hoop votes no," Pops said. "That make it one yes, one no, and . . ."

"And two abstentions," Mr. Tetley put in for him. "Manny?"

The barrel of a third baseman stared through Timmy. "For what Hoop say, I say no, too. He's got the good wheels for our game, but he's still white shit."

"Scrappy?"

"I feel like Mr. Tetley," said Scrap Iron Davis, the shortstop. "I vote take 'im."

"Thas the infield an' Clayton. So, Ike?"

"I think the boy gonna hep us. I vote take 'im. If he don' pan out on Sunday in Fargo, send 'im home to his mama."

"Now we got three and two. Moon?"

Moon, the third pitcher, played right field and could fill in anywhere. "We don' need him. We doin fine with what we got. No share to this white boy."

"It's you now, Merv," said Pops.

His hand was still in the bandage that Timmy's father had put on. "I be aw right by Sunday. I say we don' need 'im."

"That make it four no an three take 'im. Bofey, it up to you."

"My right arm I can hardly lift to eat, an' my left arm, it begin to ache a little, count of I go off stride comin down with it 'cause the right arm ain't natural. I be aw right Sunday for one game, can't promise no two games. So I say take 'im. He showed us some good stuff yestiday. I work with 'im, startin this evenin, on his pitchin. He might gonna hep us."

"So now we four an four an two . . ."

"Abstentions. Do either Nathan or Clayton wish to change one way or the other?"

"Up to Pops now," Clayton said.

"We have no disharmony among us. We can't be together with disharmony. I respeck you no votes. I admire you speakin out against takin a white boy along. But I gotta look ahead. Even with Merv and Bofey in good shape, we oney got eleven, even countin me to come in to catch when need be. He make us twelve. We need twelve. We allus carried twelve before. My mistake we oney took eleven this year. We got share greedy. Now we in trouble, we gotta pay. I vote we take the white boy, give 'im his chance, pay 'im half a share till we see can he really hep us or not. Now if there's any bellyachin, I wanna hear it now, get it out. Otherwise. . ."

There was no bellyaching. "Okay, Pops," said Little Hoop, "we carry 'im along."

"Shear his head and lather it good, Dan," said Mr. Tetley. "I'll do the shaving."

"Come wif me, boy." Ol' Dan led him to the hood of the Packard. "Gonna be our barber chair. Undress yosef and sit up there, we can get at you."

In his B.V.D.'s he straddled the hood of the car. While

Ol' Dan lathered his shorn head and Mr. Tetley honed the straightedged razor on the rim of the bean pot, the others gathered around as if inspecting a hack pony being fussed up for the show ring. They marveled at the whiteness of the revealed skull.

"He look more like dat albino dog a his wifout his hair dan wif it."

"Those ears a his — damn if he don' look like a silver lovin cup."

Holding still lest Mr. Tetley nick him, he looked out at yesterday's field of contest.

"He sure don' look like he did."

"Git his eyebrows, too, Mr. Tetley. They too dark for an albino."

"We will regard them as an aberration. Their function is to keep the perspiration from blinding him."

"He ain't gonna be no hep to us iffn he can't see the ball."

"Still don' think he evah be worth a damn to us."

"We gotta tan his head some to match his face."

"He done passed. Ain't that a bitch? He pass from white to black, maybe first time ever." And they yipped and cackled.

Timmy slid from the hood into their midst.

"You along," Pops said. "All we can say now, you along."

Feeling like a white glassie in a ring of black agates, he crawled into the bed of the truck and made himself a corner of his own. He changed into coveralls and tennis shoes and stowed his Saturday night clothes away. Then he came out to help Ol' Dan clean up the breakfast mess. "No, no, boy. Not like that. You cradles them plates inside the pot lika this here."

13

On the Road

————◄◆►————

The road through the countryside took them past farms where Timmy could call the dogs and bulls by name. Standing in the flatbed, looking over its cabin, his white skull protected against the morning sun by glistening Vaseline, he had the feeling of being in a strange and hostile land.

As they approached Hawley, ten miles north of Indian Springs, Pops ordered a stop for provisions. "Oney me'n Ol' Dan git out an' go in," he ordered. "Evabody else sit tight. You" — he commanded Timmy — "you stay outta sight under the tarp. Don' wanna start no talk yet we got a white boy wif us, not till we ready to play you in uniform."

Under the tarp, he peered through the cracks in the side wall at the white faces and soft flesh of the townsfolk. He watched as Pops and Ol' Dan went into the general store and the next-door meat market to stock up, never asking a price, paying cash on the barrelhead, back to the Packard through a circle of curious whites. Pops stopped at the ice house at the edge of town for a fifty-pound chunk of ice. Ol' Dan called Timmy to show him where different things were stored.

And back out again on the road, heading west toward the Red River of the North, by themselves again; the others easy in their rest and card game, Timmy alone in the sunshine. At noon they pulled up alongside a country schoolhouse, stilled for the summer. "These places allus a good stoppin place," Pops said. "They got the water pump, the outhouse, grass an' shade, an' nobody bother you this time a year." Their meal was cold cuts and beans. Pops figgered Timmy's head had had enough sun for one day and ordered him to the shade of the tarp.

Midafternoon they made camp where they would stay till Monday, after the Sunday double-header with the Slaughterhouse Nine. It was in a bend of the Red, ten miles below Fargo. Nearby was the deserted playing field of the school in the village of Yellow Sand, population sixty-two.

Their camp was shaded from the sun and shielded from the dirt road. The stream floated a few leaves in silence. Timmy gathered dry driftwood along its high-water edge, snapping and chopping it into lengths of Dan's liking. He found a little yellow-sand beach a hundred yards upstream, for their bathing pleasure after practice. He showed them his skill with the cane pole and cast the bobber beyond a multi-rooted stump and landed three five-pound pickerel for their evening meal.

"Anyway, he make a good kitchen boy for Dan."

He was hauling water up to Dan's washtub for soaking and laundering the uniforms for Sunday's double-header when Hoop yelled down at him: "Pops say get your ass up for practice. We ain't cuttin you in for no share till we learn you what to do."

He forgot his whiteness in the universal fundamentals of the game. He caught for Pops's infield practice, while Mr. Tetley was running the outfielders with his fungo. Then Pops sent him into the outfield to shag. He showed 'em he could go get 'em, coming in or going back. He was sweating easy and blowing hard when he was summoned to pitch batting practice.

Bofey instructed him from behind the mound. "Nothin but fast balls, three-quarter-arm only, down the pike. You not comin through easy. Rare back and come down *through* — pow! — you let the ball go. Come down *pow*. You gotta get your weight behind you. *Pow*. You gettin it now. *Pow* . . . Now throw me ten fast balls in a row to the outside corner on the knee . . . Pow! . . ."

His turn at bat, with Moon throwing, he did nothing but bunt — third-base line, first-base line, over and over. The bunt would be his specialty when they put him in to run the Pin Wheel. "Any reasonably competent professional can swing at the ball and hit it *somewhere*," Mr. Tetley told him. "We want you to hit the ball where we say, to make our plays. You won't be up there swinging when we need a hit. You'll be up there, our albino clown, when we come to the entertainment part of the proceedings . . ."

The last half-hour they practiced new tricks for their pepper game and made a fool out of him; best he could do was keep from getting hit by the tosses that seemed to pop out of everywhere and nowhere. "Maybe two, three weeks' practice, we can put him in the show," Pops said doubtfully.

With darkness, the fire burned low, and the stars through the leaves flickered high above. The mosquitos were fierce. Wrapped in his blanket, his shirt over his head, he lay beside the embers on his pad of burlap, too much of the day crowding back into his mind to let him sleep. But suddenly it was morning. He started the breakfast fire for Dan and filled the coffeepot and helped mind the frying of the salt side pork for the red-eye gravy.

They worked him for two hours on his base-running comedy specialties. With Moon pitching, they set up the game situation in which Timmy would come in to bat with the bases loaded and run the Pin Wheel. Pops gave him the drill. "First thing now you gotta get through your dumb skull is you are the *clown*. We is funny in our funny stuff because we is *good* at it. You different. You *dumb*. You got a thick white skull we caint get nothin through. See, so I be coachin here at third. You come to the plate. You pick up the bat wrong end. Mr. Tetley, he come out an' straighten you out which end of bat you hold. Okay, you grin an' jump up an' down, you finely got that figgered out. You dig in, you ready. C'mon, you wave the pitcher, c'mon, throw dat ball. But you never forget you a deefy, see? You don' make a sound. Now I wavin all kind of signs at you, what I want you to do. I give you the bunt sign — flesh, cap, touch the letters. Okay, that's bunt. But you don' get it, see. You step outta the box, show me you got it, but you show me you gonna swing away. I come down the line, yellin at you, not swing away, you gonna bunt. Now you get it, you gonna bunt. You know it, we know it, the otha team know it, the crowd, evabody know you gonna bunt. So the first pitch come in on you. No matter where the pitch is, up at you or in the dirt, you swing away, but wild. You swing hard as you can but you miss the ball by three feet. Next pitch you bunt it down third-base line, an' evabody's flyin. You know the Pin Wheel. You seen us do it. You got it? Okay, we try it. You go back to the bench, I signal you to come out an' bat . . ."

"This will indeed add a new dimension to our comedy," Mr. Tetley said. "The white buffoon. When you come out to pick out your bat, do a little jig showing how happy and excited you are to be called upon. When I come out, I'll explain the baseball bat to you in elaborate detail — this is the end you hold, this end up, here is the striking surface."

"Yes, sir," Timmy said.

"You can't come out with no frown on your face," Pops yelled at him. "You gotta come out smilin an' laughin. You gotta show people you the happiest fool in the world. You can't show you scared you can't get the job done."

Timmy went back and came out again, smilin an' laughin. Six or seven tries later, he got the drill through his thick white skull. Then they went to work on Wrong Way.

For this merriment Timmy would be batting ninth in the line-up, either as a pinch hitter for the pitcher or already in the line-up as pitcher — just ahead of Scrap Iron, the lead-off man. Timmy would bunt his way to first base. Scrappy would belt a line drive to left or right center, good for two or three bases. Then they would both run the wrong way. From first base Timmy would start back for home; Scrappy, confused by this reversal, would set off for third base. Pops would be screaming and waving to get Scrappy turned around, and the entire House bench would be out trying to get Speedy Deefy headed back to first. Then they would *fly* the right way. Scrappy would run a triple into a single, and Speedy would keep going with the aim of getting caught in a run-down between second and third. "Nothin people like better than seein some smart-aleck base runner get caught in a hot box," Pops said. "With you dodging back an' forth, they gonna laugh theirselves sick."

"I'm pretty darn good at running out of the hot box," Timmy told him.

"Don' really matter. We got the game won by then any-ways. Main thing is make 'em laugh at this crazy white clown we got runnin for us."

"Speedy Deefy, the White Crow," said Manny. "Damn if I ain't comin 'round to think he can hep us, dumb as he look out there, his crazy jiggin an' grinnin."

After the noon meal, the whole team was going into Fargo. Pops would make pay-off arrangements and be interviewed by the baseball writer for the *Forum*. The players would get a night out in Dark Town, the only substantial Negro neighborhood in the two thousand miles of woods, prairies, plains, and mountains between the Twin Cities and Spokane. Its attractions included a general store, a picture show, three pool halls, a café, a dance hall, four churches, and a happy welcome by its five hundred inhabitants.

"Not you, Speedy," Pops said as Timmy was getting dolled up with the others. "You gotta stay'n keep camp an' take care of Merv."

"You give yourself away," Busy Ike said. "Maybe we can fool them white crowds on the field, but no way you gonna fool the colored folks we gonna be sashayin 'round with, likker runnin free."

He had fancied himself fox-trotting a cute colored girl around the dance hall. "That's not fair, Pops."

"Lotsa things ain't fair," said Pops, turning away.

"But, sir — maybe I could go in with you to find a doctor to come out and treat Merv."

"No physician of white — of white persuasion, shall we say? — gonna give a good God damn about his Oath of Hippocrates to come out here to apply his healing arts to a sick nigger!" Mr. Tetley's flash of anger set Timmy back a step.

"We got a healin woman there," Pops said. "I see her."

Merv spoke up from his pallet under the willow tree. "Bring me some a that moonshine likker, what I need to hep me sleep."

"There some here in this fruit jar for tonight," Ol' Dan said.

Merv nodded. "Make me feel better, here alone, missin the good time."

Timmy cut the bandage from Merv's hand and cleaned the sore with peroxide and had him soak it in hot salt water in the old tin lard pail . . .

It was lonesome alone with Merv — but the pleasant lonesomeness that comes with being snug and having responsibility for the place. "I'm good at cooking fish, Merv," he said. "I know where I can catch us a mess of little rock bass, big as your hand, sweet and tender."

"Fish fine with me, Speedy."

He squatted on the old stump and caught eight hand-sized rock bass down among its roots with a dropline baited with pork rind. He cleaned them and brought them back fresh-packed in wet grass. It was coming on dusk, and he built up the fire. "Be back in ten minutes," he told Merv and ran the dirt road to the potato field he had spotted coming in. He helped himself to a baker's dozen of new potatoes no bigger than golf balls.

"Boiled new potatoes and fish, you can't beat it."

"Where you get them potatoes? You steal 'em from that farmer's field? Pops don't 'llow no stealin from fields. We asks and we buys. We take no chances gettin folks up in arms that we be stealin their fields." Merv was getting himself all worked up about it. "Suppose that farmer come stormin in here lookin for the niggers stealin his potatoes?"

"He won't miss em, Merv. Nobody 'round here bothers if somebody samples a few potatoes or ears of corn when it's ripe."

"You better not let Pops hear you was out a-stealin."

"We'll eat up all the evidence," Timmy promised him. They washed it down with boiled coffee with canned cow and sugar in it. After supper, Timmy cleaned and bandaged the infected hand for the night and put leaves on the fire to make a smoke against the mosquitos.

Merv's forehead was hot, but he pushed away the cool cloth Timmy laid upon it. "Bring me that bit a likker they leave for me." He gulped it down. "Missin all that good time they be havin," he muttered and lay back, turning his back to Timmy.

There was no comfort on Timmy's thin pad. His night thoughts were of his humiliations. His trial and their reluctant vote to carry him along now seemed an inquisition. The way they had drilled him to come out jiggin an' laughin . . . the humiliation of his ineptness in their pepper game tricks . . . Pops's command to stay in camp . . . He saw himself as a spatter of white birdshit on their black brilliance . . .

Then he rolled over in anger and resentment. Damn their eyes! He had come to share and help and be one with them on a road of adventure to which he was born. And they . . . damn their black souls!

He sat up. The fire was out. Merv was sleeping. He sank back alone in the strange darkness. He pulled the tarp over his head and tried to feel the snug comfort he felt in his own bed, in the privacy of his room, in the shelter of his home, in the town of his life. The lines of Kipling came to him:

> "His cot was righthand cot to mine," said Files on
> parade.
> "He's sleeping out and far tonight," the Color Sergeant
> said.

And then the lines of a poem he had learned in the third grade:

I remember, I remember
The house where I was born . . .

Then, as so often in his bed at home as he lay twixt wakefulness and sleep, there came marching along fragments and snatches of rhymes and rules, of poetry and facts — of things he had been required to memorize in school and confirmation class and of other things he had learned by heart for the fun of it. Now they surfaced as they would, amiably and without jostling, to replace his night thoughts of humiliation and lonesomeness:

Genesis, Exodus, Leviticus, Numbers, Deuteronomy, Joshua, Judges, Ruth, First and Second Samuel, First and Second Kings . . .

A straight line is the shortest distance between two points.

Then out spake brave Horatius,
The captain of the gate:
"To every man upon this earth
Death cometh soon or late.
And how can man die better
Than facing fearful odds
For the ashes of his fathers
And the temples of his gods?"

But I say unto you that whomsoever looketh on a woman to lust after her hath committed adultery with her already in his heart.

If ye break faith with us who die
We shall not sleep, though poppies grow
In Flanders fields.

Why is He called the Holy Ghost? Because He is Himself holy and because he makes us holy by working faith in us and appropriating to us Christ and his salvation.

A country dog came into town,
His Christian name was Runt
Piddling was his specialty
And piddling was his stunt.

The square on the hypotenuse of a right triangle is equal to the sum of the squares on its legs.

For Thine is the Kingdom, and the power, and the glory, for ever and ever. Amen. What is meant by the word "Amen"? That I should be certain that these petitions are acceptable to our Father in heaven, and heard; for he has commanded us so to pray, and has promised to hear us. Amen, Amen, that is, yea, yea, it shall be so.

Suddenly, overriding all of these random bits, came in marvelous rhythm the names of all the way stations and flag stops on the Northern Pacific main line from St. Paul to Seattle . . . St. Paul, Minneapolis, Anoka, Coon River, St. Cloud, Pelican Rapids, Wadena, Staples . . . One summer afternoon in the depot, waiting for Grandpa Tim to finish some business and get back to an ancestral reminiscence, he had learned them by heart from the timetable. Now, long after he had given up hope of being called upon for this information, they were running along as steady and reassuring as the clickety-clack of wheels on the track, and he felt the snug security of being in the upper berth of a Pullman car on the overnight run home from a trip to Minneapolis . . .

14

The Man from Gilt Edge, Tennessee

In the morning Pops and Ol' Dan came back in the Packard. The healing woman had brewed a bitter herb medicine for Merv. It seemed to do him good, but he was of no mind to do anything but rest in the shade of the willow tree and watch the river go by.

Pops also brought the new advertising signs that would be put in the barbershop windows and tacked to the telephone poles in the towns they would be playing across North Dakota to the Missouri River and Mandan.

THE MARVELS OF BASEBALL
The Original
COLORED HOUSE OF DAVID
versus

NEW: THE DEMON OF THE BASES
SPEEDY DEEFY, THE WHITE CROW

His nervousness at being billed as a special attraction was abated somewhat by knowing that he would be playing before the big crowd in Fargo only in his running specialties, for entertainment, not with the money riding on him. Then, as casually as if he were expressing the hope it wouldn't rain, Pops told him: "You be ready to come in an' throw low strikes, case we need you. Bofey gonna pitch the first game only, rest his sore arm, mean you gotta be ready to relieve if somethin happen. Moon pitch the second game, mean you take his place in the outfield, be ready to relieve him, need come up. Never tell."

"How much will we have riding on these games?" he asked.

"Sept for the Mandan Cowpokes, where we got special bets, an' the big rodeo crowd in Billings, this the biggest pot we play for all year — six, seven hunnerd, maybe eight."

His chest was not big enough to contain his heart. "Oh, gosh."

"We give you good defense. Keep the ball down an' on the plate, you figger to get by. We may need you just 'bout every game till this man I sent for git here from Kansas City, no tellin when."

Helping Dan get the noon meal for just the four of them was something to do, but he couldn't get it off his mind that he might have to go out there tomorrow and throw $700 worth of low strikes.

Merv was picking at his plate. "What kinda good time evabody have last night?" he asked Ol' Dan.

"Like all the times we play here," Dan said. "Dancin an' the girls an' the hootch."

"I wonder that girl, her name Ellen, she wore a yellow skirt an' blue stockins last year, you see her there this year?"

"I don' pay no 'tention to any which one. I sit back to the music an' see 'em all."

"We had a time," Merv said. "She dance wif nobody but me an' took me home to where she sleep."

"Busy Ike, they couldn't get enougha his playin and blues shoutin, stomps an' ol-style music them folks up here some um 'em never did hear before."

"Tonight, too?" Timmy asked.

Dan nodded. "Sattiday night. Yeah, yeah, last night they just git warmed up for Sattiday night. But we go git 'em, bring 'em back here to sleep it off. I reckon it gonna be three, four a'clock in the mornin we git 'em all rounded up an' in the truck."

"With seven hundred dollars, maybe eight, ridin on the game, you would think," Timmy said, afraid for his own ability to throw low strikes, "that they would get a good night's sleep."

"They be ready. This do 'em good, relax 'em. Oney real break the whole summer wif our own people."

"You can't play this game on water," Merv said and went back to his pad under the willow tree.

"What time do we go to the ball park tomorrow?"

"High noon. We leave here at high noon."

That afternoon he toiled with Ol' Dan at the washtub, whomping the dust and sweat out of the uniforms in the soapy water, scrubbing grass stains on the washboard, and rinsing the uniforms in the river. By late afternoon, the uniforms — grey blue with orange lettering — were hanging like paperdoll cutouts on the lines between the trees.

"Let me throw to you for a while, Pops," Timmy said.

"You ready now. You don't need no throwin till warm-up time tomorra."

"Please, Pops."

They went to the school diamond, and he threw hard — pow! pow! — for ten minutes.

"Thas enough," Pops said. "Don' leave your arm out here when you go to town to play."

The sun was sinking below the trees across the river when Pops and Ol' Dan drove off to the whirl of Dark Town and "left the world to darkness" — and to me and Merv, Timmy thought as he got the camp ready for their night.

Before full dark he swam and floated in the river until he felt tuckered out enough to sleep through his worry for tomorrow.

"Speedy boy?"

"Yes, Merv?"

"You be bringin me that new jar of moonshine to be heppin me git some sleep? I 'preciate you bein good to me. Speedy. You reckon ahm gonna die a this fever?"

Timmy felt his forehead. "You're sweating a little now, Merv. The aspirin an' the moonshine are breaking the fever. My dad said you're going to be just fine in two-three days."

"He a doctor man, he oughta know. I been thinkin 'bout down home when I's a boy . . ."

"Where you from, Merv? Tell me about your home."

Merv shook his head. "Ain't been home in a long, long time now. Since I was hardly no more'n a boy, jes sixteen years of age. Never go back no more. Don' even know me back there no more, nor not where I am, nor not *if* I am, nor nothin 'bout me . . ." He held out his cup and swigged it down. "Oh, yeah. Oh, yeah, make me feel I ain't dyin." He held it out again. "That surely do me good."

Timmy watched the grip of the fever soften. He propped the jar handy to the cup and minded the fire and settled down beside him, covering their heads with their shirts against the mosquitos. "I never heard your full name, Merv," he said.

"Merv ain't my name, somebody else's name," the sick man said in the voice of a dead man talking through his shroud. "My name's my secret. I tell you, you might tell somebody else. This big jail farm, acres an' acres, cotton an' sorghum ten miles to the river. The trusties, they had the shotguns on them doin the work. But yonder on the hill an' in the wagons, half mile away, they had the guards wif rifles, case a trusty get rushed, lose his gun, the rifles cut 'em down. Many a man died there in the sun, beat to death, some um 'em. Bury 'em right there on the farm, dig a hole somewhere, bury 'em. Nobody knew. They say in the report they escape. No way a knowin.

"Oney thing we had, Sundays, they let us play ball in the yard. Got prouda us, bring in teams to play us, let white folks come in an' watch us, see how happy we is, havin a good time playin ball. We not 'llowed to talk to nobody, say nothin. Play ball. Playin ball all we had. Act up, you gone, I mean *gone*."

"Dear Jesus," Timmy prayed under his shirt, "help him get well and be free forever." Aloud he said: "That's where you learned to play ball?"

"Man there, useta play for the Indianapolis Clowns, taught me the fine pointsa pitchin, all we had to do but work 'an sleep."

"How did you get the name Merv?"

"With a *y*, spell with a *y*. Full name, Samuel Booker T. Mervyn — M-E-R-V-Y-N . . . He a man, maybe fifty, been there 'bout all he could remember, like I was gonna be. For no what for but some argument in the pool hall. He got sickly, but they kept workin 'im, like a sick mule till they drop, more where they come from. One day he cough blood in the sun an' die. It was near sundown, we ready to go in.

"They call for the Cap'n. He come on his mule. He say

they gonna bury 'im right there. I say save me supper, I stay an' dig his hole. Time you come back, I got his hole ready for to lay 'im in. He say you do that, I be back. That black dirt, it dig easy, I dig it deep, slant it deeper to one side. I know I be better dead than be caught. But this chance, the oney chance I evah get to walk free, I take it. I lay Mervyn in and git in the deep side an' covah me ovah with loose dirt, all but my arm an' head, till I pull 'im ovah on top of me, leavin me oney a breathin hole, an' lay there an' wait, thinkin I be better dead than be caught, they gonna beat me an' put me in the box a month an' weld the iron to my legs. They come an' the Cap'n say, where the boy? where the boy I leave here? Someone say, they practicin ball for Sunday's game, he they oney pitcher now, he musta dug 'im his hole an' gone to practice. Someone say, yeah, he be pitchin battin practice. So the Cap'n say, covah 'im ovah an' put the sod on top. They do an' they go. I scrape me a breathin hole 'tween me'n Mervyn an' lay there till I know it's full dark an' fight my way out, bury Mervyn back and lay the sod like before. They ain't gonna know till mornin I gone an' I gotta be long gone away or they git me wif the dogs, but I know 'bout dogs, I useta run coon dogs down home, an' I take to the woods, circlin an' circlin back, till I can climb me a tree an' jump a tree an' make my way to the river. I swum me out in the big current downstream till near dawn, usin a log to keep me up all the way, an' ovah to the Tinnissee side, an' run down a paved road 'tween the cotton, where no dog can track me . . ."

"The Count of Monte Cristo," Timmy murmured, rising on his elbow to marvel.

". . . an' hep mysef to some work clothes like evabody wear from a sharecropper's line an' steal me a chicken to take to de railro' tracks till I can breathe easy, lotta people look like me a-ridin the freights. Took me near a year to work mah way to Kansas City, till I hear 'bout this team an' Pops take me on, he need a pitcher to back up Bofey . . ."

"This year?"

"Las year. This my second year wif the Original Colored House of David. I established now. I nevah tol' nobody till now. I tell you case I gonna die, you a writin man, you write my mama . . ."

"You're not gonna die, Merv" was all Timmy could think to say, looking down at the shrouded head. "You'll be back in the line-up in a few days."

He saw the head shake a negative. "I feel sick in my bones . . ."

"What's her name? Where do I write?"

"She Annie Moore. Write her to Gilt Edge, Tinnissee."

"Gilt Edge? Like gilt-edged money?"

"Thas right. She on a farm outta town. She go to church there, come to the store. They know her. She nevah miss a Sunday, nor me neither when I's a boy, long years ago. They nevah knew 'bout the trouble I got in when I run off to fin' work in Arkansaw. Don' tell her 'bout my trouble, she be 'shamed . . . Tell her I a good boy playin ball."

"When was that? When you left home?"

"In Twenty-one . . . Maybe she gone now, maybe nobody lef to know or care."

"If I have to write, maybe I'd better write in care of the church. What was the name of the church in Gilt Edge?"

"Called the Lo, I Am with You Always Runnin Water Baptis Church."

" 'Lo, I am with you always, even unto the end of the world.' "

"Thas it, thas it. This you secret, oney if you need it, like I said. Don' you be tellin Pops and the others a worda this, 'bout my trouble, 'cause if you do, they be in trouble with the law, knowin I 'scaped an' takin me in. I choose you to tell, you a white boy they won't bother none."

"But you're not going to die, Mervyn. We're gonna get you well in a day or two."

The good hand emerged from the shroud with the tin cup, and Timmy refilled it.

"Willis," Mervyn said. "My mother called me Willis."

From out of a snug place in memory came a prayer from the Christmas carol Timmy loved best, and he sang it to Willis and the stars. " 'Bless all the dear children in thy tender care, And fit them for heaven to live with thee there.' "

"Thas good," Willis said. "Thas good."

A solitary cloud swallowed the moon, and the stars seemed to Timmy to shine more brightly. But sleep hovered over a jungle of worry and hurt. The hurt for his loss of Donna got tangled with fear of failure on the field and his belief that Mervyn (Willis Moore) was going to die and what he would say in his letter, c/o the Lo, I Am with You Always Running Water Baptist Church, Gilt Edge, Tennessee.

15

The Seven-Hundred-Dollar Pitch

The ball park was that of the Fargo-Moorehead Twins, of the Class D Northern League, who were away at Crookston. The grandstand overflowed its good-natured humanity into standing room along both foul lines clear out to the fence. The pregame excitement — hawkers selling peanuts, popcorn, chewing gum, and soda pop; people pushing to get to the ticket windows and through the gates — was intense. Timmy was trembling with it.

They had driven in uniform from the camp, because colored were not permitted to use the visiting-team clubhouse. Filing past it on the way to their dugout, Timmy was glad they would be going back to their camp and a swim in the clean river after the games. The clubhouse smelled of old pee and white sweat.

Timmy caught Bofey's warm-up while the rest of the team put on their pepper game. The crowd laughed, cheered, and clapped for the dazzling performance. There was friendliness coming out from the crowd, but the enemy players, circling the backstop area to watch, were talking ugly. "Those coon are half ape." "Looky that nigger's arms, almost drag on the ground." "That fancy nigger stuff ain't gonna get 'em nowhere once Lefty starts knockin 'em on their black asses."

"Pay them no nevah mind, son," Bofey said when they were lined up along the third-base line for the National Anthem. "We got ways to take care a ourselves." No Nubian gladiator ever stood more proudly or more afraid in the Colosseum than Timmy — his head shining under a glisten of Vaseline — stood that day between Bofey and Mr. Tetley.

With Merv back in camp, the bench of the House for the first game consisted of Ol' Dan, who would coach at first base; Pops, who would coach at third and, if need arose, come in to catch with Mr. Tetley moving to first base, and Timmy. For the second game, with Moon pitching and Timmy in right field, Bofey would be on the bench.

Once, two summers ago, Uncle Hans had taken Timmy to see an exhibition game between the Slaughterhouse Nine and the Fargo-Moorehead Twins. Only a few of their power-hitting regulars of then were in today's line-up — guys with big bellies who hit steers on the head and disemboweled hanging hogs for a living. They had recruited good college players and hired a barnstorming pair of brothers, Lefty and Mickey Vondell, to pitch and catch. Former minor-league players, they now bummed around playing as paid ringers for town and semipro teams.

The first game was a breeze for the House. Scrap Iron, Manny, and Busy Ike led off with hits, and Mr. Tetley slammed one out. Before the inning ended, they had batted around and scored six runs. At the end of the fourth, they were up 10 to 0. Bofey was unfathomable. He would show the college kids his fast ball and dipsy-doodle them with curves. The butchers would lunge ahead of his curves and stand there looking as a fast ball tailed in on them. The catcher was the only batter he respected and he walked him twice, to a rolling thunder of boos. He threw contemptuous junk against the pitcher. The home team called for the ball again and again, but the umpire could find no trace of spit, Vaseline, mud, or abrasion upon its cover.

Lefty began to throw at and behind the House batters. "This gone 'bout far enough," said Busy Ike. Pops came down the line. "Easy, now, easy. We don' wan no trouble up here." Ike danced away from a pitch at his shins, fell away from a high hard one at his head, and then swung hard at a pitch over his head. The bat slipped out of his hands and went spinning out toward the shortstop. "Scuse me," he said to the catcher. "Tell your pitcher next time it take his legs off." Next pitch, Ike popped a bunt down the first-base line, ran past the charging first baseman, and had a clean shot at the pitcher, off balance at the bag to take the throw. Instead of crashing into him, Ike stopped short, doffed his cap, and let himself be tagged out. The crowd whooped its derision for Lefty and applauded Ike's restraint. Under the noise, Ike smiled at the pitcher and said: "Mr. Tetley gonna come up next. You throw at him, he ain't gonna step aside. He gonna make *ham*burger outta your honky ass."

"That's enough now," the first-base umpire said, pushing between them. "You boys play some clean baseball or you ain't playin none."

Lefty couldn't see the plate through the red of his hate. After he walked Mr. Tetley on four pitches, the Slaughterhouse boss took him out to cool him down for the second game and relieved him with a hard-throwing college boy, who was genuinely interested in testing his best stuff against the best batters he had ever faced.

In the seventh, Pops called for the Pin Wheel. Clayton

doubled. Manny singled, but Clayton stayed at second. The crowd buzzed its anticipation of the fun ahead. Moon popped a Texas Leaguer over the shortstop's head to load the bases.

"Okay, Speedy," Pops said, "hit for Bofey and do your stuff."

Timmy, a clown's grin on his stiff face, his head shining, jigged out to the plate, and stepped into the box holding the wrong end of the bat. He was unprepared for the wild laughter of the crowd, but inspired by it. His bench was laughing as hard as the crowd while Mr. Tetley struggled to teach him which end of the bat was up. Then he stepped out of the box to try to figure out the signs Pops was giving him. At last he had it right, he was going to swing away. Pops came down the line to take the bat and show him explicitly that he was being called upon to bunt. He pantomimed his understanding; okay, he was going to bunt. The first pitch was high and outside, and he swung wildly at it. Down the line again came Pops. "How I gonna get it through his white skull, he gonna bunt?" Okay, okay, now Speedy's got it. The next pitch was a perfect hard strike, but Speedy stepped back in terror and ran toward his bench and had to be coaxed to stand back in. He took a ball high. The next pitch was in there, and he tapped it out toward the mound. The pitcher had no chance to catch Clayton, flying with the pitch, at the plate: no chance to force Manny at third; now he turned to snap a throw to first, but Speedy had the ball beat. He wheeled inside the astonished first baseman toward second. Now they had him in the hot box. When the throw passed his head, he reversed toward first. The rattled pitcher, backing up the first baseman, took the return throw in time to see Moon breaking for home and fired to the catcher. Moon slid in safe under the tag, and Speedy turned second and headed for third. The catcher's throw had him beat a country mile, so he dug back toward second. The throw hit him in the rump, and he dashed back toward third while the short-stop and second baseman collided in their scramble for the ball. The desperate throw was into the dirt past the third baseman's lunge, and he danced home free, pausing to thumb his nose at the rattled infield. All four runs had scored on a bunt. The crowd laughed and clapped for the fun of the show.

Moon pitched, and Speedy went to right field. In the ninth, he and Scrap Iron teamed up perfectly on the Wrong Way. Busy Ike caught the final out of the game in his back pocket.

Moon started the second game on the mound with Speedy in right field. Lefty, cooled down and with his rep on the line, pitched well. It was a tight game for six innings, but the House broke out in the seventh and, with a 6 to 1 lead, turned on another spectacular Pin Wheel that scored two more runs before they went down for the inning. Pops called the change: "So now we gonna give these folks they money's worth an' we gonna see kin this boy throw us some strikes." "Our bread's on the table," Little Hoop protested, but Pops shook him off. "Speedy go to the mound, I go catch, Mr. Tetley go to first, an' Nathan go to right."

He was not a clown now, but a pitcher. He couldn't swal-low, and he couldn't spit. He threw the first pitch into the dirt: the second high; he aimed the third; the butcher lined it into center. He threw a wild pitch and walked the next batter for two on and no outs. One of the college kids hit the ball hard down the third-base line. Manny came up with it marvelously on the bag and threw to Little Hoop for the double play. The next butcher golfed a low strike against the left center-field wall for a triple. A college kid lined a drive into Scrappy's glove. No thanks to Timmy, only one run had scored.

"Don' be sendin that boy back out there, Pops, the way they whackin his stuff," said Manny. "It's our money on the line, not his."

"This boy can't throw for money. He just a showboat clown," Little Hoop put in.

It was as if he were a horse, a mule, a piece of property they could use or get rid of without regard to his wishes, needs, or feelings. He felt his resentment blaze up.

Pops shook his head. To Timmy in the privacy of the dugout: "Git on out there, boy. You put the tyin run at the plate an' Bofey gonna come in and get 'em out."

"I'm not pitchin your game, Pops," he said. "I'm pitchin all my stuff. Two fingers for the curve, three for my screwball."

"You pitch what I call, you hear? And remember," Pops called after him as he walked into the sunshine, "you is a deefy."

Little Hoop picked up the ball and was waiting at the mound to slam it into Speedy's glove. Then he made a big show of wild pantomime that he was telling this dumbo to get tough and get those batters out. But his words were mean and heavy: "Now you listen what I say, white boy. I say you choke up an' lose us this game, I gonna take my belt to your white ass we get back to camp."

Timmy gripped the ball and felt like smashing it into the saturnine mouth. Little Hoop tensed as if to strike first.

"Hey, out there," Pops called from the plate.

Speedy grinned and waved his arms wildly, chasing Hoop

out to his position. The crowd seemed to sense the fallibility of the clown. It yelled its derision and sent out a roar to encourage its butcher boys and their ringers to knock him out of the box.

Breathing deeply before each pitch, Timmy threw his first three warm-up pitches down the pike, coming down and through hard — pow. For the fourth he motioned Pops the curve, for the fifth the screwball. They moved just right.

It depended on his first pitch to the batter. If he got it where he wanted it — throwing hard, not aiming it — he would be all right. He shook off the fast ball; Pops jabbed it down again angrily; he shook it off again — and again. Okay, Pops gave him number two, the curve; Timmy shook it off. He wanted to test himself with the screwball, the most difficult to control. He felt cold and loose as he stared in at Pops and waited for number three until Pops gave it to him. Now he had it. Now could he do it? You could do what you knew you could do. He did not *know* he could throw the screwball; he *knew* he had to try. Why was he cursed with knowing the latter without knowing the former?

He stepped off the rubber, which was not rubber at all but a spike-chewed piece of pine. He looked at it and looked at the sky. Timmy had become Speedy Deefy, a real fool standing in real sunshine with real Vaseline on his unreal shaven head. A real ape was swinging a real bat waiting for him to throw the real ball.

There was no encouraging word from the infield. He fixed his eyes on Pops's right shoulder over the outside corner of the plate, took a full wind, and came down turning his wrist to let it fly. It looked like money from home to the batter, who dug in and swung with might. The ball spun in toward the small of the bat. Trying to check his swing, the batter topped a little roller down the first-base line to Mr. Tetley for an easy out. "A seven-hundred-dollar pitch," the huge man said.

Timmy could see Pops's grin inside the wide laugh of the mask. Pops gave him number three again, but Speedy jumped up and down to show him no, no, no. Speedy wanted to let this smart-ass college boy take a look at his curve . . . He *knew* . . .

They got two hits and a harmless run off him, but he struck out a butcher along the way, and Busy Ike ended the second game, as he had the first, by catching a lofty fly ball in his back pocket.

Speedy Deefy ran leaping and jigging out of the sunshine toward the privacy of the dugout. Among those in the grandstand aisle who had crowded to the screen to get a closer look at the black wizards were a Mutt and Jeff pair of drunks. Hollering and clapping their hands off, their tribute seemed to be mainly for him. Speedy touched his cap to them, but Timmy betrayed no recognition of Uncle Hans and Grandpa Tim as he sunk into the dugout and covered his white skull with a towel.

"C'mon, Speedy," Ol' Dan said. "Hep me get the bats in the bag."

He sat in his corner of the truck going back to camp with the towel over his white skull. He went down to the river and swam hard upstream half a mile and floated back down, washing away the dirt and sweat of the day.

They were laughing and cackling in the pleasant shade, drinking home-brew and shots of moonshine while waiting for Dan to boil the corn and cook the ham and greens.

"Hey, Speedy, they tell me you the star of the show," Merv called from his willow tree.

"Then he scared us he gonna blow a five-run lead," Manny said.

"So I go out to give 'im the ball" — Little Hoop was laughing as he told it — "an' I tol' 'im I gonna personally whup his white ass if he don' settle down an' git 'em out."

"That what settle you down, Speedy? You 'fraid of a whuppin?"

"We can anticipate that an inexperienced boy is going to make some mistakes," Mr. Tetley said. "And he did."

Timmy helped himself to a bottle of brew and sat among them but not with them.

After supper, they all dressed up and drove away in the flatbed to strut their stuff one last time in Dark Town. "I gonna get some more a that healin woman's medicine for Merv," Pops said, climbing into the Packard with Ol' Dan.

"A quart of moonshine will do him more good," Timmy called.

"You been good to me, Speedy," Willis Moore said as Timmy got him ready for the long night.

16

The White Girl in the
Ice-Cream Parlor

Only Pops and Ol' Dan got up for breakfast. Before reporting for his chores, Timmy renewed his white skin in the ever-renewed river. His sweat of yesterday, mingled with yesterday's river, was now, he reckoned, on its way to salt the ice in Hudson Bay.

He filled his plate and cup and refueled his dark interior with the goodness of food. The scattered forms of his team-mates, pooped from yesterday's double-header and three nights of excess in the town, were like rag dolls scattered by a naughty child. But, as Pops said, "Let 'em sleep it off. They got nothin to do anyways but drive thirty miles an' make us a new camp." It would be on the Sheyenne River near a town named Norberg where they would play a twi-lighter with the town team on Tuesday.

"But you an' me, Speedy, we gonna hit the road, you drive me in the Packard, make a big swing over to Valley City an' back to where we camp tonight. Gonna put our posters up an' make arrangements in the five towns we play till the

Sunday double-header in Valley City. That gonna make us seven games we play 'tween now and Monday week, so we got our work cut out. I got the map here, where we gonna go today."

Timmy studied the map. "Good." He was going to like this day's work, driving the Packard through the countryside, seeing the towns and diamonds where they would be playing. "Looks like we've got a good two hundred miles to cover. We better get going."

"Git yoursef ready."

"I am ready."

"You gotta be in uniform, put new Vaseline on your head. You gotta be Speedy Deefy in these towns. I show you off an' you go 'round tackin up the posters, put 'em in the store windows."

The vision of a pleasant day became the humiliation of the clown. "But, Pops, I can't see why I can't just —"

"You colored now, boy. Like us. You can't put on no white-boy airs, you travel with us. 'Sides, we need you to drum up the crowds — the more that come, the more we make."

West of Fargo, in the wide valley of the Red River of the North, the land stretches out to the plains. The black gumbo soil, the leavings of fifty thousand years of glacial retreat and recurring flood, rewards its methodical tillers with heavy crops of sugar beets and rich feed crops to sate the beasts that become just about the primest beef and pork on the earth. From the grain elevator and water tower of one town you can see ten miles ahead to the grain elevator and water tower of the town coming at you forty miles an hour on the section-line road.

Now, with the distant grain elevator and water tower of Norberg rising ahead and the plume of their dust rising behind, Pops expanded on what was expected of Timmy: "You gotta be careful now, we play these small towns, four or five hunnerd people sittin close, some standin right behind our bench — not a dugout, a bench, a *bare* bench in the open . . ."

"I know, Pops, I know. I played with the Beavers and the high-school team on a bunch of fields like that."

"You *don'* know. Why you tell me you know when you don' know what I'm tellin you? You gonna listen me or you gonna stay in camp an' catch fish?"

"I was brought up in this country, Pops. It's the one thing I do know, this part of the country."

"This country you know so well, born and brought up, you know it as a white boy, not as a colored boy. You gonna find out it not be the same to one as it be to the other. You gonna find you be in a strange land, a long ways from home. To them you be a nigger. You gonna act like a nigger, you hear? You no king-a-the-roost white boy no more. You gotta know your place, what colored can do an' can't do. You understand what I say?"

"These are nice people out in these small towns, Pops," Timmy protested. "They're glad to see us."

"They may be nice as pie, but they still *white*. I know white. Same here as they are down home. Reason we get by so good up here is we don' in-ter-ject oursevs. We come by oursevs, we stay by oursevs, we pay for what we get, we play ball, we take their money, we go. We don' in-ter-ject, you hear me?"

"We know our places," Timmy said.

"Now you got what I'm sayin. An' you be careful. You can't hear me or them, no matter what they say. I show you by sign. You grin an' you do it. You keep grinnin no matter what they say, you jes a happy colored boy happen to have white skin. You got to *perform*, boy. To hep us, you got to be parta the act. Give 'em what they pay to see . . ."

"But, Pops, you're *ball*players. First and foremost, you're ballplayers. They come to see you play better ball than they've ever seen before."

Pops shook his head. "Baseball been the biggest parta my life, all these years. I started playing in the barehanded days. Caught barehanded behin' the plate, not under the bat like now, but a step back on the first bounce. But Negro ball, some a the best players in the whole histry a the worl' — I seen 'em all, Satchel Paige, Cool Papa Bell, an' many more . . . There's nothin in it but a few dollars here an' there, till you go back to farmin or roustin or shoe shinin. So then I hear about the white House of David, they let their hair grow an' barnstorm around."

"The *white* House of David? Aren't we the *original?*"

"Original *colored*. We the first to copy ourselves after them — long hair, beards, but not their religion. We fake our religion to draw people in. We mostly jes plain Baptists. But they found theirselves some special religion outta the Bible. They come from up outta Michigan somewheres, some kinda settlement they started where they live together, work to-gether, pray together . . . You know what they be most famous for?"

"Their traveling ball team?"

"Nope. Makin jelly. I hear someone say they the greatest jelly makers in the whole wide world."

"There's a lot of great fruit country in Michigan."

"So we look at it if they kin let their hair grow an' draw crowds to see 'em play ball, so kin we. But up here, up North. Down South, we no special draw to colored folks, an' white folks got their own ball. White only. So we swing up this way, spring to fall. First year, we play straight ball, show 'em our best. But it's too good for 'em, their teams got no chance

137

wif us. Then we see they come early to watch our infield drill and our warm-up pepper game. So then we make a show of it, like Wrong Way an' Ike catchin fly balls in his back pocket. But it's more than the show they come to see. It's us as *clowns*. See, it's aw right for whites to come out an' see colored as clowns that know their place. That way they don' have to see us as people. Nor as ballplayers neither. If they gonna see us as ballplayers, they gonna see we better ballplayers than they. That don' swallow too good. If we be better ballplayers, why don' we get our chance in the big leagues where the money is? They can't take us serious or they see how wrong they are in their hearts. We gotta be clowns they can laugh away and say how clever them niggers is with their tricks."

The summer serenity of the fields, the green lushness of the bountiful harvest to come, seemed to deny what Pops was saying about the people who enjoyed their bounty.

"It's humiliating," Timmy said at last, "to have to be a clown to make a living."

"It beats choppin cotton," Pops said.

Pops got out his black book and studied where he was and who he was going to see about the arrangements in Norberg. "These towns up here, they all alike. I get the next town we gonna play mixed up in my mind with the one we just played. The towns are the same an' the faces in them are the same, made from the same white dough."

"Oh, no!" Timmy protested. "When you get to know them, you'll find that they're all different . . ."

"Looka here,' said Pops as they came to the outskirts of Norberg. "I could say it by heart." He cupped his hand to his mouth for a megaphone and called out the passing charms of Norberg like the driver of a rubberneck bus: "An' on your left, ladies and gennelmun, is the Consolidated Cooperative

Grain Elevator, tallest edifice in the great city of Norberg. Now we passin the town water tank, an' here come the depot . . . Every town up here got the same thing. An' a main street where they got the stores, a bank, an' the post office . . ."

"And an ice-cream parlor and a picture show . . ."

"They all got three churches . . ."

"Four, if there's enough Catholics . . ."

"An' a school . . ."

"Both a grade school and a high school . . ."

"They all got big elm trees on the streets where people live. Same kinda houses, all with their woodsheds an three-hole shithouses. What you mean, oh no, they're all different? Ain't a dime's wortha difference 'tween them. Nor the people neither. Know one, you know 'em all."

Timmy was going to argue that the people in these towns might seem alike to strangers but were richly individualistic to those, like him, who knew them to be fine, upstanding, hard-working, God-fearing, fair-minded . . . But Pops told him to pull up in front of the farm-implement dealer on the edge of Main Street. It did occur to Timmy that in every town he could think of, the farm-implement dealer was located at the end of Main Street, near the hardware store.

"Man in here, fella named Mr. Winberg, he the one I deal with in this town. So you be takin the posters down the street with the tack hammer. Put 'em on the poles an' in every store window they let you. 'Member, you a deefy."

"How do I ask them if I can't talk?"

"Grin an' jig an' make signs like a happy coon."

Timmy put the tack hammer and tacks in his back pocket and a stack of posters under his arm.

"You gotta take the ink pot an' brush, too. Write in the Norberg North Stars. Game is 6:00 P.M. Tuesday. When you get done both sides a the street, you come back here an' I show you off to Mr. Winberg."

At the second pole, two or three youngsters hopped around him to examine his uniform and see what he was up to. He pointed to the sign and to himself that he was Speedy Deefy, the White Crow, the Demon of the Bases. Quickly joined by three or four more, pretty soon a dozen of them, the kids chanted him down the street and into the stores, yelling that here was the white coon from the nigger baseball team coming to play the North Stars.

"Don't you be using that word *nigger* in front of him," the lofty woman in the Buster Brown shoe store scolded. "You'll hurt his feelings."

"He can't hear nothin, Mrs. Johnson," their leader shouted. "You can call him anything you want. He can't hear nor talk back."

"When Otto came by this morning to tell about his trip to Fargo, he told about this albino coon he saw but didn't mention he was a deaf-mute."

If this were happening at home, Timmy was thinking, he would scatter the kids with swift kicks in their asses. He grinned and jigged for Mrs. Johnson, and she laughed and put the poster in the window. "Crazy kids," she said as they romped away with him.

They knew Speedy Deefy in the barbershop. On the sports page of the Fargo *Forum* was a photo of him running out of the hot box in yesterday's game. "Otto seen 'em yesterday," the barber told his customers. "He went to Fargo and seen 'em, said them niggers put on the funniest show he ever did see."

"I'm gonna be there with bells on tomorrow evenin."

"Said this white coon is as hard to catch as a green fart."

"Wouldn't miss it for the world."

"He's as white-lookin as you or me."

Timmy grinned his thanks and jigged his way out to the street.

A Girl of his Dreams had been taking form and rising like a wispy golden goddess in the dark aching void where he had adored and lost the vision of Donna. In the morning quiet of the cool ice-cream parlor, suddenly disrupted by the swirl of noise that pranced in with him, he beheld her behind the soda fountain. There she was!

Her braids of golden hair were wound into a crown to keep them free of the cold ambrosia she scooped for mortals from the ice-cream barrels. Her smock was stiffly starched to contain the precious overflow of her bountiful breasts as she leaned forward to scoop; the alabaster of her arms and face and throat were but the visible proof of the entirety of her womanly perfection. Her lips were made for nibbling cherries away from their stems and for kissing. Her eyes were as blue and merry as the waves of a playful lake. There was, withal, a presence of calm confidence that she would soon bequeath her priceless virginity and eternal love to a worthy One and Only.

To me!

He would amuse her now, learn her name, write to her when he got back home to reveal himself as the renowned Tim Nelson of Indian Springs, get acquainted, become engaged . . .

He smiled his love for her and pantomimed himself as Speedy Deefy and his errand. The snotty kids were shouting that this was the white coon with the nigger ball team, etc. "Be quiet, you kids!" She silenced their pesky leader with a quick slap to the side of his head and confronted Timmy. "Now what is it you want in here?"

A fat man in a white apron, the proprietor, flopped from

his stool behind his fortress cash register into which he was plunking the coins for the day's change and sailed into the commotion like a blimp. "What is this, Julia? What's going on here?"

Ah, Julia.

"The kids say he's a deaf-mute nigger from the ball team that's coming to play here tomorrow. He wants to put a poster in the window. He sure doesn't look like a nigger to me, does he to you, Mr. Swanson?"

Julia, care of Swanson's ice-cream parlor, Norberg, North Dakota. "Dear Julia, you will remember me as Speedy Deefy . . ."

Mr. Swanson took in the situation. "He's a nigger all right. What they call an albino. I heard about him from Otto. Tell him, sure, we'll put up his poster. Good for business. A lot of the folks will be coming in after the game. Now you kids get out of here! If you can't show me your nickel, get out! You know you're not allowed to hang around here without a nickel to spend."

He shooed the kids out and returned to his stool and the counting and plunking of the nickels and dimes and quarters.

Timmy looked after the moon-faced Scrooge and blessed him for a minute alone with his dream girl. He dipped his brush and, to amuse her, leaned forward on the counter to complete the poster, pretending with extended tongue to labor over the formation of the letters. She sniffed to see if he stunk and stepped back with a frown of aversion. No laughter? Not a smile?

She picked up the poster as if it were a soiled handkerchief and flounced the few steps to place it in the window. Suddenly he remembered Robert Herrick's little poem of how his seventeenth-century Julia moved when she walked:

142

That brave vibration each way free,
O how that glittering taketh me!

One of the kids in their English class had asked what "brave vibration" meant. Their teacher, Old Mrs. Morken, had shut off the giggling with hostile finality: "It means that she walked like a slut." Now Timmy's Julia of the twentieth century returned to frown at his little giggle. "That's it, then. Get out!"

But the dauntless Speedy Deefy of today, out in the world, put his coins on the counter and pointed to the sign above her golden crown that touted a two-scoop chocolate soda for fifteen cents. He gestured humorously to show his dry throat and need for sustenance.

"Mr. Swanson," she called. "He wants a soda. Do we serve niggers in here? His money's on the counter."

Fifteen cents on the counter deserved contemplation. "Don't see any harm in fixing him a soda, long as nobody's here anyway. But he's got to eat it standing up. Wouldn't be right to let him sit at a table in case the dry-goods ladies come in a little early."

Timmy, smiling raptly, stood mute through this exchange and while she scooped and fizzed the soda. Then, with uppityness, he seated himself at a table and waited for her to serve him.

"No, no," she yelled and ran around to grab him by the arm and hoist him to his feet. "Over here!" She tugged and motioned. "You stand here!"

He shrugged and raised his palms and jigged obediently after her. He sucked up the nose-tingling chocolate fizz without taking his eyes from her. She washed her hands in the basin faucet without taking hers from his. While he spooned the ice cream, she dried her clean-again hands. With final noisy suction, the last of the soda went up the straw. He set the glass down and raised his eyeballs to show the rapture of his enjoyment. As quickly as it had darted out to slap the noisy boy, her hand snatched the soiled glass. Her left hand pointed him sternly to the door. Then, as his smile faded, she threw his glass into the trash can. "Get out of here before somebody sees you in here, you dirty white nigger." The loathing on her fair Nordic face revealed the ugliness she would not have put into words had she known they could be heard. Through the surge of red rage — anger? shame? hate? — he saw her beauty as the mask of evil. Then he smiled, for his had been the briefest love affair of any he knew about in life, literature, or legend. Oh, the cycle of fool's paradise and wretch's hell he had been spared!

Outside the pack of kids picked him up, and he grinned and jigged between telephone poles back to where Pops was going to show him off to the farm-implement dealer.

Upwards of five hundred town and farm folks paid two bits each to see them clown to an easy win over the Norberg North Stars. Pops rested bofe of Bofey's arms, and Speedy played right field for five innings. With two out in the fifth, a likely fly ball came his way, and he tried Ike's trick of catching it in his back pocket. When the ball hit his back, he made like it knocked him sprawling and then jumped up and down rubbing the pain in his rump while the runner circled the bases for a free home run. "Thas good, thas good," Pops said. "We keep that in the act for games like this." Speedy pitched the last four innings, throwing hard and easy; he showed the rubes his curve and screwball just for fun and practice.

While Pops and Ol' Dan went to the Packard to count the take from the implement dealer, Speedy trooped with the others toward the truck. But there was Julia, helping out in the Ladies' Aid lemonade stand. He darted away and spun his nickel on the counter. One of the ladies, Mrs. Johnson from the Buster Brown shoe store, laughed and filled a paper cup. "That was a good show you boys put on," she said, quite forgetting he was deaf.

He raised the cup in toast to each of the ladies and to Julia, then slowly turned his hand and poured its untasted contents to the ground. He tossed the cup into the heavens and with a mute's raucous whoop sprinted away to join his kind.

17

A Man of Considerable Erudition

"A nicely mannered white boy like you," Mr. Tetley remarked about midnight, "scorning those dear sweet ladies. Why, they could have been your mother and sister!"

They were on their pads on a breezy knoll away from the others. Timmy had buried the chicken bones and corncobs following their feast and had made Merv comfortable in his sack by the fire. The edge of sarcasm in Mr. Tetley's remark seemed unfair. Hadn't he . . . ?

"They had it coming," he said and found himself getting hot in the ears about it as he related his story as clown in the town and the ice-cream parlor.

"But you were not personally humiliated." Mr. Tetley took a swig of moonshine from his silver flask and settled back to gaze beyond the starlight. "For you it was just a tiny taste — a little glimpse — of what it's like to be black in your white world. It takes me back to my first real . . ." But he shook his head slightly and closed his eyes.

"Your first real what?" Timmy asked.

"Humiliation. It was my first trip away from home, too . . . I got to thinking about it the other morning when you came into our camp in your Sunday suit . . ." From out of the huge cavern of his chest came the gentle rumble of laughter. "It's funny . . . it occurred to me then how much alike we were — you leaving home for the first time to join our little black world, and I leaving the black bosom of my family in New Orleans to venture into the white world . . . Eleven years and a thousand miles between us, headed in different directions to different destinies and yet" — and the little laugh came out again — "somehow alike."

"Funny? What's funny about it, Mr. Tetley? After all, we're both . . ." Both what? What they both were was . . .

Mr. Tetley looked at him and said it for him: "From families of some means . . . not poor boys . . . and traditions . . . and education . . ."

"I knew from the first," Timmy said into another long pause, "that you were a man of considerable erudition."

Another rumble of easy laughter. "What a fine way to put it! Most white people have a different term for it — 'edjicated nigger.' "

"Ohh."

"Oh, they do . . . But, anyway, yes, I am that all too rare phenomenon . . . and came by it naturally, not because of any particular determination or bootstrap effort on my part . . ." The deep vowels and soft consonants of what he was saying were set in cadences of unfamiliar charm to Timmy's northern ears. On the diamond and in the camp, his fancy diction was exaggerated and edged with irony. Now it seemed to revert to an earlier time of his life. "My father was — is — the pastor of the largest African Methodist congregation in New Orleans . . . My Grandma Daisy is publisher of the leading black newspaper, the cultural leader of

147

the Negro community . . . She organized the first Negro Shakespearean repertory company in America — or anywhere else . . ."

"And your paternal grandfather . . . William P. Tetley the First . . . What was he?"

Mr. Tetley said nothing for a long spell. Then he said: "It's getting late."

"But," Timmy protested. "You were telling me about your first . . ."

"Humiliation. Oh, *that* . . . it's not much of a story."

"You said it reminded you of me."

"I said you reminded me of it. Well, like you, I had obtained parental permission to leave home for the summer . . . to try out for the Birmingham Barons, one of the better professional Negro teams . . . Anyway, I was on this train, in the colored coach, all dolled up in my Sunday best. The white coaches and Pullman cars were plush and elegant — silver and linen in the dining car. Ours was an old windowless mail car that had been fitted with bare benches. At major stops, a white hawker would board the colored coach and permit us to line up to buy summer-sausage sandwiches, candy bars, and paper cups of weak lemonade for a dime a throw. I didn't feel that I *belonged* there, and I felt no kinship or fellowship with the other passengers. Others were wearing their Sunday best, too, probably going back home for weddings and funerals, so it wasn't only my dress that set me apart from them. It took me a while, bumping and swaying in my corner, to realize that I felt shame for them — not so much for their disgraceful treatment, but for their amiable, shuffling acceptance of it.

"Along in the afternoon, I got in line to buy a sandwich and a cup of lemonade. I gave the hawker a quarter and said, 'Keep the change.' Suddenly it was still and tense. For a moment I didn't know why. The hawker's red neck flamed, and his dirty hands became white fists. He looked me down from my straw skimmer, silk necktie, coat and vest, to my tan shoes. 'Boy,' he said, 'you stan raht thay. Now heah's yo nickel, boy.' He flipped it to the floor. 'Now, boy, you gonna stoop'n pick that nickel up. Heah me, boy?' The brakeman came up behind the hawker. 'What we got us here? A bad nigger?' 'This city nigger think he kin tip a white man,' the hawker replied. Then to me he said: 'You heah what I tell you?'

"I looked around for the nickel. 'I heard you.' 'You heard him what?' the brakeman demanded. 'I heard him, sir,' I heard myself saying.

" 'We oughta feed this boy to the railroad bulls,' the brakie said. 'You know what railroad bulls do to bad niggers like you?' 'No, sir.' 'You gonna fin' out raht quick you don' stoop'n pick up that nickel,' the hawker told me.

"So I shuffled over to the nickel and stooped and picked it up and shuffled back to my corner."

"Ohh," said Timmy.

"It was a trivial, everyday incident . . . Nobody got beat up . . . or locked up on a chain gang . . . or lynched . . ."

"And then? Then what?"

Mr. Tetley took a final nip from his silver flask. "I went on to Birmingham and became Mistuh Tetley of the Barons."

"But now, Mr. Tetley. What are you doing way up here . . . with us?" Timmy asked.

Mr. Tetley thought about it for a while. Then he said: "Thinking."

18

Their Red Brethren

The silver-plated shaving mirror hanging from a thorn on a crackleberry tree elongated his nose and receded his chin and showed him that his face was still white. Damn, if he hadn't got to thinkin of hisself as black. In the last few days — now that they were zigging north and zagging west on the back roads between towns on the way to campsites and performances — he had come to feel black in a black universe. Black was the home universe from which, like the space adventurers in *Amazing Stories,* they descended into the sudden whiteness to cavort before the ridiculous but harmless inhabitants.

Pops took to the back roads to avoid passing through towns. He guided them to remote and secluded campsites both to avoid trouble and to keep people from seeing them out of uniform. Only Pops and Ol' Dan — and Speedy Deefy on advance ballyhoo trips — conducted business with the whites and went into stores and farms to buy provisions. The others went as a tight band into the whiteness, performed their baseball wizardry, and soon were back again in the black universe of their camp.

The weather held good. They had easy games as they circled north to the little towns — Pillsbury, Cooperstown, Dazey — that took them to Valley City for the Sunday double-header and a $500 crowd of two thousand.

Pitching the first game, Bofey's good left arm went bad. A dull ache in the third inning became sharp pain in the fourth. Pops and Mr. Tetley went to the mound, and Pops signaled for Speedy to come in to mop up.

"It stiffnin up like the right arm did. I kin git 'em out . . ."

Pops shook him off and took the ball. "We gotta rest you up for Mandan. Speedy, he kin do it for us here."

Bofey told Speedy: "Git 'em on low strikes, sept that number-four hitter, curve him. He be way out in fronta your slow curve."

Timmy nodded. "Okay, Bofey. I'll get 'em."

"Be still, you deefy!" Pops pretended he was talking to Bofey. "Now I give you this ball, you jump up an' down, ack like you be too scared to pitch. You run off, I come an' get you back, you is scared *white*, unnerstan? White!"

Speedy jumped up and down in tantrum and fled toward the bench . . .

They breezed through both games and put on a good show. The question that hung in the air: Would Bofey be ready for the Mandan Cowpokes?

Timmy got Pops's okay to drive the Packard and was behind its wheel when they broke camp next morning and headed out. "Mind you now, be quick for the turns I call, they be sharp and they come at you sudden," Pops instructed. "This place we goin, shouldn't take too long, if I can remember rightly where it's at, halfway out in nowheres 'bout twenty miles either way from bofe where we play in Farmersburg this evenin and in New Stockholm tomorra evenin . . ."

"The New Stockholm Swenskies."

". . . so we get a nice two-day camp outta it at a little country church where they don' come but on Sundays and for buryin. There's a li'l river go by where you can get your swim an' catch us some pickrel —"

"What's the name of the river?"

"Don' know it got a name."

"It must be the Mouse River. It's up here somewhere. These cricks and rivers out here, they're not flowing north and east to the Red, but south and west to the Missouri. Might be some trout in them." They were working their way north and west of Valley City in a swing that would take them through Devils Lake to Minot for a Sunday double-header.

Half an hour out, making the ninety-degree turns that Pops called out — north and west and north again on the uncharted section-line roads — Timmy had no sense of where they were or how they would go, but only a helmsman's faith in his pilot. The top green of the wood pastures, restless in the steady wind blowing cool and dry through the hot sunshine from the northern plains, and the vastness of the tawny undulating winter wheat heightened the sense of voyage on a calm ocean. Timmy liked being out front with Pops and Ol' Dan, away for a while from the fierce competition and arguing, bickering, wrangling, whooping and cursing of the acey-deucey game on the floor of the flatbed.

In midafternoon, by luck or by instinct, Pops called the final turn, skirting the edge of a small town, that got them to the churchyard and their best campsite since they had left the Sheyenne. The white church was beside an elm-shaded picnic grove with tables and a big stone fireplace, and a pump into a deep and cold well. Behind the church were two threeholers (Ladies Only and Gents). Beyond the grove, away from the river, were the tombstones of the mowed and tended graveyard. There was no sound but the wind in the trees and the calls and songs of a hundred near and distant birds. They pulled in and stretched their lean-to canvas between the wet-footed willows by the river.

By three o'clock they were in the picnic grove lolling and dozing after the huge helpings of Ol' Dan's chicken-okra gumbo and rice, and the cherry pie Pops had bought at the bakery in Valley City.

Contentment, Timmy was thinking through the translucent pink of his eyelids, was in knowing — not just being vaguely aware, but *knowing* — that there was no place you would rather be than where you were . . . a full belly and an hour of ease away from the rest of the world . . .

"Holy smokes alive, God *damn!* Who dat comin in on us?"

They sat up or turned to prop themselves on their elbows to follow Nathan's gaze through the sunshine to the intrusion. It was a band of itinerants in a steaming flivver. The driver jumped out to twist off the radiator cap and let the steam blow free. By the beaded band on his forehead, by his long black hair, by his bare feet and ragged denims, they knew him to be an Indian boy of perhaps fifteen summers. As he turned toward the pump with a bucket, he looked over and saw the fierce array of black strangers in the shade. There was fright on his face as he motioned to his chief.

The chief, perhaps the boy's father, got out and stared at them. He was a short, slim man of about forty with a bloody rag bound round his head. This red man motioned to the young one to stand fast by the flivver and to its occupants to sit tight. He strode unsteadily forward. The break in his stride, they saw, was because of the lack of a heel on one of his worn-out cowboy boots. He stopped halfway and looked in upon them. Pops motioned his people to stay and strode to the parley.

"We don't aim to bother you none," they heard the red man say, wobbling a little. "We need some water an' we'll be movin on."

"No bother to us," Pops said. "This place as much yours as ours."

More yours than ours, Timmy was thinking. We're black strangers in your land. He realized how fearsome they must appear to the Indian and blessed Pops for his smile and his reassurance: "We just a travelin baseball team passin through. Don' pay us no mind."

"Much obliged," the red man said and motioned his band to come to the pump. They kept piling out of the flivver like in a two-reel comedy. First a woman carrying a baby and leading a tot. Then three kids from five to eight — and two more half-grown.

"One little, two little, three little Indians," Timmy sang softly. "Four little, five little . . ."

Finally, the old grandma squaw hobbled into view, clutching a brown paper bag. It was Little Hoop who observed that the bandage on the chief's head had once been the hem of her faded green-flowered calico skirt.

"In all my years of observing the extremities of poverty, and of being inspired to elude their toils," said Mr. Tetley, "I'll be dipped in shit if I ever saw any sorrier-looking folks than these Indians."

They nodded their comfortable agreement. "It makes you count your blessings," he went on, stroking his full belly and admiring the ash on his cheroot, "to be born a Negro in these great United States of America."

"We seen hard times like that when we was kids down home," Nathan spoke up.

"Specially that year the boll weevils et up all the cotton in the county," his twin affirmed.

They watched as the boy pumped a battered bucket of water and poured it into the intestines of the expired flivver. The children, pumping for each other, drank greedily from their cupped hands. The chief brought a tin can of water to the mother, who tilted it for the baby. The grandma took half a loaf of bread from the brown bag and divided it into equal parts for the kids and the mother. The mother soaked her share in water and fed her baby. There were no crumbs left over.

"We got more'n we need," Ol' Dan said.

Pops nodded. "Speedy, you hep Dan dish 'em up. Git that corn bread an' sorghum left from breakfast. Make 'em up that crocka lemonade . . ."

But Hoop was on his feet to object. "Not so fast here. Now just a minute . . ."

Timmy, already on his way to help Ol' Dan, turned like a ferret on Hoop. "Not you, nor anybody else, is going to stop us feeding these people."

"We gotta feed 'em," Ol' Dan said, coming up alongside Speedy. "I couldn't sleep nights again, seein them big hongry eyes . . ."

"What did I say about not feedin 'em? You ain't heard yet what I got to say. What I say is that Pops an' you is talkin like you can hear. We got strangers in camp. You be a deefy, you act like a deefy."

"But these are just Indians," Timmy protested. "And they're starving."

"Rule 'bout deefy don' say nothin' bout just Indians or whether they be starvin."

"Thas right," Manny said. "Rule say he can't hear, he can't talk. We use signs only."

" 'The quality of mercy is not strained,' " said Mr. Tetley.

"That's Shakespeare," Timmy said.

"Who talkin about strainin mercy?" Hoop said. "I'm talkin 'bout how we know these Indians don't go shootin off their mouths in fronta white folks sayin this famous Speedy Deefy, this albino, he ain't nothin but a fake."

"The boys are right," Pops decided. "We got the rule, we keep it. You come on back here. We start over."

Speedy grinned and jigged back to Pops, who pantomimed elaborately, reinforcing his signs with the words he was trying to get through the albino's dumb white skull: "Long time, no eat, see? You go dish 'em up plates . . . Start with little ones, get them big hongry eyes off'n me . . ." Speedy, now he got it, he grin an' jig an' gather the children to the table . . .

When they saw the preparations being made for them, the woman began to weep and her husband stared out over the stones of the graveyard. Mr. Tetley returned from foraging in Dan's pantry with two cans of Carnation. "These two little fellas," he said to the mother as he punched two holes in the tops of the cans, "will find this, when diluted with water, as delicious and nutritious as mother's milk itself."

Soon the kids and the grandma were scraping and slurping from the heaping tin plates. The mother was nursing the baby by letting it suck the warm milk from a sopping rag while she and the tot took alternate spoonfuls from a common plate of the gumbo.

The chief was restraining the Indian boy to wait for what was left after the little ones were satisfied.

"Let 'im get his plate," Pops said. "We got plenty for all."

The boy grinned and dug right in.

"You, too," Pops said.

"Much obliged," the chief muttered, wobbling like a

156

drunk. Clinging to the pump for support, he keeled slowly and gracefully around it to a dignified sitting position.

Speedy crouched beside him, trying to get him to understand that he had medical supplies and would doctor the wounds on his head. Moon, who helped Timmy with the nursing of Mervyn, was assisting. "You gonna be all right," he told the chief. "This albino boy here, he gonna fix you up as good as new."

"Got dizzy," the chief said into his hands.

The woman had given the infant to the grandma to come to her husband. She had seemed a tired drab in rags; now, her black eyes alight, nimble in her unencumbered movements, she was a good-looking woman — or anyway, you could see that she once had been. "Dizzy," she said, trying to get him to his feet, "dizzy from nothin to eat for two days. Dizzy from getting beat up by those measly cops." He tried but slumped back. "Henry," she said softly, "please come and get some food in you. Then this white boy here —"

"He's a albino, ma'am," Moon explained. "He can't hear nor talk, but he's got heap big medicine. He's like our doctor."

"The car," the chief muttered, "gotta get it runnin. Gotta get there tonight."

"We can't get there tonight," the woman said. "We've got no gas. We've got no money. We've got nothin to go on."

"We've got this far," he said.

"Where you bound for tonight?" Moon asked.

"Turtle Mountain Reservation." She motioned to the north. "Still a hundred miles."

"Gotta get outta this county by dark," the chief said. "He gonna throw us all in jail."

Speedy signed for the woman to take the dirty bandage off the chief's head; he'd be right back to fix it up.

"Do what he say," Moon told her.

"What did he say?" she asked.

"He say you be takin that dirty bandage off, he be right back with his medicine to fix it up."

Timmy sprinted over to the lean-to where Merv was propped against a tree. In the fluster of concern for destitute strangers, Timmy's time to nourish and doctor their own invalid had slipped past. "What all that ruckus goin on up there?" Merv looked feverish again, and his forehead was hot and dry.

"A poor Indian family. We're feeding them." He poured the last of the healing woman's brew into Mervyn's cup. "I've got to put a fresh bandage on their chief. He got beat up by some measly cops."

"They runnin from the law?"

"I don't know what they're running from."

"They gonna bring the law down on us." There was fear in his near-delirium. "We don' wan no law messin wif us."

"They're just trying to get home to their reservation." Timmy soothed him and freshened the cooling pad in the ice water in his tin pail and placed it on the hot forehead before sprinting back to doctor the chief.

While Ol' Dan got his lathering brush and razor and a pan of warm soapy water, Speedy and Moon got the chief to his hands and knees with his head under the pump. The cold water flushed away the blood clots on the wounds — one on his forehead, one behind his ear, and one on the crown. Speedy set about cleaning them and closing them with tape. He did it well. In fifteen minutes, he had the wounds dressed and protected by ten yards of neatly wound gauze. The chief, much refreshed, sat down before a steaming plate of gumbo.

The sound of children's laughter was rising from the picnic

grove. Mr. Tetley had one chocolate-smeared kid on his lap and two bigger ones on his knees. Clayton and Nathan were juggling baseballs and making them disappear in flight and reappear from the most unlikely places, including their hind ends.

Speedy darted down to the flivver where Manny, who knew a thing or two about machinery, was working with the boy. He had got the damn thing running again. "Lucky we had an extra can of radiator solder," he told Timmy, forgetting he was a deefy. "They gonna have to add water once in a while, but ol' tin lizzie, she gonna get 'em there."

Hoop came down with the two-gallon can of gasoline they carried for their own emergencies and poured it in the tank. "Oughta get 'em to some town where they kin git some more."

"Trouble is," said Timmy, also forgetting he was a deefy, "they don't have any money to buy it with."

"We takin up a collection," Hoop said. "Ain't you voted Pops to put in your share?"

Timmy went back to the grove to see about it. "We voted a dollar each outta shares," Pops said.

"I assumed I had your proxy and voted you in," Mr. Tetley said.

Speedy grinned and jigged to show his approval.

Suddenly every human-related sound but the mindless chugging of the flivver was silenced by the dust-raising stop of a black Buick sedan on the road out front. As two men with holstered revolvers stepped out and came toward the black and red itinerants, Timmy could hear again the calls and songs of birds and the wind in the trees. One of the lawmen was a shrimp of an old man wearing a blue shirt and a gold star, the other a young strapper wearing a grey shirt and a tin star. Speedy and the other men of the House, without word or signal, stepped forward to put a black barrier between the law and the red wayfarers.

Astonished, the lawmen stopped and glared eyelessly from the shade of the broad brims of their Stetsons at the black array.

Pops, an old hand at parley, ambled forward: "Evenin," he said in noncommittal greeting.

"Vot in de name of shit and Shinola have ve got going on here anyvays?" Old Gold demanded in the familiar rising-falling Scandinavian inflections of that part of the country.

"I'll be ding-danged, Charley," quoth Young Tin, as he tilted his hat back and recognition lighted his broad Norsky face, "if we ain't run smack dab into the darkie ball team I was telling you I seen at Valley City."

"Oh, is dat who it is out here?" And Old Gold tilted his hat back. "I couldn't figure out for the life of me who the heck you fellers were," he said to Pops. "I hear you got a pretty comical bunch of baseball players."

Pops nodded. "You got us figgered right."

"I understand you vill be playing for de folks in New Stockholm tonight," Old Gold said.

"Tomorra. Tonight we play in Farmersburg."

"That white one there," said Young Tin, "he's that albino I was telling you about. Deaf as a post, but can that boy ever scoot!"

Speedy stood tense and mute.

"What might we be doin for you?" Pops asked.

"You boys are fine," said Old Gold. "Ve haven't got vun single complaint against you fellers. It's dose Indian beggars ve been following to check up on."

"They not botherin us none," said Pops. "We get along

fine 'n dandy. What they done wrong, you come lookin for 'em?"

"They're just no-good thievin Indians, that's all," Young Tin explained affably. "We gonna see they haul ass outta Republic County by sundown."

"Uttervize, you see, ve got to lock 'em up."

"If it isn't presumptuous," said Mr. Tetley, ambling his naked-to-the-waist bulk to the front, "may I ask the nature of your charges against our red brethren?"

"He's that big catcher that hits the ball a ton," Young Tin explained to Old Gold.

"Two of my deputies — dere not regular deputies, but I svare 'em in as de need arises — dey caught dese Indians in Republic City last night, stealin and beggin and scarin folks half to death."

"That's the one back there. Hey, you with the bandage on your head," Young Tin called to the chief. "Front and center."

The chief stepped forward. "We do not steal," he said.

"He sure as hell was going to steal," Young Tin felt obliged to explain. "They caught him after dark in the alley behind the stores on Main Street."

"If you vasn't up to no good," said Old Gold to the chief, "try to explain vy you try to make a run for it ven dey tell you to halt."

"I ran to get away from their clubs," the chief said.

"These Indians, they'll twist it every time," Young Tin explained. "The reason they clubbed him was because he run for it."

"If I may ask you, sir," said Mr. Tetley to the chief, "what were you doing behind the stores after dark?"

"Looking for food," the chief said.

"We got reports from all over town that these Indians were on the loose," Young Tin said. "The old lady was begging door-to-door, scaring people half to death."

"If I had've been dere, you bet your boots I vould have locked 'em up last night," Old Gold said.

"On what charges, may I ask?"

"Lots and lots of charges if dey vas needed — attempted burglary, beggin on the street, wagrancy . . ."

"Being off the reservation," Young Tin added.

Mr. Tetley again turned to the chief. "What, may I ask, were you doing off the reservation?"

"Looking for work picking peas and beans for the cannery. Me and my wife and big kids, we can make five-six dollars a day, help tide us over the winter."

"Shit," said Young Tin, "these lying Indians don't know what honest work is."

"But I vasn't dere, you see," Old Gold continued, "so my deputies took it on demselves to let dem go on de condition dat dey get out of de county by sundown today. So den I figgered ve better check up on dem, you see, to make absolutely certain dey get out of my yurisdiction, so nobody can criticize me dat I let dem run loose in Republic County."

"We can't take a chance of having them become wards of the county," Young Tin amplified. "Surely you boys can understand our position."

"Certainly, certainly," Mr. Tetley said. "How far is it to the county line?"

"Headed north, up toward the reservation, it's a good twenty miles."

"They've got a car that's running, gasoline, money, and food," said Mr. Tetley. "By sundown they'll be three counties away."

"We figure sundown here the same as suppertime, six

o'clock," Young Tin said. "You unnerstand that?" he demanded of the chief. "Six o'clock you out of the county. Unnerstand?"

The chief nodded. "These people, they save us."

"This is just a taste" — Young Tin tapped the bandaged head — "what you're gonna get if we ever catch you in Republic County again. You hear me?"

"Ve vill count upon you boys, seeing you is so friendly vit dem, making absolutely certain dey get started out of here in plenty time to make it out of Republic County by six o'clock dis evening, den?"

"You have our assurance," Mr. Tetley said.

"It was nice seeing you boys close up like this instead of in your uniforms," Young Tin said.

"I'm hoping I can get avay to take my missus to vatch you boys play ball in New Stockholm tomorrow evening," Old Gold called as they stomped away. The Buick roared away in a cloud of white man's dust.

The red folks piled into the flivver. Grandma got in the middle, and set her brown paper bag, now bulging with Ol' Dan's leftovers, between her legs. Each kid fitted into a place just big enough. The chief, the boy, the mother, and the infant enjoyed the roominess of the front seat.

"Much obliged," the chief said. The mother's words were lost in the chugging of the flivver and the chorus of *good lucks* and *take it easys* from the House.

"Hurry up an' get into uniform," Pops ordered. "We done fritter away the whole afternoon."

19
House Call

———◆▶————

The dusk in which they had left the field of the Swenskies with $87 in winnings had deepened into moonless dark in their sanctuary on the Mouse River. Timmy hurried to Merv. The aspirin had not broken his fever; he was hot and dry and out of his head. He was gasping and groaning and fighting off white demons. With Moon's help by lantern light, Timmy laved him with cool water and raised him so that he could see the campfire and the forms of his comrades. Ol' Dan nourished him with warm broth of chicken softened with saffron, and Timmy got him to swallow aspirin powdered in hot lemonade. He seemed some better; he rested his head, and a calm settled on him. Busy Ike, musing over his guitar, hummed and sang bits of happy songs from way down yonder and long ago . . .

Goin all around the wur-rold
To find my Sweet May — May-ree . . .

. . . She ain' no bumble-bee
But she sure make some sweet honey for me . . .

Timmy went down to the river and soaped the Vaseline from his white skull. He dove into the quiet pool and floated and watched the gibbous moon rise above the trees. It seemed to him he was floating in time instead of water, way back to when his ancestors had worshiped the White Goddess.

Busy Ike must have seen her rise, too, for he was struck by her beams:

> *You caught the Santa Fe, I caught on behind;*
> *You caught the Santa Fe, I caught on behind.*
> *I caught ya, pretty momma! Lord, you make*
> *   moonlight man go blind!*

It was coming on ten o'clock now and time to bed down for an early-morning start up new roads to Devils Lake. Pops came to Merv with the nightly tin cup of moonshine. He gulped and gasped: "You boys good to me." Then, God damn it! he puked everything up.

Timmy cleaned him up and laid him back and smoothed an ice pack over his eyelids and brow. In the circle by the dying fire, Timmy proclaimed: "We've got to get a doctor — now, tonight."

"You crazy, man? Where we gonna fin' us a doctah?"

"Down home, we could get us a doctah," Clayton said. "They come if the boy is sick enough."

"Down South," said Mr. Tetley, "they think of us as valuable property. Up here, shit! They think of us as untouchable apparitions that live on sunshine and watermelon. A sick nigger better go in his hole and die like a poisoned rat."

"This is my part of the country," Timmy said. "I know

165

these towns. I can find a doctor, and I can get him out here."

"Where you gonna do that?"

"In New Republic, the town we skirted coming here."

"How you gonna get 'im come out here?"

"He'll come. My father came, didn't he?"

"C'mon then," Pops said. "You take me to 'im, I do the talkin."

Timmy stood up in the watchful circle. "No."

"What you mean no?"

"What he means," said Mr. Tetley, "is that he wants to conduct the delicate negotiations involved on a white-to-white basis. But he can't do that without coming out of character as Speedy Deefy, the White Crow."

"Zackly," said Little Hoop. "An' right smack dab in the town where that sweet sheriff man beat up the Indians."

"Mosta them people in that town, they bound to seen us play, one town or 'nother 'round here. They know you," Pops said. "You fin' me the doctah, I'll do the talkin. You play Speedy like always we go to town."

"They won't know who I am," Timmy said. "Wait a minute, you'll see." They watched him climb into the flatbed and return dressed as he had been the morning he had come into camp to join them, the boy's cap of last year concealing his dumb white skull. "Okay?" he said and felt like crying for his lost identity. "I'll come back with a doctor."

"Git goin then," said Pops. "Be careful, you hear me?"

"I know these towns," said Timmy. Then he turned back and went to Merv's side and, after a moment's thought, picked up the tin pail.

The only lights on Main Street were from the drugstore and its ice-cream parlor and the picture show. The drugstore would stay open to catch the folks coming out after the second show. But there should be another lighted downtown window, marking the telephone company's central switch-board. He found it around the corner next to the post office.

The lone operator was an old lady, who peered through glasses so thick they looked like they had windows in them.

Timmy set his empty pail down. "Ma'am," he said, "we've got a sick man out at our rig a few miles down the road. Could you ring up a doctor for me, please, ma'am? He's running a fever from an infection."

"Only trouble is the only doc we got right here in town is Old Doc Thorson, and he's a vet. Most folks go into Devils Lake for their doctorin, but some go to Old Doc for farm accidents and the like. He'll set a bone, but he won't do no cuttin.'"

"Where will I find him?"

"If he's not out someplace with a sick horse, he's always home this time of night. Let me see if he answers."

She plugged in and cranked the call. "There's a young fellow here with a harvest rig, Doc. They've got a sick man they want you to go take a look at. I don't know where it is. Down the road a few miles. Why don't I tell him to come by your place, the two of you decide?" She gave Timmy directions to his house on the edge of town. Timmy picked up his pail and thanked her.

Amid the glowings of a hundred fireflies between the leafi-ness of the trees, a plain old kerosene lantern beckoned Timmy up the walk to the porch swing on which Old Doc was creaking his evening ease. He raised the lantern to cast its yellow light on Timmy. "How come you come here to drag me out in the middle of the night?" He set the lantern on the porch rail. He was a long-nosed Norwegian, somewhere between sixty and ninety. He stood tall, his huge hands swinging like scoops on the ends of steel cables. Timmy explained about the man on this crew with blood poisoning that looked like he was going to die if he didn't get help soon, tonight. Then he came to the tricky part: "I was just going by, stopped in to get a drink of cold well water from the church pump, and they asked me, please, would I drive into town and find a doctor."

"God ding-dang it anyway. You no sooner think you've got yourself a nice clear night of good sleeping ahead of you than something like this has to pop up to spoil everything. Don't know what I can do for him anyways . . . Them doctors couldn't even save Cal Coolidge's kid from dying of blood poisoning . . . This ain't no charity case, is it?"

"They've got cash money," Timmy assured him.

". . . Gotta charge same as for a night horse or cow call . . . Three-fifty plus five cents a mile coming and going . . ." He fortified his lower lip with a forefinger of Copenhagen from his snuff box and hollered into the house that God ding-dang it anyways, he had a three-fifty sick call and might be up half the night, not that anybody gave a whoop in hell whether he got an honest night's rest or not . . . "I'll follow you out."

The erratic blue-white glints of the carbide lamps on Old Doc's old Moon behind him seemed to Timmy to be the eyes that would see through his pose as a white boy who had happened to be passing by. He began to worry that he should have gone in as Speedy Deefy and let Pops do the talking and take the chance that a doctor would come out to tend a sick coon. No, he knew the towns and the people up here. It took a trick to get him out. Another trick was called for. He pulled up on the road in front of the turn-in and walked back to wait for Doc to pull up behind. The whole House was up waiting. Timmy pointed to their shadows around the lantern swinging from a branch. "He's up there, Doc," he said. "I'm already late, so I'll be getting on my way."

168

"You're the one that got me out here. You're the one agreed on my fee and mileage. How do I know they're gonna pay up what you agreed to?"

"They're as good as gold, Doc," Timmy said and got back in the Packard and drove down the road. Around the bend, he pulled off the road, shut off the lights and engine, sprinted into the cemetery, and worked his way back to and into the flatbed, unheard and unseen by the palavering shadow-casters around the lantern and the refreshed campfire.

In a minute he emerged as Speedy Deefy into the circle. ". . . Can't understand about that boy, why he'd lie to me 'bout some harvest crew, why he didn't tell me it was that team of colored ballplayers. Why, shoot, I was in Farmersburg to see you play. Saw him, too, that albino there" — spotting Speedy in the circle — "running like a scared rabbit."

"I presume that our white Good Samaritan made the assumption that you would not knowingly leave home and hearth to treat a sick colored man this time of night."

Doc looked Mr. Tetley up and down. "A regular doctor wouldn't, and I can't blame him. Thing is, folks wouldn't want to be doctored with the same instruments that had been used on a colored man. But I'm just a vet, and a sick hog or cow or horse I stick with a needle has got no way of knowing — nor doing anything about it anyway — if the hog or cow or horse I stuck before him was white or black or spotted. It don't make a dime's worth of difference to me neither whether it's a white cow or a black horse. I stick them all with the same needle . . . Long as I get my three-fifty and mileage, it's no skin off my nose. Tell you the truth, this is the first colored man I was ever called out on. Couldn't rightly say one way or the other whether I'd've come if I'd've known. Pony up your three-fifty plus ninety-five cents mileage, and I'll see what I can do for this sick man of yours."

"We pay when we see what you gonna do for him," Pops said.

Old Doc shook his head. "Thing is, maybe I can't do nothing for him. Depends how far the infection's gone. If I don't get my money . . ."

Mr. Tetley stepped forward. "We must insist that you see our patient, doctor."

The old man was not intimidated, but he conceded: "Reckon I can't take your money without I take a look at him."

Speedy stepped forward, tugging and gesturing this way, this way.

"He just an old country vet," Little Hoop was heard to say. "He ain't no doctah."

"This ain't no white man neither," the old man said, holding the lantern to inspect his patient. He opened his bag, stuck a thermometer in Merv's mouth, and went to work, his huge hands deft and firm as he probed the wound and felt for the spread of infection. He came away shaking his head. "Nothing more I can do, nor anybody else. No use lancing it or bleeding it now. You got plenty aspirin? Give him two aspirins every four hours to break the fever, plenty of water. Keep his arm hot and his head cool. All to do now is hope he can fight it off and get well. But this blood poisoning . . . You got a very sick man here. Only thing else I know to do is take him to the hospital at Devils Lake . . . Doubt they can do much either . . . if they take him. I don't know . . . They don't take Indians . . . That'll be four forty-five."

Pops counted out the money. "Obliged you came out."

"I wish to God I could give him some medicine or work some kind of miracle, but there ain't no medicine for what ails him, and I ain't no Jesus. If it was a horse, I'd say put a

170

bullet in his brain and haul him off to the glue factory."

The old man stomped away in the puddles of yellow light cast by his lantern. "Wish to God I could help him," he called back.

"That ain't a real bad man," Clayton said.

"We risk gettin in trouble, lettin 'im go to town, folks findin out we runnin some kind of fake with that albino shit," said Little Hoop. "An' we is nothin but out nearly five bucks."

"Take it out of my half shares," Timmy said.

"We all pay," Pops said.

"Just don't put on those white-boy clothes again," Mr. Tetley said. "Not till you go back to your own kind."

Timmy cooled Merv's head and made him comfortable for the night and laid his own pad beside him. The steady wind had blown the mosquitos away. The moon was high and bright above them. "You're going to be all right in a day or two," he whispered into the dying man's ear.

"The doc he say so?"

The lucidity of the question made Timmy look hopefully into the moonlit face. "He said you're going to be just fine."

20

Born in Slavery

━━━◄◆►━━━

That evening's game was some forty miles to the north, in Devils Lake. They would be coming back south before heading west to entertain in Harvey and Anamoose on the way to the Sunday double-header in Minot, so Pops decided they would camp where they were on the Mouse River another night. That way, they could give Merv another day and night to fight off his fever. Bofey, one of whose arms might be needed to quell an uprising in Minot, would stay in camp and put heat and Sloane's liniment on his own shoulders and tend to Merv. Pops, Ol' Dan, and Speedy would take the Packard to ballyhoo in Harvey and Anamoose and meet up with the others at five o'clock for the game in Devils Lake.

There was a good gravel road from the second crossroad all the way to Harvey, so Timmy didn't have to look sharp for the section-line turns Pops called on back roads.

"Mister Dan," said Timmy, as he addressed him out of respect for his age and his position as chief cook of the

Original Colored House of David, "some of the guys were saying you were born in slavery and are darn near a hundred years old."

"Born in slavery," said Ol' Dan, nodding, "but" — shaking his head — "don' know my zact age."

"Be a shame to get to be a hundred and not have a big cake and people singing happy birthday to you. Maybe we can figure out how old you are."

Ol' Dan shook his head. "Don' know how."

"Were you ever sold? Maybe there's a record of your sale."

He shook his head. "Not me. I's *given* away. See, Missus Sloan was then a widow woman livin in Savannah wif her sister, Missus Hopper, 'nother widow woman. She die, I b'long to Missus Hopper, stay right on. By then I got what dey call a *house* look, I take care just 'bout evrything. Thas also when I get married to Dee Dee, she b'long to Missus Hopper, so we together, start havin our chillun."

"When was that? What year?"

"Fifty-five, 'member dat. Missus Sloan die in Fifty-five."

"How old were you then?"

"Grown man. Musta been 'bout twenty."

"Where were you born? What's the first you remember about your parents?"

"Just a kid growin up, workin in the sawmill. Sloans, see, own a big mill in pine country south of Savannah. Then he die. See, thas when Missus Sloan sold my papa an' mama an' li'l sister. Oh, she cried to do it, say what a shame to break up such a good family. But she a widow woman, gonna move in wif her sister, gonna keep me, give me a house look . . ."

"When was that? What year?"

"In Fifty. Never saw or heard of 'em again."

"How old were you then?"

"Mostly grown." He shrugged. "Was chasin me a girl,

name of Sadie, but they — she live down the road on the rice farm — they keep her under lock an' key. That man, he kept houns an' ran horses, they say he keepin her for hisself to play wif."

"So maybe you were fifteen or so."

Ol' Dan nodded. "That be 'bout right."

"Okay, fifteen in Fifty would make twenty in Fifty-five. So you musta been born in Thirty-five."

"Reckon so, 'bout then."

"So that would make you . . . ninety-three now."

" 'Bout right. 'Cause, see, it was in Seventy-nine, Missus Hopper die, an' we — my oldest boy, he got a job out west in Kansas City, he send for us to come, need me to cook in this fancy restaurant where he openin oysters. The Savoy. Been there ever since. Still put in time there winters, helpin out when they get big parties in."

"You were about forty-five then?"

" 'Bout right."

"What month were you born? Remember that?"

"Nobody kin remember when he was born. But" — he smiled to remember it — "my papa an' mama used to say bofe me an' my li'l sister was New Year's babies, a year apart. They have us after the drinkin an dancin celebration on New Year's Eve."

"September, then? You and your sister were both born in September?"

"That time a year."

"Okay, so we'll say you were born September first of 1835. What I'm going to do is write it all out, how all the facts show that to be your birthday, which means you will celebrate your hundredth birthday on September first . . . in 1935."

"If I make it, thas close enough. The folks at the Savoy gonna give me a big party, I know 'cause they're proud of how old I am an' how long I been there . . ."

"Evabody in town gonna come to that party," Pops said. "White and colored."

"You know what I hope?" Timmy said.

"You gonna be there, too?"

"That, too. But what I hope is that Missus Sloan's white soul is frying in hell."

Ol' Dan shook his head. "She a nice widow woman. You got no call to judge her."

*

Batting ninth, Speedy made the first and third outs in the first inning as the House scored eleven runs against Satan's Pitchforks of Devils Lake. Speedy went all the way on the mound, resting Moon, throwing as loose as for batting practice. After the sixth, Ol' Dan mentioned that they ain't got no hits yet, so Pops tol' 'em let's go git us a no-hitter for Speedy. The infield stabbed and gobbled up every line drive and ground ball, and the outfield speared and swallowed every liner and fly ball. The most remarkable aspect of Speedy's perfect game — twenty-seven up, twenty-seven down — was that he got it without a strike-out. Nobody could remember that happening anywhere, ever. Mr. Tetley hit seven home runs, and six was the most anybody could remember. So it became a game to remember in a blur of tank-town games. Final: Satan's Pitchforks of Devils Lake, o; the Original Colored House of David, $95.

Out of town a ways, at a lakeside roadhouse, which was the spirituous home of the Pitchforks, their colored money was good for a fifty-pound chunk of ice, two gallons of moonshine, and a dozen quarts of home-brew.

After their cackle of wonderment at a no-hitter without a strike-out and Mr. Tetley's seven home runs, which end to end, somebody figured, would have gone half a mile in the air, Timmy in their corner in the flatbed told Mr. Tetley how he had figured out Ol' Dan's hundredth birthday.

"There are still a good many old folks back home that were born in slavery," Mr. Tetley remarked. The others chorused yes, yes, still some around. "My grandma," said Manny, "she still livin." "Bofe sides a my family, I still got slave kin livin," said Scrappy.

"Your Grandma Daisy?" Timmy asked Mr. Tetley. "Was she?"

"Not quite. Her mother, a slave, was freed by her owner, my great-grandfather, shortly before Daisy was born. So . . ."

"Tell me about it, Mr. Tetley?"

The big man tilted his silver flask and shook his head.

"What I hear," Scrappy was saying, "times were harder for some after slavery than before."

"Still are, some places . . ."

Busy Ike had been tuning his guitar. "Heah we go, boys, like down home on the chain gang . . . *Take this hammer . . .*"

"Whanh!" they all yelled, coming down with their hammers.

Take this hammer (whanh!)
Carry it to the captain (whanh!)
Take this hammer (whanh!)
Carry it to the captain (whanh!)
If he ask you (whanh!)
Am I runnin (whanh!)
Tell him that I'm flyin (whanh!)
Tell him that I'm flyin (whanh!)

Speedy came down as hard on the "whanh!" as any poor devil on the gang.

21

Among Friends on the Mouse River

―――――◆▶――――

"He don' eat nothin, want nothin but water," Bofey reported.
Merv raised his head and managed to sit up. "You git a good
take?" It was a hot still night, oppressive by the campfire.
Before Merv could lapse away again, Timmy and Moon got
him to his feet and helped him to the grassy knoll over the
river where there might be the comfort of a breeze. They
made him a fresh bed and an ice pack for his brow and got
him to swallow the aspirin and his hot lemonade. The new
moon would not rise until midnight. "See stars up there I
ain't seen since I's a boy down home," he said. "Some a 'em
is fallin. One there now . . ." The moment passed into a
sudden gasp and a deep groan.

Timmy dozed beside him, rising between naps to cool the
hot head and refresh the dry mouth. Every breath was a deep
gasp in and a soft groan out. It was the silence in the still
night, not yet dawn, that awakened Timmy. There was no
breath, no pulse. He never before had touched a dead man.
He covered the face with the towel.

He lit the lantern and carried it to the lean-to, where Pops and Ol' Dan were sleeping.

They built up the fire and all gathered around to hold council.

"We'll bury 'im here at sunup," Pops said.

"We can't do that," said Timmy. "We could get into trouble. We've got to get the coroner to certify the cause of death. I don't know just how that works, but I know the sheriff who was out here for the Indians could tell us what we have to do to get him buried."

"We gotta hit the road in the mornin," Pops said.

"Where they gonna bury him up here? They got no colored cemeteries up here," Moon said.

"No need to get the law messed up in this," Little Hoop said. "We bury 'im an go our way."

"Next of kin?" Mr. Tetley asked. "Is there any kinfolks that should be notified of his demise?"

"He come to us outta nowhere," Pops said. "He don't say nothin 'bout where he from or why he come. He come to me an' say he is a pretty good ballplayer, done some good pitchin, can we use 'im."

"He probly been in some trouble, way it allus seemed to me," Scrap Iron said. "He was close-moufed 'bout who he was an' where he came from. Never mentioned no folks to me, close as I was to him."

Not as close as I was that night by the river when he pledged me to keep his secret and write his mother.

"Forget your white-boy concerns about how we're going to handle the demise of our brother," Mr. Tetley told him.

"Be diggin a grave up here over the river," Pops said. "Cut the sod away so we can lay it back over him. Mr. Tetley gonna conduct the service, an' Busy Ike, he sing the hymn."

"I've got a Bible,' Timmy said. "My mother made me take it."

"Goes to show," said Mr. Tetley, "that mama knows best."

At sunup they wrapped the body of Willis Moore, known to them only as Merv, in his blanket and rested it in its grave.

"In the name of the Father, the Son, and the Holy Ghost . . ."

"Amen, amen," they chorused.

"We consign our brother to the earth and pray thee, dear Jesus, to take him into Paradise with thee until the Day of Resurrection when thy faithful shall be united with thee and the heavenly hosts forever and ever. Amen."

"Amen. Yes, Lord. Amen."

Mr. Tetley read the Twenty-third Psalm and then these words from Ecclesiastes:

> Or ever the silver cord be loosed,
> Or the golden bowl be broken,
> Or the pitcher be broken at the fountain,
> Or the wheel broken at the cistern;
> And the dust return to the earth as it was,
> And the spirit return unto God who gave it.

As the first pale rays of the sun lit his face, Busy Ike played and sang the funeral hymn:

> Just a closer walk with thee. . . .

> In this world of toil and snares
> If I falter, Lord, who cares?
> Who with me my burden shares?
> None but thee, none but thee.

They covered him over and replaced the sod and scattered the remaining dirt, and no eye could see the place where he was lying.

Going through a little town on the way to a new camp near Harvey, Timmy told Pops he had to stop at the post office. He jigged in as Speedy and mailed the letter addressed to Mrs. Annie Moore, c/o The Lo, I Am with You Always Running Water Baptist Church, Gilt Edge, Tennessee.

Dear Mrs. Moore,
Just a line to inform you that your son Willis passed away peacefully from a fever caused by an infection. He wanted you to know that he was always the good boy you brought him up to be. He died among friends and was given a proper Christian burial. God bless you and keep you.

A Friend

22

Mr. Tetley's
Patrick Henry

———◄◆►———

In Harvey, Pops got a long-distance call through to the
Kansas City Monarchs. He came out glum. "That pitcher
they gonna send us to Minot, he didn't pan out. So now they
got another, but best he kin do, comin by train, is meet us in
Mandan — Monday *after* our double-header with them Cowpokes . . ."

"I be ready," Bofey said. "Gimme the ball, I be ready."
But they knew he was whistling Dixie. He couldn't raise
either arm over his head without crying out loud.

They got settled down behind the schoolhouse in Harvey
in time for their noon meal. Afterward, Mr. Tetley pointed
his cheroot at the idle playground equipment. "It has been
many years indeed," he said to Timmy, "since I went up and
down on a seesaw."

"Teeter-totters, we call them. But you're gonna have to sit
about halfway down if I'm gonna get you up in the air."

It was pleasant in the shade, up and down, up and
down . . .

"Your Grandma Daisy," Timmy said. "You were telling me about her Shakespearean company. How she . . ."

But Mr. Tetley looked up while he was going down and shook his head and said, "Yes, the story of how I became a man of considerable erudition, as you put it . . . It is, as you have surmised, an interesting — perhaps a compelling — story. I've been expecting you to pump it out of me the way you have pumped our comrades. Except for hearing him relate it to you, I would not have known that Little Hoop's grandmother was a daughter of the great Apache chieftain, Cohise . . ."

"She married a Negro cowboy and . . ."

"And my impression is that you knew more about the unfortunate Merv than you told us."

"I promised to keep his secret."

"What's your secret?"

Timmy shook his head. "No, it was buried with Merv."

"I mean yours. You. Who are you? Who is this strange kid we picked up in some dinky tank town . . . What's it called?"

"Indian Springs. I don't know what you mean, Mr. Tetley."

"Your story? What is it?" Going up, Mr. Tetley looked down at him. "It is not just happenstance that you are on the road with us."

"Heck, you know all there is to know about me. I don't have a story. I was born and brought up in Indian Springs. My father's the town doctor. My mother was a Catholic who turned Lutheran. My Grandpa Tim is the station agent at the depot. My Uncle Hans runs the family farm. I've got a sister who's married to the department-store people in Detroit Lakes. My brother is a no-good frat man at the University of Minnesota. I'll be a senior in high school this fall. Then I'll go to the university."

"And what course of study do you intend to pursue?"

"Medicine, I guess. My dad was disappointed that Freddy didn't have a head for math and science and couldn't even get into medical school."

"It is your father's wish, then, that you follow in his professional footsteps?"

"He takes it for granted."

"And why is it that you do not want to be a doctor like your father?"

"I didn't say I didn't want to be a doctor like my dad."

Mr. Tetley sniffed that away. "I don't think that who you are wants to be a doctor like your father. You know who you are, just as I know who I am. Do you suppose" — and he seemed to be asking it of the sky — "that's why we're here together, going up and down on this seesaw?"

"Teeter-totter. I sort of know — but, no I don't — I don't know what you mean, Mr. Tetley."

"None of us has anything to do with who we are — whether we're white or black, smart or stupid, big or small, male or female . . . But who we are determines what we must do. People who don't know who they are don't know what they must do. But take you, for example. Since you knew you must, somehow, join us, I can conclude that you know who you are."

"Q.E.D."

Mr. Tetley nodded. "*Quod erat demonstrandum.* So?"

Timmy found himself, incoherently and in broken swatches, telling the story of his lineage according to Grandpa Tim and Uncle Hans.

"Do I correctly surmise," Mr. Tetley asked, "that you believe in the truth of the ancient fables of the God of Fire and the White Goddess spun for you by your Grandpa Tim?"

Timmy frowned his uncertainty into the heat of the day.

(He would have smiled affirmation in the light of the moon.) Then he remembered: "In our ancient language, we put it like this, 'Flanmora, flanmira; flanmira, flanmora.'"

Mr. Tetley repeated the words, like a chef tasting another's broth, in the hope that their sound could convey their content, but shook his head.

"It means, sort of, that you cannot believe without understanding and that you cannot understand without believing. Or," he added after a moment of thought, "is it the other way around?"

"It's like the baseballs of our game," Mr. Tetley suggested, "no front or back or up or down, but round and true."

"Grandpa Tim taught me that there is no such thing as . . ."

"As?"

"As eternal truth . . ."

"No eternal truth?"

"One time he was telling me that when a person is born, there's a new star in heaven, millions and millions, one for everybody. When you do wrong on earth, a devil of the God of Fire touches your star with a black torch. When you make your amends with the White Goddess, she sends an angel with heaven's own dew to polish it clean. But if you do not make amends, your star falls out of heaven in a streak of fire and your spirit will have no throne and will wander without rest or comfort throughout all eternity. On a clear night, you can look up to the heavens and watch the stars of the damned fall from heaven.

"I was about twelve then, I guess, and I told him that they were just meteorites. He told me he was telling me the truth as it was then. He said the truth changes. He said the only eternal truth is that there is no eternal truth."

Many an idle summer day after that, looking at the changing clouds, and many a wakeful night, Timmy had turned and bent it every which way until it came to him that the eternal truth must prove its truth by changing.

"Because there is no eternal truth," Timmy found himself telling Mr. Tetley, "my grandpa taught me that the greatest curse and evil of civilization is the written word."

"A curse? The written word?" Mr. Tetley looked up. "Who would I be without it?"

"The way my grandpa saw it was that all the wars and hate on earth are caused by people believing that old written words of truth are still the truth. He said look at the nonsense people live by and die for because it is written down in an old book. He said the written word took away the greatest freedom of all, the freedom to know and speak and live the changing truth . . ."

The old man's words, fumed with moonshine and wafted on smoke from his pipe, were set in Timmy's memory as indelibly as if chiseled on stone or engraved on bronze.

Mr. Tetley smiled down. "Nevertheless . . ."

"I love that word — 'nevertheless,'" Timmy put in. "I think it's my favorite word. Nevertheless . . ."

"Nevertheless," Mr. Tetley went on, "without the written truth of the past, you would have nothing to think with about what the truth for you is now. We all *think* in words, you know. In your case, you would be just a loony kid with a headful of yarns made up by your grandpa and uncle."

"*Flanmora, flanmira,*" Timmy told him. But the thought that he was a loony kid stung. "They all call me Timmy," he blurted out. "Not Tim or Timothy — *Timmy*, like I was a kid who would never grow up."

"With me, it was the other way around," Mr. Tetley said, seeming to talk more to himself than to Timmy. "There was about me as an infant and growing boy — or perhaps it was an unexpressed sense in the household — that my destiny was to some kind of greatness. It was a family attitude that precluded nicknames and diminutives — not Bill or Billy, Will or Willie. At home it was always William, except that sometimes I was referred to or called by both my given names, or first name and middle initial. 'See here, William P.,' Grandma Daisy would say, 'you get on back to that butcher man an' tell him he knows very well he is not going to divest himself of his old fish on my kitchen.' Or, my mother with a friend: 'And William Pierpont won first prize in the Elocution Contest with his reading of Patrick Henry's liberty or death speech . . .'"

"Do you remember how that goes?" Timmy interrupted. "Did you learn it by heart?"

Mr. Tetley looked up through the years gone by. "Let's see . . . well, it begins, I remember this, it begins . . ."

Holding his foot on the end of the seesaw to hold Timmy's end up, he stood to face the Assembly, thrusting his right hand at its lofty president:

" 'They tell us, sir, that we are weak — unable to cope with so formidable an adversary . . .' Let's see . . . then it goes on about we're never going to be any stronger or better able to fight than now and, besides, we have no choice . . . no 'election,' he called it . . . 'Besides, sir, we have no election. If we were base enough to desire it, it is now too late to retire from the contest. There is no retreat but in submission and slavery. Our chains are forged. Their clanking may be heard. The war is inevitable, and let it come.' And then there's something about why stand we here idle. We may cry for peace, but there is no peace. Then, of course, into the ending . . . 'Is life so dear, or peace so sweet, as to be purchased at the price of chains and slavery? Forbid it, Almighty God! I know not what course others may take . . .'"

And Timmy, from his lofty position, joined him in the last grand cadences: " 'But as for me, give me liberty, or give me death!' "

"Hurray, hurray, hurray!" Timmy shouted.

Mr. Tetley smiled as he lowered Timmy to the ground. "It hit them all," he said, "the same as it hit you now, those words did. The men hollered and stomped and waved their fists, and the women wept and cried amen, yes Lord, yes Lord, amen."

"Because," Timmy said, "they knew blame well you weren't talkin about the Yankees and the British."

"They knew what I was talkin about," Mr. Tetley said.

Scrappy came ambling over to tell them that Pops said to suit up, a picture-taker from the Minot newspaper was there to give them some ballyhoo for the Sunday double-header. "What you guys been batting the breeze about? We hear you hollerin liberty or death."

Timmy slid down the teeter-totter. "We've been having our ups and downs," he said.

23

The Phonograph-Needle Pitch

———◄◆►———

Moon had an easy time against the Harvey Haymakers, and Speedy didn't have to throw hard the next evening to set down the Anamoose Antelopes, so they were both ready to bear down against a good team of town toughs and pro ringers before the good Sunday crowd in Minot. Moon breezed his game, but Speedy was hit hard. The good hitters creamed his fast ball and slugged his roundhouse curve and screwball. He gave up twelve runs, but the House scored fourteen to save the game.

"And this team ain't got near the hitters them Cowpokes is gonna come at us wif," said Pops. "Nor the pitchers neither . . ."

"Don't you worry none," said Bofey. "If I ain't ready by Mandan, I'm gonna make us a winnin pitcher outta Speedy. I teach him all I know — all!"

"Are you going to impart the secret of your dipsy-doodle pitch?" Mr. Tetley inquired.

"Nevah you mind what," said Bofey. "Just quit worryin 'bout them Cowpokes."

On the way south down to Mandan, they had five easy games ahead of them in Russo, Garrison, Turtle Lake, Sweet Grass, and Sterling. Bofey tried his right arm for two innings in Russo and his left arm for two in Garrison and the stints did bofe arms in. All the team could do was hope that complete rest and Sloane's liniment would bring one or bofe of his arms around in time to pitch, at least in relief of Speedy, against the Cowpokes, who would be loaded for coon.

After the Turtle Lake game, Pops gathered all hands around the fire to talk about the chances of their losing to the Cowpokes all they had earned since Fargo.

"You wasn't wif us las year, Mr. Tetley, nor was Clayton an' Nathan, nor Speedy neither, so let me tell you 'bout these boys we playin. They ain't no pushovahs. First, you gotta know their manager, Longhorn Stevens they call 'im. He play good ball somewhere long time ago, then he go into bronc bustin and rodeo work an' make a lotta money, so now he got this big ranch, but the one thing he love more'n anything else, his ball team, an' he put together a pretty good one, an' he drill 'em. They run an' throw to the right bases. They peck, peck, peck, an' they blast, blast, blast. They kin score. We allus play 'em winner-take-all, which gonna run seven-eight hunnerd. Here four-five years ago, Longhorn an' his players challenge us to ten bucks a man in side bets. So we been takin their money, usually 'nother hunnerd an' forty a game. This year, wif Merv passed, we oney got twelve, countin me an' Ol' Dan, so it'll go one-twenty in the side bet each game. We allus took their money, an' we can't come limpin in now, cryin to back out. They tell us take our black asses outta town an' don' come back. They gamblin men. They pay, they gonna spect us to pay. Longhorn he rather beat us an' take our money than be President of the United States of America . . ."

"Let's see, now," said Mr. Tetley. "If we win both games, we go away with a thousand dollars, more or less. If we split, we go away with half the gate, say four hundred. And if we lose both, we go away with nothing minus two-forty."

"Zackly. Thas why we gotta do no worse than split. Thas why we gotta shoot our wad in the first game an' scramble any way we can to win the second. We gotta jump on 'em early an' hol' tight late. So Moon, we start Moon, an' he hum — man, he *hum* — as far as he can go — the first game — maybe start the second. Then Speedy come in, give it all *he* got the resta the way. Maybe Bofey can work an inning or two. Our game is gonna be outrun 'em an outscore 'em . . ."

Timmy gulped air, not so much breathing it as chewing it to get it down.

Now Bofey spoke up. "I say we kin win 'em bofe. Maybe some miracle happen next three days, I kin work in relief, but thas nothin we kin count on to put in the strongbox. But I can hep one way. I kin teach Speedy my secret pitch. Man who taught me, I promise him I don' teach no other pitcher till he dead an' he ain't dead yet, but Speedy he don' really count because he be leavin us, an' he gotta promise me anyways, he aint gonna use it again nor tell nobody till I'm dead and gone. Me 'n Mr. Tetley work on him wif it tomorra, see if he kin get it. If he do, we kin win bofe games. We give the ball to Moon in the first game, his job to pitch an' win it. If he need relief an' I not be ready, Speedy kin go in an' curve 'em crazy. Speedy start the second game wif Moon behin' him, an' we take 'em bofe. Depends, kin Speedy get the hanga the secret pitch, control it an' throw strikes, 'tween now an' Sunday. In the mornin, I see what I kin teach him. Maybe he be ready to try a few in the games 'tween now an' Sunday . . ."

Pops nodded. "This a big thing you do for us, Bofey, teachin your secret pitch."

"If Speedy can make that ball do just half of what Bofey can make it do," said Mr. Tetley, "we're going away with Mr. Longhorn's long green."

In the morning, Bofey said: "Bring your mitt, Mr. Tetley. Speedy, put on your ball pants an' spikes, git your glove, an' folla me behin' the schoolhouse."

Never did a novitiate more wonderingly follow his high priest to the hidden temple of the God of Fire than Timmy followed Bofey to the deserted playground behind that country schoolhouse.

"First thing now," said Bofey, as he unhooked his belt buckle, onto which was welded his lucky silver dollar. "Take off that cheap Boy Scout belt you been wearin and put this on, nice'n snug. Next thing, you gonna need these." He handed Timmy a pack of steel phonograph needles. "Dump 'em loose in your back pocket. Okay, looka here an' do what I do. You just fired in a pitch an' you standin here on the mound, waitin for the catcher to toss it back. Okay, you waitin an' you put your right hand on your hip, hookin your fingers in your back pocket like this, a natural move. You gotta do this all the time, whether you gonna use the secret pitch or a reglar pitch. This move, your right hand on your hip, waitin for the toss, it gotta be a natural move, what you allus do. Now you show me that. Take your wind, make your pitch, come through — pow — now you straighten up an' put your right hand on your hip, hookin your fingers in the pocket. Okay, now again. An' again. An' again. 'Tween now an' Sunday, evry pitch you throw, you make that natural move, somethin you allus do. Okay, now you gonna use the secret. You standin on the mound waitin. Now you gonna ease your long fingers deep in your pocket an' get a phonograph needle 'tween fingers. Like this now, looka here. See, I got the needle. Now I raise my glove to take the toss from the catcher. Like this, see? So now I turn the needle to my lucky-silver-dollar belt buckle an' press the point into the seam, just enough to make sure it gonna hold till it hit the mitt or is hit by the bat. Then it fall away and is gone in the dirt."

For the next hour, over and over in front of Bofey's chirping and scolding, Timmy worked on the preliminary moves and getting the needle set in the seam. Mr. Tetley sat in the shade in silent watchfulness.

When Timmy was despairing of ever getting it down pat, Bofey said, "Now you gettin it. Now you gonna start throwin the ball. Now looka here how you gonna grip the ball, same way evry time. Behin' your glove, you put the tips of your two throwin fingers on the seam, the needle 'tween 'em, like-a this. You gonna grip it that way no matter which pitch you gonna throw, fast ball, curve, or screwball, the three pitches you got. Now looka here what gonna happen. You throw your fast ball. It gonna be spinnin in on the right-hand batter. You git enough spin an' speed, it natchurly gonna tail in a little. Now the weighta this here needle gonna make it spin nearly like a curve ball. Your fast ball now gonna ack like your screwball, it gonna *break* in. Now when you throw your screwball, it gonna ack like a big roundhouse curve, it go sweepin in. An' your curve ball gonna come in from way high an' go sweepin down to way low an' outside. Okay, you throw a few, nice'n easy. It ain't gonna do much till you throw hard. But I tell you this, I seen an' tried 'em all — spitter, Vaseline, mud ball, emery ball, evry trick pitch there is — an' none works so

much spell on a ball as this here phonograph-needle pitch. An'
the beauty is, no one evah know how you do it, 'cause it never
be there when they call for the ball an' it don't mark the ball.
Now you got the secret an' you keep it till I die or say okay
. . . Now throw some . . ."

Making the moves, setting the needle, throwing easy to Mr.
Tetley, Timmy found the ball was not much charmed by the
spell of the needle. "Thas okay, thas okay for now, I kin see
it takin the spin. Now you kin throw hard to Mr. Tetley
twenty pitches, no more 'cause your arm gotta work four-five
innings tonight and tomorra an' be ready Sunday, just enough
to see how it take the spell when you throw hard . . ."

Throwing hard, he could charm the ball; the weight of the
needle gave off-center momentum to its spin. Watching the
fast ball break like a nickel curve, the curve ball float lazily
until it zoomed down toward the dirt, the screwball float out
and cut sharply in across the plate, Timmy felt supernaturally
empowered, as if he were indeed the agent of an ancient god
interfering in the struggles of mortals.

When the ball hit the mitt, the needle fell away. It came
back to Timmy — as to a baffled umpire in a game — un-
blemished by the cause of its bedeviled flight.

"They don't break as crazy as yours," Mr. Tetley said to
Bofey, "but they break crazy enough to drive a good hitter
crazy and a weak hitter crazier."

"Thas enough now, thas enough. He got it good enough
he can try it a few times tonight. Try it once on each batter.
Mr. Tetley calls the pitch as always, what Speedy throws —
one finger fast ball, two finger curve, three finger screwball.
If you want the phonograph-needle pitch, you finger your
mask. If Speedy wanna throw it on his own, he pull his cap
down after he get the sign . . ."

"One thing, though," said Timmy. "Aren't the batter and the umpire gonna be wondering where all these needles are coming from?"

"My role in this deception," said Mr. Tetley, "is to plow them into the dust of the diamond with a sweep of my spikes."

"Thas why I bring Mr. Tetley into the needle part of the secret," Bofey said. "So he kin cover 'em up. Me, workin it, I don' use only enough to get me a strike-out when I need it."

"How many will I need?"

"I figger you gonna use right about fifty needles agin them Cowpokes on Sunday."

"When the ball is hit," Timmy asked, "what happens to the needle?"

"It be scattered to kingdom come."

24
Wetter Water

In the town of Sweet Grass, in the home half of the seventh with Speedy Deefy on the mound and the crowd laughing and cheering the play, all hell broke loose from the heavens above. The wind blew, and the people squawked away like hens when the shadow becomes the hawk. A lightning bolt hit the livery stable, and the fire reared up against the storm. When Old Thor up there rumbled new breath to hurl new blasts — blast on blast on blast — you could hear the screaming of the stallion and the buggy mares and the hoarse and vain imprecations of the fire chief to his volunteers. The hail flayed the wheat for miles around.

It was still raining when they oozed back to where they were camped behind the horse corral of the farmer who managed the Sweet Grass Studs. The only dry stuff they had was the money in the strongbox in the Packard and Busy Ike's guitar in its iron-strapped case. The lean-to they had set up for shade had flown into the corral. Their bedding, clothing, and cooking and eating gear were in the mud.

"I go settle up an' ask 'im can we sleep in his barn for the night," Pops said. He slopped off toward the lights in the big white farmhouse.

They stood in the rain and watched it come down. Damn if he didn't believe, Little Hoop remarked, that the rain falling on them was wetter than the rain falling on the white folks. Mr. Tetley made an analysis of the moisture he wrang from his shirt — tasting it, weighing it in the palm of his hand — and nodded judicious agreement. This definitely was not H Two O; it had the heavy wetness and peculiar penetrating quality of H *One* O; it made a man wet inside as well as outside . . .

"How you reckon they *do* it?" Busy Ike wondered. "To get wetter rain to fall on colored than on white?"

"They all white up there," Little Hoop said. "Jesus, Mary, John, an' Moses — they all white. Bet when we get there, we find one cloud say White Only an' another say Colored."

"Whose side you reckon the Devil be on?" Clayton wondered. "They say he be black. Maybe he make them fires hotter for white sinners than he do for us."

"Thas our only chance," Little Hoop said.

The rain had let up when Pops came back with the money and the news, short on both. "He say he don' 'llow no bums ever to sleep in his barn for fear they set a fire or agitate the horses. But he say his hogs gone to market, we welcome to use the hog shed yonder in the pasture . . ."

"That's mighty white of him," Mr. Tetley remarked.

"An' we can build us a fire where they render the lard an' dry us out. But you ain't heard nothin till I tell you this: he say we play only seven innings, he only pay us thirty-three dollars a the take, which come to forty-five. He say times gonna be hard around here, he don' know how much wheat he lost to the hail . . ."

"Seven-ninths of forty-five is thirty-five," Timmy pointed out. "How come he pays us only thirty-three?"

"There was oney one out in the seventh when the game was called."

25
Words in the Wind, Pictures in the Sky

They all had cleanup jobs the next morning. Timmy's and Mr. Tetley's was to rinse and wring the uniforms and stretch them to dry on the blueberry bushes at the edge of the pasture woods. Scrappy and Ike were scrubbing them in the tubs by the hog shed. Clayton and Nathan would lug a soapy batch the half-mile across the pasture. Timmy and Mr. Tetley would sluice them in the watering trough by the windmill. After they had spread a batch on the bushes, they would stretch out beside them in the morning sunshine.

The wind and the windmill, old partners in the pumping business, were working amiably sixty feet up in the high sky. The gearbox and pumping rod slammed and rattled and creaked. The cold water, tasting of its iron, splashed into the watering trough from which ten head of cattle could drink at the same time.

Timmy propped himself on an elbow to see if Mr. Tetley was awake. "Busy Ike was telling me you could have a lot of good years left playing for the Barons," he remarked. "He said Shoo-Fly . . . Was that really his name?"

"Shoo-Fly Williams . . . taught me all I know about the tools of ignorance . . ."

"What tools, Mr. Tetley?"

"Mitt, mask, belly protector, shin guards . . . Catching's a hard way to make an easy living."

"How come they called him Shoo-Fly?"

"His snap throw to second from his crouch was like shooing a fly away from his ear."

"Busy Ike said that Shoo-Fly wanted you to stay on, take over as manager . . ."

"The offer's still good . . ."

"Shoo-Fly was the one who started calling you Mistuh Tetley."

Mr. Tetley had a smile for the memory of it. "I had been playing semipro ball in New Orleans for a manager named Toothpick Jones, who scouted for Shoo-Fly. On his say-so, Shoo-Fly sent for me to try out with the Barons . . ."

"And on the train, in the colored coach . . ."

Mr. Tetley nodded. "I told you about that, didn't I? Anyway, Shoo-Fly gave me a uniform and called the other players: 'Boys, this yere high-society dude from Noo Orleens is gonna be tryin to take my catchin job plum away from me, and I hope he gonna do it cuz soon I gonna be fifty yeahs ol'. Now Toofpick Jones, he send 'im here by the name of Big Boy Billy Tetley, what they call 'im in Noo Orleens, where he play in some one-ball league. Now you seen he kin move quick for his size an' he hit the ball hard an' Toofpick say he kin make it wif us, which we still gotta see. But he be a funny one, not no ordnary ballplayer like you an' me. This high-society dude, not dry behin' the ears, he tell me he don' wanna be called by no name like Big Boy Billy, he gonna be called by his whole name, which be William P. Tetley the Second. Now we gonna show this boy we respeck him. We gonna call him Mistuh. His name be Mistuh Tetley. Maybe we get people to pay their way in to see this high-society Mistuh Tetley hit the ball downtown.' " Mr. Tetley smiled about it. "The high-society dude from New Orleans, Mistuh Tetley, was my act, with my uppity airs, like yours is Speedy Deefy, the albino clown."

"Baseball is what gave me a chance to become a member of the Original Colored House of David," Timmy said. "And it was what got you out in the world . . .

"Out into the white world," Mr. Tetley said, nodding. They were stretching a shirt over a blueberry bush. "Your white world." Now it was up to the sun to finish drying that batch. Mr. Tetley stretched out and looked up at the windmill. "Into a life and world you know nothing about" were the words that went upward so softly that Timmy had to prop his head on an elbow to get his ear close enough to hear them going by on their way into the sky. "No more than you know anything about Negro baseball. You'll go back to your white world and brag how you played ball with a Negro team. But you don't know nothin . . . nothin . . . I left home and played professional Negro baseball for ten years . . . one of the best with the best . . . I don't mean the best colored ballplayers . . . I mean the best *ballplayers* . . . I mean players you whites — with all your reverential regard for the legendary and statistical achievements of your heroes — have never heard of . . . nor ever will . . . You know about the fast ball of your great Walter Johnson, but you don't know that a black man named Red Ant Wickware who, like Walter Johnson, was born and reared in Coffeyville, Kansas, was faster than Johnson . . . Pitching for the Mohawk Giants, he defeated Johnson and a team of white major-league all-stars, striking out seventeen . . . You never heard of Red Ant . . . or of Cyclone Joe Williams . . . Pitching for the Lincoln Giants, he beat Rube Marquand and the New York Giants . . . He beat Grover Cleveland Alexander and Philadelphia when they were the National League champions . . . He pitched against and defeated the best white pitchers of the century, including your Christy Mathewson . . . But you never hear of Red Ant or Cyclone . . . or String Bean Williams or Rube Foster or Cannonball Dick Redding . . . or me . . . or a hundred others . . . You don't know there was a time, long before my time, when whites and blacks played professional ball on the same teams . . . You don't know you whites now have a rule that says no more than four players from one major-league team can play an exhibition game against a black team, so it can't be shown that a black team can beat a white major-league team . . .

"Ten years of Negro professional baseball in an America you know nothing about . . . tramping the streets of a northern city looking for some colored family to take you in to lay down your head . . . not knowing where to go to take a pee or get a drink of water . . . You don't know about the life of a Negro in your beloved America . . . You don't know and don't want to know . . . any more than you want to know what goes on in your prisons, because if you knew, you would have to quit mouthing your noble principles of liberty and justice for all . . . endowed by your Creator with certain unalienable rights . . . you'd have to give them up . . . or make them true . . .

"What you know about is jiggin coons and darkies beatin their feet on the Mississippi mud . . . how we loved Ol' Massa . . . the uppitty nigger and the Negro Who Knows His Place . . . the gentle voices calling Old Black Joe . . . the Darktown Strutters Ball . . . Booker T. Washington and

George Washington Carver and the glory of pulling yourself up by your own bootstraps . . . You don't know nothin . . . nothin . . . nothin . . ." He sighed to a halt like a locomotive coming to rest at the depot.

As he leaned back to look up into the sky where the words had gone, Timmy got a flash of Uncle Hans and Grandpa Tim as he had last seen them — like the Mutt and Jeff comic-strip characters — three sheets to the wind, waving and cheering from the grandstand in Fargo. "I have been thinking . . . the stories they told me . . . how much this is . . . traveling from town to town, playin ball, puttin on a good show for the yokels . . . how much it's like what my ancestors did in olden times. But I see now it's all bullshit," he heard himself saying, and now Mr. Tetley was leaning to hear his words, "the stories they told me. They're all bullshit that have nothing to do with the real world out there."

Mr. Tetley, sitting up, lit a cheroot and considered Timmy's words. He lay back and blew smoke into the blue. "No," he said, "those stories they told you, they're not bullshit. Those stories and the stories you've read and the poetry you've learned by heart . . . They are the Timmy that became Speedy Deefy . . . That's what we're made of — flesh and bone and the stories we know."

"Flesh and bone . . ." He watched the marvelous workings of his hand as he opened and closed his fingers against the sky. He felt as he had as a boy running home in the dark from Grandpa Tim's shanty, believing the *sidh* were rustling the leaves over the path. "The stories you know," he asked at last, "where do they begin?"

Mr. Tetley opened his eyes. The question seemed to agitate him. He got up and went to the gush of water and drank a handful and splashed his face. He looked up at the windmill and walked around the trough before turning to Timmy. "My great-grandfather owned my great-grandmother."

Mr. Tetley's back was to the sun, and his shadow was on Timmy's face. "That hurts your white conscience, doesn't it?" Then he shook his head. "But it shouldn't. You didn't have a damn thing to do with it. And neither did I."

"But *we* did. White people . . ."

Before leaning back again, Mr. Tetley reached over and polished Speedy's white dome with his black hand. "One thing you've got to get through that fanciful noggin of yours," he said, as much to himself and the sky as to Timmy, "is that none of us — not you nor me, nor white nor black, nor Jew nor Gentile — none of us chose our ancestors nor had anything to do with what they did. So we have no reason for shame nor right to pride in who they were or what they did. Do we?"

But Timmy's pride in his ancestry could not be poofed away like his boyhood belief in the fairies.

"Do we?" Mr. Tetley raised his head, but Timmy was still trying to get a handle on his pride in his ancestry and his shame for the white man that had owned Mr. Tetley's great-grandmother. "But only in ourselves — what *we* are and what *we* do . . . and what we pass on to *our* descendants. My great-grandfather, for instance . . ."

"Yes," said Timmy, eager to get on with the story. "Who was he?"

"Education and freedom. He laid those two burdens upon me."

Timmy could not believe that he had heard right. "Burdens, Mr. Tetley?"

"You can't just *have* them — like toys to have fun with while they last. You've got to *use* them. Take *care* of them. They're *tools*."

"To make a better living," Timmy affirmed. "And bring

your kids up right and come and go and do and say as you please."

"You think of them as toys," Mr. Tetley said scornfully. "Like playthings that Santa Claus put under your Christmas tree. For your pleasure while they last! The mitt and the mask can earn me a living . . . the tools of ignorance. But education and freedom are the tools of . . ." There was nothing to see in the blue into which he was staring, but he was seeing something.

"Of what, Mr. Tetley? The tools of what?"

"Of thought."

Timmy sat up to think about thought.

"It's hard work," Mr. Tetley said. "And it can be painful."

Timmy lay back again. "You're thinking about your great-grandfather, aren't you? The one . . ." *who owned your great-grandmother.*

"No," said Mr. Tetley, "I am thinking about what to do with the rest of my life."

"But you said that it was he . . ."

"He's part of it. A big part. He got us started in the printing business . . . words . . . education . . . He couldn't marry her, of course, but he declared her a free woman . . . what they called *libres gens de couleur* . . . freed slaves . . . there were a good many of them in New Orleans, long before your famous Emancipation Proclamation . . . He came to New Orleans from Vienna in 1853 to take over the printing plant his uncle had established years before. Along with the shop, he inherited the old man's slaves . . . including Bella . . ."

"Your great-grandmother?"

"She was born there, the daughter of Markey and Mary."

"Your great-*great*-grandparents! Gosh, I don't know who any of mine were."

"So much for your ancestral pride," Mr. Tetley remarked.

"Poof," said Timmy, blowing it up to the sky.

"Markey took care of the horses and the stable and drove the carriage and delivery wagon. Mary was the cook, Bella the housemaid . . ."

There was no sound but the clanking of the pump, the splash of water, and the caw-caw-caw of a wandering crow.

"A crow never caws just once," Mr. Tetley remarked. His eyes were closed. Timmy closed his and kept his mouth shut.

"It was on Marigny Avenue, near the wharf . . . The yellow brick building was both plant and home . . . The apartment was on the second floor, the type cases and presses on the first . . . the slave quarters in the basement . . . I walked by and around it last winter . . . Its arched entrance and windows are boarded up . . . the ruins of the stable are filled with trash . . . That's where Daisy was brought up . . . in the apartment . . . born free . . . Daisy Klein . . . brown skin but with the same grey-green eyes and black ringlet curls of her father . . . By the time she was ten, she could read and write better than white children after eight grades of public or parochial schooling . . . Soon she was setting type as skillfully as the succession of itinerant printers, mostly drunks, Abraham hired to keep the shop running as New Orleans sacrificed its young men to the Confederate cause . . . Daisy gradually took over as proprietor . . ."

Clayton and Nathan, swinging the tarp between them, dumped their sudsy burden in the trough.

"This gonna be the las load," said Clayton. "We leave you the tarp, fetch 'em back clean an' dry."

"Iffen you git rested up enough while they be dryin to make the haul," Nathan added with pleasant sarcasm.

"There are no disturbing ancestral memories in the pod those two peas came from," Mr. Tetley remarked after them.

"Nathan wants them to go back to farming, and Clayton wants them to try out for the Monarchs next spring," Timmy said. "Whatever they do, they're going to do it as twins."

"If, while discussing their future with you, they ask your advice, tell them to go back to the farm. Nathan can't hit a pro curve, and Clayton doesn't have the good arm."

They rinsed and wrung and spread the batch. "So there you have it," Mr. Tetley said, at their ease again, "the story of how I became a man of — how did you put it?"

"A man of considerable erudition," said Timmy. "Of education and freedom . . . thinking about what you're going to do with the rest of your life . . ."

"Grandma Daisy is old . . . If I don't take over as editor and publisher, she's going to sell the newspaper . . . So here I am . . . on this road . . . playing funny ball from town to town . . . thinking it over . . ."

"Whether to take over the Barons or take over the newspaper?"

"Mostly . . . what *kind* of a newspaper . . . a plaything or a tool . . ."

"Of thought?"

"And where thought takes you. So there you have it. You've pumped it out of me."

"Not all of it. You're William P. Tetley the *Second* . . ."

"That's not a story you tell to pass the time."

"But it's not fair to tell half a story." He reached up to finger a dangling pants leg. "And these uniforms aren't but half dry either."

"Billy. He came to the shop as Billy Tetley, an itinerant journalist and printer in the days after so-called Reconstruction. He was then about thirty, and Daisy was twenty . . ."

"And they fell in love?"

"Worse. They got married."

"He was a . . . a . . . white man, too." While he said it, Timmy added one-eighth for the great-grandfather and one-fourth for the grandfather and figured that Mr. Tetley was three-eighths of white origin.

"From up North . . . from a New England family of teachers and preachers . . . That's what made it still worse in New Orleans. But it was even worse than that . . . He was a follower of Karl Marx."

"A *Communist!*" It was as bad a word as Timmy knew.

"Like Jesus, he believed in separation of church and state . . . 'Give unto Caesar that which is Caesar's . . .' But he also believed that Jesus was a radical . . . 'Come unto me, all ye that labor and are heavy-laden . . .' So he set out for the South, where the heavy-laden were laboring . . . and where the dream of Emancipation had become a nightmare of repression . . . More terrible, in some ways, than legal slavery, because it was a mockery of law and was enforced by terror and torture . . . Anyway, he didn't have romance in mind when he came to the shop on Marigny. He had his eye on Daisy's newspaper, *The Delta Sunshine.* It was a religious rag she had started."

"Rag!" Timmy protested.

"Badly written, poorly edited . . . a circulation of a few hundred . . . She and a few Negro preachers, semiliterate, wrote stories and essays — Parables of Joy, they called them — to bring the comfort of salvation through Jesus in the next life to ease the suffering in this one . . . When Billy picked up a copy by chance, he saw instantly that he could work in parables of Communism . . . of political and economic justice . . . of protest and revolution . . . Soon Daisy Klein was listed as publisher and William P. Tetley as editor . . . He made it *his* kind of newspaper . . . Because it was cloaked in harmless Sunshine Christianity, it was not immediately perceived as a threat to white supremacy by the few white people who might have seen it . . ."

"So they fell in love and got married," said Timmy, eager to get on with the story of their romance.

"They couldn't get married legally, of course. But when their son, Abraham . . ."

"Your father!"

". . . was born . . . It was in 1875 . . . Billy insisted that he be christened Abraham Tetley, which probably would not have caused much stir . . . But in the next issue he listed Daisy *Tetley* as publisher and wrote a paragraph announcing a new joy in the form of a son in their sanctuary of Sunshine Christianity. Daisy was both proud and terrified. What she was afraid would happen *did* happen. On New Year's Eve of 1875 the hooded horsemen clattered up Marigny. They smashed the windows and wrecked the presses and soaked Billy in oil and strung him up and set him afire as a warning to all nigger lovers."

"Ohhh . . ."

"So that," Mr. Tetley said calmly, "was the end of *that*."

"Of . . .?"

"Sunshine Christianity . . . of parables of protest . . . Daisy Tetley sold the building on Marigny and moved the shop to Congo Square . . . began to publish *The Oracle* . . . a moderate and respectable voice of the Negro community . . . got my father married to a preacher's daughter . . . prospered . . ."

"And now you . . ."

"Hoo-eee! Hooo-eeee!" From across the pasture came Ol' Dan's hog call that noon dinner was hot and waiting. Timmy wigwagged that they had heard and were coming.

". . . you're thinking."

They gathered the uniforms from the bushes and piled

them on the tarp. "What happens to people who know stories is more important than what happens to the people in the stories," Mr. Tetley said, as he picked up the front corners. Before picking up his corners, Timmy went back and disconnected the pump. The trough was full of clean water for the cattle.

26
Full Shares

Timmy perfected his use of the phonograph-needle pitch on the rubes in the tank towns between them and the showdown in Mandan. In these easy games, Pops would save their arms by pitching him and Moon half a game each. Working on the setup moves and the amount of wrist-turn on the curve and the screwball, Timmy used one or two needles on each of the twenty or so batters he faced during his stint. The rubes swung at the changes of its speed and degree of break without squawking. They thought the albino's pitching was another example of the baseball wizardry of the colored clowns.

"Don't think you get away with it this easy in Mandan," Bofey warned him. "Them pros seen plenty a crooked pitchin. They gonna be callin for the ball. The ump he gonna be lookin for spit, mud, Vaseline, an' scratches an' rough spots on the ball."

Crooked! The secret pitch was crooked — illegal, against the rules of the game, *unsportsmanlike!* Timmy had a vision of Baby Elton, his favorite hero of Henry Barbour's stories about young gentlemen athletes of the prep schools of the East. "I assure you, sir," Baby Elton would have said, "that you have come to the wrong place to enlist a participant in this infamous skullduggery."

On the Friday night after the evening show in Starberg, they were camped in a country churchground halfway down to Mandan. After supper, in the darkness by the embers, Timmy found himself asking Mr. Tetley about it. Were not the rules and sportsmanship of the game the same for everybody who played it? Because there was money on the line and they were playing against strangers up here in the white North, did they have the right . . . ?

Little Hoop, stretched out nearby, came at him through the shadow-casting flickers of light. "You sayin, boy, that you too good to use some nigger trick to win for us? Against your own kind? That what you sayin, boy?" he demanded.

"I didn't say I wouldn't," Timmy said. "I was just . . ."

"He say we teachin him to be a crook," Moon put in. "Him an' his fine white ways, like he too good for us."

"Me being white has nothing to do with it. It's just the way I was . . ." He damned himself for being a fool but felt a compulsion to say it: ". . . brought up."

Little Hoop grabbed his shirt and jerked him to his feet. "Once before I tol' you I gonna whup your white ass. I gonna do it right now. You gonna go out an' throw how Bofey learn you to throw or —"

In a flash of anger, Timmy flung Little Hoop's hands off him. He had had all he could take of their black superiority. "You ain't man enough to make me do anything!"

"Come back here from the fire. I show you am I man enough."

"You damn right!" said Timmy.

"Let 'em fight it out, the bad blood they got between 'em," Moon said.

Timmy was unbuttoning his shirt. "How do you want it?" he demanded. "Marquis of Queensberry — or catch-as-catch-can?"

The tension was broken by the hoots and laughter of the House: "Now I heard it all!" "Go git 'im, Speedy, with your mark a the queen." "Careful a that boy, Hoop. He gonna belt you wif his mouf."

Pops was laughing, too. "Thas enough, boys! You crazy, Hoop? You gonna risk one a the two arms we got? Dan, bring out that jug, a cup all around to settle us down. An' you boys shake hands now. We gotta be together."

"I don' shake hands," Little Hoop said.

"Neither do I," Timmy shouted at him. "And when I use Bofey's pitch, it ain't 'cause I'm afraid of you."

"Shame on bofe of you," Ol' Dan said, splashing the moonshine in their outstretched cups.

"Where's my cup?" Timmy demanded.

"You don' drink no moonshine," Ol' Dan said. "You still a boy."

Pops tossed Timmy a tin cup. "Tonight he git a taste. Like his grandpa let 'im have on the Fourth of July."

Way back then, on the Fourth of July! It seemed a lifetime ago to Timmy as he raised his cup for a sip. "Something else I want to tell you guys," he said.

"You got something stuck in your craw, boy, spit it out," said Little Hoop.

"Now's the time," said Pops. "Throw some sticks on the fire."

"I don't like this white-boy shit I've been getting from some of you," Timmy said into the light and shadows. "I want to be treated as an equal!"

This was considered in uneasy silence. Some looked to Mr. Tetley for response, but he was lying back and gazing up into the dark sky as if he had not heard. It came from Scrappy. "You ain't our equal. You ain't our equal as ballplayers, but mainly you ain't our equal 'cause you be here just for *fun*, a white boy pertendin to be one a us up here workin for a livin. Thas what we *here* for, workin for a livin. This double-header we got in Mandan, we win it, it's meat on my family's table for a month this winter. Thas what we're playin for," he said to the others, "meat on our table this winter. This Speedy boy, son of a rich white man, he playin for *funs*. The money don' mean nothin to him."

Timmy spoke up again: "I want full shares, the same as everybody else."

They thought about it. "He didn't come with us on full shares," said Moon. "He come on half shares, does he earn 'em."

"I've been figgerin half shares," said Pops. "In my books I got him down for half shares, startin with the take from Fargo. What you boys think? We go around, each have his say."

"I say if he does us a good job, an' win his game in Mandan, we give 'im full shares a that game," said Manny.

"I say if he be pitchin in my place, he take *my* shares," said Bofey.

There was a chorus of noes. "Whether he throw another pitch or not, Bofey gets full shares the whole trip," said Pops. "We talkin 'bout Speedy. Who else got a say?"

"In my opinion," said Mr. Tetley, sitting up, "there is merit in his claim for full shares. He's worked hard for us and done his best for us. With Merv's passing, we would have been in sore straits without him. Now our chances for an additional one thousand dollars to go into our shares depend upon how well he can throw the pitches Bofey has taught him. So . . ."

"I agrees wif Mistuh Tetley," Scrappy put in. "But not full shares clear back to Fargo. I say start 'im on full shares back to Minot. Thas when he start takin ovah. Kin you figger it back to Minot, Pops?"

Pops nodded. "I kin figger it any way you boys say. Unless I hear diffrent now, thas the way it gonna be. Anybody got a say, speak up wif it."

There was no dissent. "I pass the jug again," said Ol' Dan.

"What about the white-boy shit?" Timmy persisted.

"Shee-itt," said Little Hoop. "You ack like a man, we treat you like a man."

Timmy laid his pad next to Mr. Tetley's. "It was in my craw," he said. "I had to spit it out."

Mr. Tetley tilted his silver flask. "Our young Sir Galahad, whose strength is as the strength of ten because his heart is pure, will put aside his code of schoolboy sportsmanship . . . He will use a trick learned from a crafty old professional, who has guarded its secret to survive in a hard world, to help put meat on our tables this winter." His soft laughter rumbled out of him.

"I'm on full shares now. It's my duty to use it."

"It is also your duty not to get caught using it," Mr. Tetley said, taking another swig. "If you get caught at it, the law of the game calls for your expulsion from it. If you get kicked out of the game, we will lose it. But if caught, you will not be dishonored, either by your teammates, the opposing players, or the umpire. If you use the pitch effectively, opposing players and the umpire will be positive that you are breaking the law of the game. Catching you at it becomes part of the game. It is their duty to catch you, and your duty to deceive

them." He spread his roll and took a final swig of the moonshine and stretched himself and closed his eyes.

*

They broke camp at three o'clock Saturday afternoon for
their game in a town called Benton's Bend on the Missouri
River north of Bismarck. Pops decreed that both Speedy and
Moon would rest their arms. Each of the others would go out
to the mound and pitch an inning or so as best he could.
Everybody had a good time. With one out in the ninth, Bofey
went out to pitch. He tickled the crowd by carrying bofe
his gloves to the mound. He floated the first pitch in left-
handed and then drilled in a pretty good strike right-handed.
Left and right, left and right, he got both batters out on
grounders.

"How's it feel?" they asked him in the truck on the way
to Mandan.

"It hurt," he said, "but there's worse things than pain."

Timmy was standing in the night wind behind the cab
of the flatbed on the way to Mandan, out where the West
begins. He had a farm-country boy's awe of the West. It was
an hour past full dark when they caravaned through downtown Bismarck and crossed the Missouri. He gazed down
upon the black water and ahead at the scattered lights of
Mandan and the black hills beyond. He tingled with the
ancient excitement of invading an unknown kingdom.

Pops navigated them through the darkness, south along the
west bank and into the hills on unmarked roads, stopping now
and then to peer for the boulder or lonesome pine that would
mark the next turn. Timmy felt that their destination was lost
in the night. But Pops came at last to the LONGHORN RANCH —
KEEP OUT sign and the wheel ruts that took them to the

215

deserted sheds and corral, used for roundups and branding. Longhorn Stevens, their host and enemy, had assured Pops they were as welcome as the flowers in May to the shelter, water, and cook shed with its huge stone fireplace. Timmy pitched in to help Ol' Dan with the fire and the gear. Soon they were taking their ease and enjoyment of chicken and corn in the light and comfort of the fire and the lanterns.

27

Meat on Scrappy's Table

Toward noon, getting into uniform after a lazy breakfast, they heard the drum of hooves on the sun-baked trail from the hills. Longhorn Stevens came galloping into camp. He reared and wheeled the long-tailed pinto and sat grinning down at them through its dust:

"One of muh boys said he seen you a-crossin the bridge last night, so I knowed you'd made it in like gypsies in the dark."

Like gypsies in the dark last night, Timmy thought, but now ballplayers in the sun. Rubbing a dab of Vaseline on his fresh-shaven dome, he felt the pride of being a pro. He also felt a sharp pang for tomorrow when he'd be going back. But it was a long time until tomorrow.

"Came a-riding by to check on our ay-range-ments with yez," Longhorn went on, addressing Pops, who had stepped forward for the palaver. "You know that center-field wagon gate? You park behin' it an' come in that-a-way. One of my boys gonna be there to let you in. Otherwise Old George, he make you pay to come in. Old George, he's not a-handin out any comps today. Oney the players, the boys in the band, the two umps, an' the marshal an' his two deppities gits in free. All else pays — four bits for grownups, a dime for kids under twelve, two bits for standing room, regardless of age."

Pops nodded. "Spectin a big crowd?"

"Reckon we gonna jam-pack three thousand of 'em in there. They're comin for blood." He grinned his delight. "*Your* blood."

"What kinda gate we be playin for?" Pops asked.

"Old George, he figgers the total gate at round-about eleven hundred simoleons. But!" — Longhorn raised a hand — "Old George done ruled the player shares cuts off at seven hundred. So the town's gonna make four hundred — plus peanuts, pop-corn, and sody-pop — for to buy a new fire engine."

"This Old George," Mr. Tetley asked. "In what official capacity does he issue his edicts and rulings?"

Longhorn looked at Mr. Tetley. "You're that new big catcher we been hearin about. Well, Old George he been mayor since Ninety-eight, an' he'll keep on bein mayor till he pushes up daisies."

"So we be playin for three-fifty a game?" Pops asked.

"Plus our usual." Longhorn looked at him sharply. "You boys ain't gonna welsh on our usual side bet, now is ya?"

"We oney got twelve this year," said Pops. "Countin me an' Ol Dan an evabody."

Longhorn pointed at each as he confirmed the count. "So that makes it one-twenty a game on the side."

"Four-seventy each game," Pops agreed.

"You boys wanna round it off to an even five hundred dollars a game?"

Pops nodded. "Figger it rounded."

"You got some new faces, too," said Longhorn. "I didn't

218

see him, nor him, nor him" — Nathan, Clayton, and Mr. Tetley — "last year. Nor him neither, a course" — pointing his quirt at Timmy — "your deef-mute white coon."

"Crow," said Mr. Tetley.

"Same difference."

"You got pretty much the same team as last year?" Little Hoop asked.

" 'Bout the same." Longhorn grinned devilishly. "Oh, we got two pitchers you ain't seen. A young fella named Fritz Green just outta high school in Spokane, been playin American Legion ball, gonna turn pro come spring. *And* Johnny Baugh. You hearda him? He pitched twelve years for Seattle in the Pacific Coast League till two years ago. Now he's jobbin around, playing town ball."

"We figgered you'd be beefin up for us," said Pops.

"Now lookee here, boys. One a the reasons I ride out here to tell you 'bout. My cook wagon's gonna come out here to barbecue us a side a lamb an forty chickens while we're a-playin ball. An' win, lose, or draw, we gonna have us the ding-dangest whoopee party you boys ever seen. Anybody wanna tell me that me an' my boys caint eat'n drink with darkies on my own ranch, let 'em come an' try'n stop me, Old George included. Some folks 'round here, they don' believe in ay-sociatin with darkies."

"Niggers," said Mr. Tetley.

"Same difference," said Longhorn and hit the pinto a lick and galloped off.

"What I be tellin you 'bout this man?" said Pops.

"A gentleman of the old school," said Mr. Tetley, watching his dust, "whose white ass we are going to beat out of one thousand simoleons."

*

219

The sky was high, the sun was hot, and Old Glory was drooping on the center-field flagpole when they trooped into the park through the wagon gate. Speedy and Ol' Dan, carrying the bat bag between them, were at the end of the file down the right-field line to their dugout on the third-base side of the infield. The people seemed to put out more heat than the sun. These three thousand fans seemed *closer* than the five thousand at Fargo. They seemed to go straight up into the air from the field like a wall of grinning white masks. When Speedy and Ol' Dan set the bag down to change hands on it:

"Here's that albino. He's deef an' dumb, too."

"They say albinos don't have hair anywhere."

"He sure don't look like no nigger."

"They say his ma was a light-skinned whore in New Orleans, made a hundred dollars a *night*."

"That am-bye-dextrous pitcher a theirs, they say we might not see him. He's got sore arms."

"We paid to see him. They oughta *make* him pitch."

"Tell you one thing, these coons play clever ball."

Timmy smiled because Speedy could not hear these bits of white shit from the stands. He felt good — strong and limber and *good*, confident he could make Bofey's secret screwball sizzle in on the right-handers, out from the lefties.

"Aw right now," said Pops in the privacy of their dugout, which had its own drinking fountain and a toilet back of the bench. "We gonna go out there an' give 'em our pepper drill, an' Speedy — this be his last day — he gonna git in it. Mind now," he said to Speedy, "you don' try no tricks you can't handle, jes be a clown."

Speedy skipped and jigged in the bewildering display of thrown and batted balls. His bafflement and clownish agility as balls popped at him from hands that didn't have balls in them tickled the throng. At the climax of the juggling display, all six balls hit him on the rump as he scrambled to gather them in one at a time. The team came in sweating.

"A new dimension of comedy," Mr. Tetley said, mopping his face.

"Must be a hundred degrees out there."

"More. Gotta be *two* hundred."

"Drink plenty a water," Pops said. "We gotta long day's work out there."

Now the Cowpokes had the infield. Timmy was watching Fritz, the young left-hander, taking his warm-ups on the first-base side. He would go six two and two hundred pounds. He came up stylishly high with his right leg and threw with easy poise. He looked like a nice guy from a good family. If this were a back-home town or high-school game, Timmy was thinking, they would get together afterward and swap stories about crazy things they had done as kids . . . As Speedy, he saw him as a white giant from a world he would never know.

"He gonna throw *hard*," Bofey observed. "But his curve ball — looka there! — he come in sidearm an' turn his wrist clean over, gonna hang comin in."

Both teams lined up in front of their dugouts for the National Anthem. The Western Stars Hoe-Down Band took the crowd of lit-up men and their tolerant ladies and restless kids into the lowest swells of "O say, can you see?" and up to the highest notes of the rockets' red glare and the land of the free. "This a great landa ours," Speedy heard Ol' Dan say. And born in slavery, Timmy thought.

Pops came back to the dugout from the meeting at the plate with Longhorn and the two umpires. "The ground rules they got here in this tight park, the main thing keep in mind, it's like we be playin on a pool table. The ball's in play all a time, off the walls. No extra base on overthrows 'less they go in the stands. You gotta play the walls, figger which way the ball's gonna come off. An' be *there*. Now we got a change in the battin order I just turn in. I want Speedy leadin off wif Scrappy hittin behin' him for the run'n hit. Now watch me close. The run'n hit sign be color, flesh, color. Okay, then we got Ike an' Mistuh Tetley's long ball an Clayt's long ball behin' him. Then come Nate, Manny, Hoop, and Moon. Now Bofey say this kid left-hander gonna be quick wif his fast ball. Question is, kin he throw good strikes? So we all gonna take one strike, two if he go to three an' one. Now watch me close, here be our signs. Flesh to color, take. Flesh to flesh, on your own. Color to color, bunt. If I do a sign twice, it takes it off . . ."

"Take on take takes take off," Mr. Tetley reminded them.

"If you got the sign, you pull your hat down. You ain't sure, you git a handful a dirt. Be *sure*. Gonna be *hot* out there. Long way to go. Go out an' come in slow'n easy . . ."

"My family back home, this game means meat on the table this winter," Scrappy reminded them.

"How many kids you got, Scrappy?" Timmy asked.

"Eleven when I leave, maybe twelve by now. Thirteen if it be twins."

"Git up there, start us off, Speedy."

"We're gonna put meat on your table, Scrappy," Timmy said and skipped to the plate as Speedy.

With the take sign, Speedy crouched lower than usual to make a low target for the first pitch. As the young white giant looked in for his sign, Timmy found himself thinking how like Astur he was preparing to attack Horatius at the bridge:

> He smiled on those bold Romans,
> A smile serene and high . . .

Without Pops's take sign, Speedy would have swung at the streak of white. It tailed up and away for a ball. So did the next. With the take still on, the third and fourth were down the pike for strikes. Pops rubbed his nose and clapped his hands — flesh on flesh put Speedy on his own. When he heard the next pitch pop into the mitt, Speedy thought he had been caught looking, but the umpire judged it high for ball three. Speedy went for the three-two pitch and ticked a foul into the catcher's mitt.

"Now we got no run'n hit," Scrappy muttered in passing.

"It was upstairs," Mr. Tetley affirmed in the dugout. "Unless this boy settles down, or till he loses some of his quickness in this heat, you better take all the way."

Scrappy took a strike, and Pops put him on his own. He lined the ball hard to the third baseman. Ike fouled off two three-two pitches and walked.

"Ike made him throw eight pitches," said Mr. Tetley from the on-deck circle.

"You the one, big man," Pops called and clapped twice. On his own, Mr. Tetley took two strikes and two balls, making the kid work. Then he stroked a line drive fair into the right-field corner. The ball caromed out into short center. While the fielders were chasing it down, Ike raced home standing up. Clayt's long fly on a two-two pitch was caught foul in the left-field corner.

"Throw low strikes in and out an' don' waste no pitches," Pops told Moon. "This heat's a killer."

Moon got the first batter on an easy grounder to Hoop but got behind on the next two, and both singled on three-two pitches. With runners at first and third, Scrappy dove to stop a grounder up the middle, flipped it out of his glove to Hoop, who threw falling away to Clayt for the double play. Both sides went down in order in the second. Speedy came to bat in the third with one out and nobody on. Pops kept clapping, flesh on flesh, to three and two. Then he ran down the line toward Speedy, clapping his hands four times to encourage the mute. Take on take takes take off. Then he brushed his letters and touched his cap — color on color, bunt. Good! Speedy pulled his cap down tighter on his white dome. Then the white giant came in wide with his first curve ball, and Speedy let it pass and started dancing down the line. He remembered not to hear the umpire's "Steee-rike!" Bofey, coaching first, waved him back to the dugout.

"If he starts throwing that lollipop curve," Mr. Tetley said, "we're going to put meat on Scrappy's table. Next time, wait for it. When he comes sidearm, wait and wait and *wait*. Then drill it up the middle."

That first-inning run was still the only one on the board in the sixth when Moon, with two out, ran a line drive to right center into a triple. Then Speedy, on two and two, got out ahead of the slow curve and struck out. Moon had to go out to the mound, dripping wet and still blowing. The first Cowpoke doubled into the left-field corner; the next singled him home. The third hit a liner over Speedy's head against the right-field wall. Speedy sprinted for it, but the ball bounced away, and Speedy was not *there*. A run scored as the batter sped to third. Mr. Tetley caught a pop foul against the back screen, but Moon walked the next two batters.

Pops and Mr. Tetley went out to the mound to cool Moon down. Mr. Tetley looked out to Speedy, but Pops shook his head and let Moon keep the ball. Scrappy got a dribbling ten-bouncer to Hoop in time for a force at second, but the batter beat the relay to first, and another run was in. Aiming the ball, Moon threw high; throwing hard, his next pitch was in the dirt.

Pops went out again, waving for Speedy to come in. In his

concentration on the game, feeling shame for his strike-outs and dumb play, Timmy had been oblivious of the crowd. Now he responded to whoops and cheers for the Cowpoke rally and hoots and jeers for the change in pitchers by skipping in as a happy clown. He felt cold inside. Four runs in, runners at first and third with two out. Their number-five batter, the tall left-hander, was waiting at the plate with two balls and no strikes. They had three innings to get the runs back and put meat on Scrappy's table. He found himself smiling.

"You go play me some right field," Pops said to Moon and took the ball from him and gave it to Speedy. Pretending to talk to Mr. Tetley, Pops said: "Bofey say throw this left-hander your secret screwball. Don' worry about walkin 'im. Throw tough. Bofey wanna see how it act in this thin air. If he get on, throw the right-hander low strikes, hope he hit it at somebody."

"He ain't gonna get on," Speedy said into the dirt.

Looking in at Mr. Tetley's three-finger sign for the screwball, setting the needle firmly in the seam against Bofey's silver-dollar buckle, Speedy knew — he *knew* — that this freckled Cowpoke had no chance against their black magic. He took aim at the Adam's apple and back-spun it down and away. Swaying back to follow the floater in on him, the batter saw it zip out and away too late. Speedy did it again. With two and two, Mr. Tetley fingered his mask and called for the sweeping curve. The hanging curve on the fat of the bat became a sinking stone on the handle and a pop foul to Mr. Tetley. As Speedy jigged in, Mr. Tetley was there to polish his dome and mitt his rump into the privacy of their own world.

"Now, gentlemen," said Mr. Tetley, "if you will concentrate on timing this tiring boy's fast ball and waiting on his

225

curve, Mistuh Tetley will knock one downtown."

With a wet towel on his head, Speedy sat back, knowing it would be as Mr. Tetley said. And it was. Scrappy and Ike singled, and Mistuh Tetley lofted a fly out of the park and far, far away. Clayt doubled, Nate and Manny and Hoop singled, and Moon hit a long fly that scored Manny. So there were six runs in with Hoop at second and only one out when Speedy strutted out to the plate.

With two and two, he heard Mr. Tetley's deep rumble from the dugout. "Now *wait!*" Sure enough, in came the side-arm curve, hanging out there like a white balloon. Speedy got all of it and watched it sail out to the fence in left center. As Hoop trotted home, Speedy rounded second and dug for third. Pops was holding him up, but Speedy ran through him as the relay came in wide to the fence. He scooted for home. He dove headfirst under the block and got a hand on the plate, safe with a triple and an error on the throw to third.

With eight runs in and only one out, he sat back again, panting into his wet towel, and watched Scrappy get his second single of the inning.

The young white giant was now a sodden, beat-down boy named Fritz Green. Again Timmy wished he might go to him after the game and shake hands. Longhorn was teetering out on his high-heeled boots, his right hand thrust high toward his bullpen. He put his arm on the kid's shoulder and must have said something like "You gave it all you had, son." But the kid shook his head as he gave up the ball and walked off looking at his feet. Over a ripple of applause for his effort came the calls of derision: "How much you pay that punk, Longhorn?" "Go back to Spokane and learn how to pitch."

"Will he make it as a pro?" Timmy asked Mr. Tetley.

"Not unless someone teaches him to pitch instead of throw."

"Like Bofey did me?"

"Get it out of your head you're ever going to be in pro ball," Mr. Tetley told him. "You go home and shine in the schoolyard and play town ball for funs. But first . . ."

"We gotta put meat on Scrappy's table."

The Cowpokes scored single runs in their seventh, eighth, and ninth, but Speedy put down each rally without using more than three needles an inning. They won it 12 to 7.

28

"Fear no more the heat o' the sun"

————————◆————————

There was a square-dancing contest between games, and they had half an hour in the free-moving air by the truck to refresh themselves inside and out. Ol' Dan had fixed summer-sausage sandwiches and had covered the crock of ice and lemonade with wet gunny sacks. They stripped to the waist and wrung their shirts out. Pops doled out the three dry spare shirts to Mr. Tetley, Moon, and Speedy.

"I been keepin book on their batters," Bofey told the council. "So if it's okay wif Pops an' Mistuh Tetley, I wanna call the pitches Speedy gonna use this game."

Pops nodded, and Mr. Tetley said: "A judicious decision, but how are we all going to get your calls from the dugout?"

"We all gotta know," said Manny, "so we kin set up our play."

"I be sittin on the top step, an' I use *bofe* my hands. I pound the step right-handed, it's gonna be the secret pitch. One, fast ball; two, curve; three, his screwball. That means

look for the ground ball or the pop fly — outfield wanna
come in a few steps. His reglar stuff, I pound my *left* hand
on the top step. They gonna hit it harder, give 'em some room
out there. Now, lissen, the secret pitch, it takes extra effort.
He gotta *hum* it. There's no way a knowin how far he kin go
in this heat. The more runs we get for 'im, the farther he
kin go."

"We gonna get the runs," said Busy Ike.

"I don't feel pooped," Timmy said. "I feel I can go all
the way." He nodded at Bofey. "With his pitch."

"Speedy move to ninth in the line-up this game," Pops
said. "Evabody move up one. So Mistuh Tetley gonna be
hittin third back of Scrappy and Ike . . ."

"Three runs right there," said Mr. Tetley.

"Now, Speedy," Pops said to him, "you stan at the plate
an' take all the way. Let 'im strike you out. Don' want you
runnin. If you get on base, don' be tryin for nothin extra
. . . an' no clownin around out there in this heat . . ."

"Let's win it *quick*," said Busy Ike, "an' get on out to the
barbecue Longhorn's got cookin for us. If we win this, I gonna
make a song 'bout Bofey's secret pitch."

"Not if," said Scrappy. "*When!*"

As starting pitcher, Timmy saw and thought a game dif-
ferently than he did as a fielder. On the mound, he saw only
the batter and the mitt and thought only about the pitch he
was going to throw. The balletic precision of the infield play
and the running grace of the outfielders were like a picture
show that he was watching. He made his moves to cover
first or back up third automatically, as if he were watching
himself, not doing it. In the deep shade of the dugout, with
the cool towel on his head, the antics and heroics of his
teammates at the plate and on base and beside him on the
bench seemed even more remote. They had their jobs to do,

he had his. His main job, he knew after the fourth inning, was to *last*.

Johnny Baugh, Longhorn's money pitcher from Seattle, was a stocky, tobacco-chewing right-hander. Timmy heard his teammates making their judgments of his stuff: "He puts his fast ball where he wants it, but it don't *move*." "That knuckler, he uses oney when he's ahead on the count." "A *spitter* is what it is," said Bofey. "The third baseman is loadin it for 'im." "Unless they call for the ball on Speedy, we don' call for the ball on him," said Pops. "That curve a his is just a *nickel* in this thin air. *Jump* on it." But Timmy let his teammates talk and think about Johnny Baugh. Speedy stood at the plate until the umpire called him out.

The game was going well for them. Mr. Tetley doubled Scrappy and Ike home in the first and scored on Clayt's single. They got another in the second, two more in the third when Mr. Tetley socked one into the top row of the right-field stands, and two more in the fourth.

They were hitting Speedy hard but mostly at people. The Cowpokes left two on in the first and second innings and had the bases loaded in the third when Busy Ike leaped high against the wagon gate to make a third out out of a home run.

The fourth inning was tough. Speedy pitched to seven batters and had to use fourteen needles to hold them to two runs. He came in feeling like a stewed chicken. Five innings to go! He had to last.

In the dugout, Bofey crouched before him and Mr. Tetley. "The next batter up, the left-hander they call Teej. He's their speed merchant, an' he's gonna be runnin on you. They see you got no pick-off move. They all gonna start runnin on you. Don' worry about holdin 'em close. But Mistuh Tetley, when they got a runnin situation, he gonna put a fist down for a pitch-out. When he do, you gonna come in high an' wide, so he kin gun 'em down at second."

"A judicious decision," said Mr. Tetley, and they went out with an 8 to 2 lead.

Teej smacked Speedy's first pitch over second, and there he was prancing off first base. Speedy threw over to get him back, but Teej saw it coming and stepped back laughing. Mr. Tetley pumped his fist down to take off Bofey's call for a secret fast ball. Aiming high and away, with the needle already in the ball, Speedy got a glimpse of Teej breaking for second. Worrying about throwing a secret *pitch-out*, he hurried the throw. Mr. Tetley had to leap to catch it, and Teej slid in ahead of his off-balance throw.

"That run on second don't hurt us," Pops called out to the fielders. "Play the batter."

"Don't get rattled now," Timmy told Speedy. "You've got Bofey's secret pitch." Or did he? He wiped his sweating right hand dry on his pants leg before pinching his fingers on the needle. Bofey pounded his right hand twice for a secret curve to the right-hander. It swept wide for a ball. Another, a good pitch — but the batter got a piece of it on the outside corner and blooped it into short right. It dropped in front of Moon, and Teej went to third. Now Bofey wanted a plain low strike, a double-play ball. Again a good pitch, on the inside corner. The batter responded with a sharp grounder, but — Oh, damn! — it bounced just past Manny's dive for it. While he could have thrown Teej out at the plate, Clayt threw to Manny to hold the runners at first and second. With the run-and-hit sure to be on, Mr. Tetley's fist called for two pitch-outs, but the runners did not take the bait. Ahead on the count, the batter waited Speedy out and walked when his three-two fast ball, in the opinion of the umpire, sunk too low.

When Speedy stared in at the umpire, the crowd jeered. Then, whack! a double. Whack! a single. Whack, whack!

With runners on base and only one out, Bofey kept pounding for secret pitches. Speedy had trouble holding the needles between his sweaty fingers and setting them firmly in the seam. Some of them must have flown out with the spin of the ball. The harder he threw to get good spin on the secret stuff, the wilder he got. He began to feel that each pitch was a hopeless venture. Six runs were in and the score tied at 8 to 8 before Mr. Tetley's shoo-fly throw nipped a runner at second and Scrappy's return peg caught the runner from third sliding into Mr. Tetley's block of the plate.

Timmy slumped back in the dugout. The four innings ahead seemed like an impossible eternity. Vaguely, in a kind of stupor, he remembered that, way back when he was a kid, baseball was a game he loved to play.

"Git 'em back, git 'em back!" Pops was calling as he went out to coach third.

"The needle pitch is not moving for him," he heard Mr. Tetley tell Bofey. "He's throwing lollipops."

"We gotta try'n git another inning's work outta him," Bofey said. He gave Speedy a dry towel for his hands and arms. "Your moves to the needle ain't nachral. They gonna see what you up to. Take your time. Make *nachral* moves." He went out to coach at first.

Timmy went to the water fountain. "Not too much. You gonna git loggy," O'l Dan said and gave him a wet towel for his head. From out there in the sun and heat, the noise and sounds of a distant game came to him.

"You're on deck," he heard Mr. Tetley tell him. "And it looks like we're going to need your stick to stay alive and get some runs home."

"How many outs?" Timmy asked.

"How many *outs?*" Mr. Tetley's scorn was like a slap in the face. "Are you in this game, or aren't you? Poor you! You've got to go out in the hot sun and do a job! And we put you on full shares! Get on out there and pay attention to what Pops is going to ask you to do. And *jig* up to that plate, Speedy Deefy. Oh, by the way, there's one out."

Speedy pulled down his cap against the sarcasm and pranced into the sunshine. Manny and Hoop were on base, and Pops was giving them and Moon the run-and-hit sign. Moon poked the outside pitch into short right center and went to second on the late throw home. One run in and runners on second and third as Speedy looked down to Pops. Take. Then Pops came down the line again, as in the first game. Take on take takes take off. He was on his own. Get 'em home as best he could. My best skill is speed, Timmy told himself, feeling cold again; if he comes high, I'm swinging; low I'm bunting. Low! He half swung down at the ball and made contact and took off as the ball bounced high. There was no throw as he crossed the bag. When he came back, panting from the sprint, he saw that Manny was in and Hoop was on third. Bofey patted his rump.

Scrappy raised a high fly to center. Instead of going down the line, Speedy stayed on first. If the ball dropped against the fence, he would try to score from first; if it was caught, he would try for second after the catch. It was caught, and he sprinted for second and dove in ahead of the throw as Hoop trotted in. Busy Ike drew a walk, and Mr. Tetley hit his second homer of the game, this one clean over the right-field stands. Speedy trotted in to catch his breath and get a drink and dry his hands as Nate flied out. With five runs in, they were ahead 13 to 8.

"We give you cushion," Pops said. "Throw *hard.*"

"Just a minute, you guys," Timmy said from the water

fountain. "I'm gonna pitch my own game. Bofey's pitch ain't workin for me. I'm going out there and throw low strikes as best as I can. The only sign I'll take is the pitch-out from Mr. Tetley."

They all looked to Bofey, who shrugged: "On your own, okay. Fire hard and fire low. *Hard.*"

"You're on full shares," Mr. Tetley said.

"Maybe they'll hit 'em at somebody," Pops said.

He *walked* out like a pitcher, feeling like his own man again, not like a clown on Bofey's puppet string.

The first two batters got on with a walk and a single, but he got the third on a fly to center. Ike let the run score, but his throw to second chased the runner back to first. Mr. Tetley's shoo-fly caught him trying to steal. Two outs and none on! Aiming low, he walked a batter and the next singled past Nate. It's me or them, he thought in sudden red rage. The hell with aiming the ball low. Throw hard, *hard!* Get the ball in there hard. High, low, anywhere, but *hard.* Maybe they'll hit it at somebody. He loaded the bases with a walk.

Mr. Tetley called time to adjust a strap on his shin guard. It was as if he were saying, "Slow down and *pitch* to this man." "Pow, pow, *pow!*" Bofey was hollering from the dugout.

In the breathing spell, he thought out a sequence of pitches. Fast ball, fast ball, and take a chance with the screwball to the right-hander. With a one-and-one count, he bent it in on him, and it bent a little, enough to get a high fly on the right-field line that Clayt camped under for the out. Only one run in. Still up, 13 to 9. In the dugout, Manny said, "Good job."

But the House went down quickly — one, two, three — and he was still blowing when he went out for the seventh. He kept pumping the ball as hard as he could, but there was a run in and one on before he got a strike-out on a three-two call at the knees. That helped. He looked in at the left-handed pinch batter. It was Fritz, the nice kid from Spokane. Nice kid, hell! The guy he had to get. He decided to show him his curve and then low-strike him. But the curve hung fat over the plate, Fritz swung, and that ball was gone! Deep into the right-center stands. Speedy looked up from the dirt to see Pops coming out, motioning to Moon to come in from right field to hold their one-run lead. "He's gone as far as he kin go," Pops said to Mr. Tetley. "We gotta hope Moon ain't all stiffened up."

Moon came in and took the new ball from Mr. Tetley.

"Five warm-up pitches is all he gets," the plate umpire called.

Speedy headed for the dugout, but Pops caught him and turned him around and headed him out to right field. "Your job ain't done," he muttered. "Watch them bounces off that wall."

The first batter doubled off Moon, and the second singled into right. Speedy got the ball on the bounce and fired blindly toward the plate. The runner scored, and the batter went to second on the dumb throw. Moon, throwing easier now, got the next two batters on sharply hit ground balls, and they came in tied at 13 runs.

Fritz had been throwing in the bullpen since he hit his homer and was on the mound again for the Cowpokes. With Hoop on first and one down, Pops called upon Speedy to bunt him over, give the top of the line-up a chance to bring him in.

"He knows you hit his curve last time," Mr. Tetley said as Speedy went out to the on-deck circle. "Look for his fast ball."

Speedy laid off a high strike. He bunted the next pitch, in on him, but it rolled foul off the third-base line. Pops now would put him on his own. But, no! Bunt him over. Surprise them with a two-strike bunt. Okay. Fritz came in with a foolish curve. Speedy pushed it down the first-base line. Fritz looked to second but his play was to first, and his throw beat Speedy to the bag.

"Good job," they told him in the dugout.

Scrappy singled Moon home, and Ike flied deep to end the inning. So Moon went out to hold the one-run lead.

Hoop threw out the first batter. For their number-four batter, a right-hander who had been pulling the ball to left, Pops waved Clayt to the line and Bofey to left center. He kept waving Speedy toward center — further, still further — until he was in a line with Hoop. Then the son-of-a-gun reached out and slapped the ball deep into wide-open right field. Speedy saw it all the way and was in top speed after it. It seemed to be dropping beyond his speed. Should he ease up and play it off the wall? "You got room! Plenty a room!" He heard Hoop's holler, and he ran harder. He got it just off the base of the wall and tumbled into it. He leaped up, holding the ball high to show the base ump he had it. The crowd groaned.

But the fans soon had plenty to cheer about. The next batter worked Moon to three-two and then doubled to left center. The next batter went to three-two, and Moon walked him. Manny went into the hole to knock down a one-bounce shot but had no play, and the bases were loaded.

Now Pops, Bofey, and Mr. Tetley were on the way to the mound. Pops was waving Speedy to come back in. Me? Speedy gestured, me? Back to the mound? Pops waved him in. Still blowing from his long chase, Timmy doubted there was a decent strike left in his arm as Speedy trotted to the meeting on the mound.

But Pops was giving the ball to Bofey!

"Gotta have my belt from Speedy," Bofey was saying.

Pops made the pantomime, and Speedy got it through his dumb white skull. He unbuckled the belt and handed it to Bofey.

"Moon," Pops was saying, "we gonna need your glove and good arm out there in right. Speedy done his job, he kin go sit."

The crowd seemed to sense a ritual as Bofey put the belt on and cinched it tight.

Speedy took off his cap and wiped the sweat off his brow with his sleeve. "I wanna stay in," he said into the dirt.

Mr. Tetley polished his dome and put his arm on his shoulder.

" 'Fear no more the heat o' the sun,' " he quoted softly into the heat of the sun, as he walked Speedy in. " 'Thou thy worldly task hast done . . .' "

Timmy risked a smile of understanding. He knew the next line: "Home art gone and ta'en thy wages." He felt a strange pride in himself — not for having done his job, but for being a man of considerable erudition, like Mr. Tetley.

In the dark of the dugout he sat back. Bofey was throwing left-handed, arching the needle pitch in. After taking a strike and missing a strike, the batter popped up to Mr. Tetley.

The House scored twice in their eighth, and Bofey held the Cowpokes to one run. In their ninth, the House scored once more to go ahead 17 to 14. Bofey went out to pitch right-handed in the ninth.

As Timmy watched, the words kept running through his head: "Home art gone and ta'en thy wages." There was more to it than that. What?

Throwing low curve balls and in-shoots, Bofey got a ground out and gave up a single. The next batter — it was Fritz again — hit a sharp grounder to Hoop who tossed to Scrappy who leaped over the slide and threw to Nate for the double play, the ball game, and another $500.

Speedy ran out to the mound to be first to jump-hug Bofey and pound Scrappy for his game-ending throw. They swarmed back into their dugout yipping and whooping for their thousand-dollar day.

"We win it as a *team*," Pops was saying.

"Dry your face," Ol' Dan told Speedy, "an hep me wif these bats."

29
Tim

———◆▶———

The lamb and chickens were dripping their fat into the wisps of smoke rising from the sputtering embers of the apple wood in the pit. A huge blackened kettle of beans was blending the heat of the pit with the fire of chili. The long table was laden with tubs of ice and pints of home-brew and bottles of moonshine.

Timmy was dismayed. He yearned for tonight as their last night together in their black sanctuary with Busy Ike strummin his down-home blues and stomps. But the others yipped and cackled their delight and anticipation as they took turns splashing away the sweat and dust of victory under the pump.

Longhorn and a dozen of his Cowpokes and ranch hands and the Western Stars Hoe-Down Band busted in on them — by flivver, truck, and horse — before Timmy could get out of uniform.

Longhorn commanded that they gather around the table. When the tin cups were splashed half full of moonshine, he raised a toast: "Here's to you, ya black sons-a-guns. Thought sure we had ya this year, an' we scored good enough off'n ya to win, but your hitting — off the best pitchin I could buy — done us in. There's no soft spots in that line-up a yours an' ya allus run to the right bases. An' here's to next year when we gonna try you again, maybe double up the stakes an' catch up. An' now, God damn, eat, drink, an' be merry an' git that hoe-down music goin!"

With cheers and whoops and hollers they raised their cups, Timmy with the rest. He swigged the moonshine and laid into the cold beer to chase it down. The sun was still up and hot, and it was a long ways to midnight, but Timmy splashed himself another swig of moonshine.

Longhorn and Pops went to the strongbox in the Packard to settle up and stash away the winnings. Timmy looked into all the faces, but Fritz was not among them.

Longhorn, like a cow pony picking his way through the herd to a maverick, bore down on Speedy Deefy and thrust a big cigar in his mouth and flicked a match ablaze with his thumbnail and lit him up. "You white, skinny coon, you! My boys gonna be swingin at that lazy curve ball a your'n in their sleep. You'd go far in this game if you was only as white as you look."

Speedy grinned and grasped the extended hand.

Mr. Tetley polished his dome. "You know, down South," he said to Longhorn, "we've got a superstition that there's nothing, not even the proverbial rabbit's foot, that brings as much good luck as rubbing the head of a genuine albino."

In the fun and laughter of the head rubbing, Speedy Deefy grinned like the mute clown they knew him to be.

Busy Ike was tuning up to sit in with the Western Stars. Johnny Baugh and Bofey were at the end of the table, head to head, in talk about the craft of pitching.

"You know this fella here," Longhorn was saying about

Teej, who was sitting next to him. "This T.J. — Teej, we call 'im — he's my son. Gonna take over the ranch and the Cowpokes one a these years."

"He talks like that," said Teej, "but he ain't about to let loose a the reins."

"Every time I looked up," said Mr. Tetley, "Teej was on base or running to the next one."

"That big number-four hitter a yours, he kin stroke 'em wif anybody," Scrappy said.

"He near beat us with that poke to right that Speedy went and got," Hoop said.

"He wouldn't come to this bar-be-cue," said Longhorn. "Nor 'bout half the resta our guys. They just couldn't bring theirselves to eatin an' drinkin at the same table with colored. That young pitcher, Fritz Green, he wanna come, but his daddy, a big banker from Spokane, he said they would come only if we set separate tables. I tol' 'em too bad, you're gonna miss one a the best bar-be-cues a man could sit down to in a hundred years."

Ol' Dan spoke up: "We know all 'bout the color line, Mistuh Longhorn. We sprised to be settin here like this, black an' white together."

Longhorn tossed off a shot of booze and chased it with home-brew. "Tell ya, boys, a story 'bout that, what happened to me . . ." Everybody was listening. Busy Ike put down his guitar. From the end of the table, Bofey and Johnny Baugh quit their private palavering. "In my rodeo days, when I was ridin broncs an' bulls, we had this Negro cowboy travelin with us, show to show. He dressed like a clown in a red cap an' a spotted suit. 'Twas his job, when a bull throwed a rider, to git the bull to chase after him, give the rider a chance to make it to the fence, without getting gored or tromped on. He saved my ass many a time, riskin his own to save mine.

241

After a contest, many a night, me'n him we'd build our own fire an' stay up half the night, eatin and drinkin together. One day a bull hooked his shirt an' broke his back against the fence an' ripped his guts open an' smashed his head before we could get to him. Or it woulda been me layin there dead. So 'bout that time, my wife back home, she gave me my first son, so I named him Thomas Jefferson after him, the pal of my rodeo days . . ."

"T.J. — Teej," said Mr. Tetley, "for Thomas Jefferson . . ."

Longhorn nodded. "Thomas Jefferson Brown was his whole name."

"And proud of it," said Teej, "to be named for the man that saved my daddy's life."

"Some day," Longhorn said, "maybe not in my time, nor any a yours, the lion an' the lamb are gonna lie down together, like the Good Book says, an' we gonna judge a man by how good can he play the game, not by the color of the skin the Good Lord put over his insides, where his heart beats . . ."

Mr. Tetley raised his silver flask and stood up. "Here's to Thomas Jefferson Brown — and to the man" — smiling down on Longhorn — "whose life he saved."

Timmy gulped his moonshine with the rest.

Things began to blur out, and the ground started to tilt about the time the sun went down. He got himself a plate of chili beans and lamb ribs and chicken and sat cross-legged with his back against the shed and slurped the beans and gnawed at the bones and tilted his pint of beer like he knew what he was doing. Suddenly he began to cry because he had come to the end of the road. A Cowpoke gave his head another rub for luck, and he laughed like a fool.

When full darkness came on, he heard Busy Ike playing

along with the Western Stars, and then he heard him shouting the song he was making up:

> *Ahm a winnin man in all I do,*
> *'Cause ah got a secret way.*
> *Ahm a winner at love and a winner at cards*
> *At evry game ah play.*
> *Don' ask me my secret, Ah keep it to myself,*
> *Said don' ask me my secret, Ah keep it to myself.*
> *If ah tell you, you might tell somebody else.*

"You heah what he singin, Speedy?" It was Bofey beside him, a bottle between his legs. "Celebratin our secret pitch."

The last Timmy remembered was reeling toward the flatbed and falling and crawling under it on his belly to throw up and be alone.

In the bright morning, remembering everything, he crawled out from under the flatbed and got out of his uniform for the last time and took his first hangover to the pump and washed the sweat and dirt of his last day and the vomit of his last night away with the cold water from the deep well. Then he shaved his white face and put on his B.V.D.'s and shirt and tie and last year's Very Best suit and packed his grip and rolled his things in his slicker. He walked across the road down to the river to watch it go by until the others were up and it was time to eat breakfast.

It came time to catch the noon train east. Pops and Ol' Dan were waiting by the Packard to take him to the depot. They would stay to meet the new pitcher on the westbound train.

The guys were lolling around as they had been the first morning he had walked in on them, the Fourth of July. Timmy tossed his grip and slicker into the back seat. Maybe,

243

he was thinking, the best thing to do is to get in and wave good-bye to them from the car.

"Hey, white boy! C'movah here!" It was Little Hoop, naked to the waist. "You forgot something."

Timmy advanced uncertainly. Hoop was holding out his old tin pail. "Oh, that!" Timmy said. "Just an old tin pail. Maybe it'll come in handy around the camp."

"This what you come with," said Hoop, "an' this what you go with."

Timmy took the pail. Hoop put his hands on his shoulders. "Pops will be payin you your shares, but we all wanna give you a little somethin for luck — an' to keep us in your mind."

Into the pail he dropped a silver dollar. One by one, each came and did the same. Bofey was next to last. "This silver-dollar buckle," he said, "it be yours to keep." He dropped it in the old tin pail.

"You'll be needing it, the rest of the way to Billings," Timmy managed to say.

"Scrappy, he gonna weld me another one," Bofey said.

"I'll keep the secret, Bofey."

Mr. Tetley was last. He took off Timmy's cap and polished Speedy's dome for the last time. He dropped his dollar into the tin pail of Timmy's boyhood. Then he extended his hand, and Timmy grasped it. "Good-bye, Mr. Tetley. I'll always remember . . ."

Mr. Tetley nodded. "*Flanmora, flanmira*. So will I. So long, Tim." *Tim!*

He turned quickly and got in the back seat. He might not be able to see to drive.

At the depot, Pops paid him his shares, which came to $119.75. It was as much as most farm hands came home with after a full summer and fall working in the fields. While he was buying his ticket, Ol' Dan bought him a two-bit cigar.

The train was on time. "You hepped us ovah the hump," Pops said as they shook hands.

His own words of farewell and good luck would have been lost in the thunder of the train anyway.

"You one a us," he heard Ol' Dan say as he swung aboard.

Number Four rushed him east the slow way they had come west. It whistled through towns where they had camped and played. Looking down from the trestle over a stream, he wondered if it was the Mouse River that flowed past Mervyn's grave.

In midafternoon, Tim started back to the lounge car to drink a bottle of pop and light up his cigar, but he hurried back to his seat to get the tin pail with his lucky silver dollars. He kept it between his legs for safekeeping the rest of the way home.